Ask Me No Questions

Louisa de Lange

ORION

First published in Great Britain in 2019 by Orion Fiction,
an imprint of The Orion Publishing Group Ltd.,
Carmelite House, 50 Victoria Embankment
London EC4Y 0DZ

An Hachette UK Company

1 3 5 7 9 10 8 6 4 2

A CIP catalogue record for this book is
available from the British Library.

ISBN (Paperback) 9781409180234
ISBN (eBook) 9781409180241

Typeset at The Spartan Press Ltd,
Lymington, Hants

Printed and bound in Great Britain by Clays Ltd,
Elcograf S.p.A.

www.orionbooks.co.uk

For my mum and dad,
Janet and Richard de Lange

MARRIED COUPLE SLAIN IN LOVER'S BRUTAL ATTACK

Spurned lover retaliates from rejection, gunning down loving parents in sleepy suburb

Shock has descended across Southampton this week, hearing news of the brutal murder of local residents, Robert and Madeleine Patterson, on Saturday. Gunshots were reported to police at 2.13 p.m. and on entering the property on Limewood Road, Bassett, armed officers found the blood-spattered bodies of local artist, Madeleine Patterson, 42, and finance director, Robert Patterson, 45, next to their neighbour, Harrison Becker, unconscious. Becker, unemployed, 46, came round at the scene and instantly confessed to the double murder. When questioned later by detectives, Becker admitted to killing the couple in a jealous rage when Madeleine Patterson ended their long-running affair.

Madeleine and Robert Patterson were both pronounced dead on site. They are survived by their twin daughters, Gabriella and Thea Patterson, 18, currently being treated at Southampton General Hospital. The twins were unaware as their parents lay dying, having been in the garden at the time of the murders with Harry Becker, 18, son of Harrison Becker.

Local residents are shocked by the seemingly un-expected crime, but described the relationship between the two families as unnaturally close. One neighbour said: 'The dad and his boy were always over their house. And she was so glamorous, it doesn't surprise me they were having an affair. I worry what will happen to those poor kids now.'

More on this story as details emerge.

Part 1

Monday, 21 January 2019

I

She was led down a long corridor, closed doors either side. Neither of the police officers said a word. One walked quickly ahead, his shoes squeaking on the tiled floor, the other following closely behind. Dressed in black, their stab vests made them look intimidating and bulky, and she stomped after them, her previously unfruitful questioning rendering her mute.

The walls were painted a bland magnolia, regular black scuff marks punctuating their progress. A single window lit the end of the corridor; fluorescent strip lights flickered overhead.

They stopped at the last door and the officer opened it. He ushered her inside.

The room was empty, except for a grey table in the centre and two brown wood and metal chairs. As she sat down, she realised all the furniture was bolted to the floor. The walls were encased with a light grey panelling, but apart from that, nothing. She was almost disappointed by the lack of a two-way mirror.

A black box was positioned on the side of the table, a small video screen showing two views: one of the whole room and the other of her face. She glanced around to locate the camera: a black dome on the far side of the wall.

The officers hovered at the door. They moved aside for a woman to enter the room. She nodded at them and they left, closing it behind them.

The woman sat down at the table and opened the beige folder in front of her. She was wearing a grey suit, a rumpled white shirt underneath. Her long brown hair was tied back severely and it didn't suit her; coupled with her minimal make-up, it made her look tired. Despite this, the woman was alert – sitting up straight in her seat, her eye contact unflinching.

The woman cleared her throat and looked at her. 'You are Thea Patterson, correct?'

'Yes.'

'My name is Detective Sergeant Munro.' She shuffled some papers and pulled out a sheet of A4. She clicked open a biro, and wrote a few details on the top. 'We are investigating a violent attack on your sister, Gabriella Patterson. I am intending to interview you. You are not under arrest and you are free to leave. However, I must tell you that if you decide to terminate this interview and leave the police station before I have asked you all the questions that I consider relevant, I will reconsider whether your arrest is necessary for the effective investigation of this offence.' DS Munro spoke without looking up, reading from the piece of paper with barely any intonation. 'Do you understand the above?' She pushed it to Thea, with the biro.

Thea looked at it with surprise. 'What's happened to Gabriella?' she asked.

'She's in hospital.' She paused when Thea didn't respond. 'You weren't aware?'

'No.'

'Gabriella was attacked on Southampton Common in

the early hours of Sunday morning – she's in a coma with severe head injuries.' DS Munro gestured towards the piece of paper.

Thea took the pen and signed it. 'You think I did it?'

The detective looked straight at Thea. 'You're a suspect in the investigation.' She stopped again, watching Thea's reaction. 'Why are you unaware your sister is in hospital?'

'We're not close,' Thea said, quietly. She didn't look at DS Munro. She picked at her nails, worrying at a piece of skin on her cuticle.

'And why is that?'

Thea continued to stare at her hands, searching for the right words.

The DS frowned. 'If I'm going to be completely honest, Thea, in cases like this, when we don't know who attacked the victim or why, we look to the family first. Especially when the family isn't – as you say – close. So anything you can tell me at this point would be beneficial.' She glanced at her notes, then back at Thea. 'You're twins, correct?'

'Yes.'

'Identical?'

'Yes.'

'And yet, you're not close.'

Thea looked at the detective. 'No.'

DS Munro studied the photo again, and Thea knew she would be taking in the exact same nose structure, same dark brown eyes, same chin, same ears. She was used to the fascination people had with identical twins. When they were younger, she found it boring; this assumption they were one: 'the twins'. Now, it was just annoying.

'You live in your family home?' the detective continued.

'If you know so much, why do you need me here?'

The detective ignored her. 'Can you account for your whereabouts on Saturday night and Sunday morning?'

Thea took a slow breath in. She felt the irritation grow. 'I was at home, working.'

'Was anyone with you?'

'No. I live alone.'

'And what do you do?'

'I'm a photographer.'

'Weddings, babies?'

'Mainly corporate shots, stock photos for newspapers, some arty stuff. A few weddings to pay the bills.'

DS Munro paused and opened the beige folder, enough so she could see inside while keeping the contents hidden from Thea.

'And what happened last Wednesday when you saw Gabriella?'

Thea looked at her. 'I think you know,' she replied.

'Don't mess with me, Thea.' The detective stared at her, her hands covering the folder. 'We haven't arrested you for this attack, but we could. This is potentially a charge of attempted murder, given your sister is lying in hospital unconscious right now, and that's a long time in prison. Now, what happened on Wednesday when you saw your sister?'

'Nothing. We were talking.'

'That's not what your neighbours told us.'

Thea looked at her, eyes narrowed. 'We had an argument.'

The detective sat back in her seat, clearly already aware and now satisfied with Thea's response. 'And what was the argument about?'

Thea paused. She knew she was trying to intimidate her. To scare her into giving something away. But Thea wasn't bothered; she'd been through worse than this. 'Normal sister stuff,' she said at last. 'It was our mother's birthday. She was angry because I hadn't left flowers on the grave.'

'This is your mother that...'

'Yes,' Thea said quickly, cutting her off.

'And why hadn't you?'

'I'd been busy. I don't dwell on what happened like my sister.' Thea met the detective's stare. 'Listen, DS Munro. You sound like a good police officer. I'm sure you didn't get to where you are by being lazy. Take a look at Gabriella's lifestyle. At the places she goes, the men she hangs out with. Speak to them about the nightclubs, the alcohol, the drugs, and I'm sure you'll find a plethora of people more interesting than me, with better motives for attacking my sister.' She tilted her head to one side, regarding the woman opposite. 'Why did you take so long to contact me?' she asked.

'What do you mean?'

'I mean, she was attacked early Sunday, today is Monday. As next of kin, you needed my permission to get her medical records, and I assume time is of the essence.' Thea stopped, a slight smile on her face. 'Why did that take twenty-four hours?'

DS Munro frowned. 'She didn't have any identification on her. It took us a while to find her bag.'

'She was mugged,' Thea said.

'We're exploring all lines of enquiry.'

Thea knew the detective was beaten. 'Fine. You do that. But for now, let me go. I didn't get much sleep last night and I'd like to go home.'

Thea stood up, waiting for a response. DS Munro didn't move from the table, then nodded.

'Thank you for coming in today, Thea,' she said. 'You'll

just need to do a bit of paperwork with my colleagues, then you're free to leave.'

Thea rolled her eyes and followed the plain-clothes officer who appeared behind her. For a moment, before the door to the interview room closed, she looked back. DS Munro was thinking, her face distorted into a determined frown, staring at the file in front of her.

And Thea knew it wouldn't be long before she saw that detective again.

2

DS Kate Munro stayed at the table, taking in the conversation. Well, that bloody didn't go well, she thought, annoyed with herself for letting her suspect get the upper hand.

Thea Patterson was clearly intelligent, confident and not easily intimidated. And she was certainly unique: a pair of identical twins couldn't be more different. No one would look twice at Thea Patterson, while it seemed men couldn't keep away from Gabriella.

Thea Patterson was almost childlike. A grey jumper flooded her figure, with short black messy hair in a bob tucked behind her ears. She seemed to take little effort with her appearance. In contrast, the girl in the photo, a society shot from a night out, flaunted her femininity – red lipstick, breasts pushed up, a short dress consisting of no more than a scrap of material, high silver heels.

Thea was prickly and slightly arrogant. And completely unfazed about being questioned in a police station. Most people would be nervous and fidgety, desperate to do or say anything to get them out, but not Thea Patterson.

She closed the file and leaned back in her chair, stretching her arms. Something wasn't right with this woman, but she couldn't put her finger on what. Perhaps it was her lack of emotion – the uniforms said she'd barely blinked when they told her about her sister lying in a hospital. Evidence of guilt? Had she already known she was there? If only things were that simple.

'Coffee, Sarge?' The plain-clothes officer stuck his head round the door.

'No, I'm fine, thank you,' Kate replied. 'I'll be upstairs in a sec, Briggs. Did she say anything to you on the way out?'

The officer shook his head. 'Nope. Face like a slapped arse all the way. Met some bloke in reception though, walked off across the park.'

'That's interesting.' DS Munro walked out of the interview room and hurried to the small window at the end of the corridor. It overlooked the large expanse of grass the officers affectionately referred to as the park, even though it was far from big enough to count as one.

She scanned the path and, sure enough, barely halfway across she could see the tiny figure of Thea, accompanied by a tall man on her left. She could see they were talking.

Another figure in the park caught her eye. She noticed him because he walked slowly, occasionally hesitating but always looking directly at the pair of them as they went. He was dressed in black and seemed to loiter in their periphery, trying to keep up but avoid being seen. She didn't think they had noticed him.

Thea and her friend disappeared out of Kate's eyeline, and just as she was considering phoning one of the uniforms to check out the stalker, the man seemed to reconsider and turn in the opposite direction. Perhaps she had been imagining it after all; perhaps she saw a potential crime in the most innocent of circumstances.

She tapped the beige file on the window, thinking about Thea Patterson. Kate had no siblings of her own, but she couldn't imagine being an identical twin and not being close.

These twins were so distant, she realised now, that Thea hadn't even asked what hospital Gabriella was in. She had made no effort to find out more about her sister's attack.

In over ten years in the police force, she'd seen the full range of responses to hearing a loved one was in hospital. Crying, hysterics; some even violent and angry. But the strange lack of emotion from Thea Patterson? Kate shook her head in disbelief. One thing was for sure: she needed to know more about this woman. And fast.

3

'What did they want?' Harry asked as they walked across the park, clear from the prying eyes of the police officers.

'You'll never get a nice girl to marry you if you carry on with those things.' Thea scowled, gesturing at the cigarette Harry was flicking away into the bushes. She threw her bag over her shoulder and walked away as quickly as she could. It was freezing out, and her sweatshirt was offering little protection from the January wind.

'It was about Gabriella,' she muttered.

'I guessed as much. What's she done?'

'She's in hospital. Someone attacked her Saturday night on the common.'

Harry stopped walking, and pulled Thea round to face him. 'Is she okay?'

'She's unconscious. They didn't tell me any more than that.' Thea walked away quickly and Harry chased to catch up.

'Did they say which hospital?'

'I forgot to ask.'

'Thea! Come on, she's your twin. We should visit. We can find out where she is easily enough.' They walked in silence for a few paces. Thea had no desire to see her sister, but she didn't have the energy for an argument. 'How long has she been back?' he asked quietly.

Thea shrugged. 'A few months?'

'And you didn't tell me?' Thea didn't reply. 'Why did the police want to see you?' Harry continued.

'They think I did it,' she said, her voice flat.

'And did you?'

'Harry!'

He shrugged, nonplussed. 'The two of you haven't exactly been on the best of terms.'

Thea looked up at him as they walked. He was looking away from her, across the park, and she saw his strong features in profile. So familiar, yet still able to tie her stomach in knots. So much had passed between them over the years. So much shared history. He was the first person she had thought to call when she arrived at the police station. She hadn't intended to but when they asked, she'd said his name automatically, reciting his number from memory.

He carried on talking. 'It wouldn't surprise me. Sometimes I think the two of you are capable of anything.'

'Fuck off, Harry,' Thea said, dryly.

They stopped at the furthest edge of the park next to a shiny new estate car, and Harry clicked it open. 'Do you want a lift home?' he asked.

She looked up at him, taking in his hair, the rogue tuft stuck up at an odd angle at the back, his stubble, contrasting with his smart shirt and tie.

'No, that's okay, I'll walk. You need to get back to work. Thank you for coming to meet me.' She reached up and tried to smooth down the spiky bits of hair. 'You need a haircut,' she said.

'I like it longer. Are you okay? You don't seem yourself,' Harry remarked, opening the car door. 'I can't remember the last time I heard you swear.'

'Just don't like police stations,' she muttered.

Harry gave her a quick peck on the cheek, pulling off his coat and passing it to her. It was an unspoken act, but the gesture made a lump form in her throat. He climbed into the driver's seat and beeped his horn as he drove off. Thea lifted a hand to wave.

She put Harry's coat on, doing the buttons up to cover her chin and nose. It engulfed her, and she stopped for a moment, taking in the smell of him – his aftershave, mixed with cigarettes. She took a deep breath. It smelt of coming home. Of feeling safe and secure and belonging. She pushed down the strange feeling in her stomach, and turned to walk the few miles back to the house.

Thea didn't mind the walking. For the first time in weeks it was a beautiful winter's day. It was cold, but the air was crisp, the sun reflecting down through the gaps in the buildings as she went.

She needed to think. She'd had a headache since yesterday, and the conversation in the police station hadn't helped. She regretted how she'd acted towards the detective; she'd been more aggressive than she should have been, but it had been the easiest way to keep her emotions in check. Hide the fear and the uncertainty behind a layer of cold arrogance. And seeing Harry had been – what? Too brief. Too sudden. She wanted to talk to him again but knew that she shouldn't.

Questions flew around in her head as she walked. Was her sister okay? How badly was she injured? Would she wake up? But she wasn't sure she had the courage to visit her in hospital, to see her face to face.

She rounded the last corner and started down the long street that led to her house. Tall elegant lime trees lined the road, cars parked haphazardly either side. The pavement was buckled from tree roots pushing through the concrete.

The houses were far apart from each other, all surrounded by large gardens and high hazardous walls. Generally, the residents kept to themselves although, as Thea had just found out, having a loud argument with your sister on your driveway meant they wouldn't hesitate to tell the police what had been going on. The neighbourhood cultivated an air of detachment and unease; nobody wanted to live near somewhere so infamous.

Thea's house stood back from the road, hidden from view by the overgrown hedge and the red-brick wall. As she walked she saw the chimney first, pushing up from the roof. It barely seemed strong enough to stay up, and it was always a worry when the wind blew and the house shook. The tall iron gates stood open; the bottom part of rusted metal stuck in the gravel of the drive. She paused at the entrance, taking it all in.

The driveway took up the front part of the house, dotted with weeds and blending into the overgrown grass down either side. Thea's trusty red Nissan Micra stood parked to the left, in front of the wooden double doors of the garage. It had always been the same. Thea's relaxed attitude to gardening hadn't done it any favours, but she remembered disappearing into the wild flowers in summer, spending hazy days out of sight, eating apples and pears pulled off the trees. More idyllic in hindsight than in reality; benign neglect had the advantage of being seen as freedom when viewed from a distance.

Double-fronted, the house had dark dirty glass staring out from bay windows, a peeling red front door, decorated with a single brass knocker, and oversized grey brickwork. A long thread of ivy multiplied across the house, a tangle of thorn bushes in front. She knew its passageways and corridors as well as the lines on her face, both an integral part of her.

She took a deep breath. Being at the house wasn't something she enjoyed, but it was important she was here. She would have to put up with the old place a bit longer.

As she stood preparing herself to go in, she saw movement out of the corner of her eye and took a step back out of the shadows of the gateway to look down the road. Two cars were parked there, with a third, a black BMW, idling on the opposite side. She could just make out someone waiting in the driver's seat. As she watched the car, two pedestrians paused next to her at the gate. They were chubby, their faces rouged in the cold winter air, their hair unfashionable and frizzy. One of them had a street map in her hand.

'Is this the place?' one asked, and the other nodded, peering past Thea. 'Do you know the people that live here?' they asked her.

She stared at them.

'Are you——?' one of them started.

'Fuck off,' Thea said, under her breath. Then louder: 'Just fuck off, get out of here.'

They recoiled and walked away as quickly as their short fat legs could carry them. 'Was that...? Well, I never... So rude...' Thea could hear them saying as they went back to their car parked on the other side of the road. She looked for the black BMW again, but it had gone.

Thea frowned, then walked up the driveway, gravel crunching under her feet. She dug in her bag for the door keys, the same old door keys, unlocking the top and bottom bolts before the middle four-point lock. She pushed the solid door open with her shoulder and was greeted by a gust of cold fusty air. It smelt of old wood, damp walls and broken promises.

Everything in her wanted to leave, to turn around and run away, never looking back. But she knew she had to stay, to find what she was looking for. It was here, it had to be. Hidden away all these years.

It was time to face her past.

She went inside.

4

Kate Munro pushed the door open to the operations room and took a deep breath. This wasn't her first investigation by any means, but it was the one that had attracted the attention of the media, and the chief inspector to boot. People didn't like it when pretty girls were attacked. People were watching, the chief had said, so she better wrap it up, and fast.

She walked to the front of the room and cleared her throat. 'So where are we today? Give me a summary.'

The two DCs looked at each another, sheepish expressions on their faces. 'Anything? Either of you? Briggs?'

DC Jamie Briggs stared at his notepad. 'We have her bag and driving licence. Now we've identified her, they're down with forensics, see if we can get any prints from them. And we know she went to Heaven that night...'

'Heaven?'

'It's a nightclub in town. Very trendy, very exclusive.' That was why she hadn't heard of it then. Briggs, with his skinny jeans and coiffed hair, seemed much more their usual clientele. Kate gestured for him to carry on. 'We know she left at approximately one-fifty a.m. We don't know where she went or who she went with.'

'Has anyone been down there?'

'No, we were waiting for you. We only know the time from the CCTV cameras in the area. She walked down

London Road alone, then up The Avenue towards the common, until the cameras lost her at two forty-six.'

'Can we see?'

DC Briggs turned his laptop round and they crowded around the screen. He moved the footage forward until the timestamp read 01.53 and they saw a sparsely dressed woman totter down the road. She was wearing a silver slip dress, spaghetti straps resting delicately on her shoulders, the material barely coming down to her thighs. Apart from a pair of dainty silver sandals and a small silver bag, she had nothing else on her.

'She's walked a long way. Do we know where she was going?' Kate asked.

'Her sister's house is in that direction — perhaps she was trying to walk there? But that's still a good mile from the common,' Briggs commented.

'What was the temperature that night?' Kate asked, and he consulted his notebook.

'Can't have been more than five degrees.'

'Christ,' Kate said to herself.

The woman on the screen wobbled away, bent over with her arms clutched round her body.

DC Briggs flipped the camera view to show the next road, Gabriella moving quickly, then disappearing out of sight.

'That's all we have at the moment,' he said, closing the lid on the laptop.

'And how long was Gabriella out there?' Kate asked.

While DC Briggs looked at his notepad, the other officer chipped in. Kate had worked with DC Rachel Yates before — she was careful and detailed, all the things that Kate liked.

'The 999 call came in at three fifty-three a.m., so we believe nearly two hours.'

'No wonder she had hypothermia,' Kate muttered under her breath. 'And we don't know who made the call?'

Yates shook her head. 'Tracking it down now.'

'SOCO?'

'Scene of crime collected anything they could from the area in the golden hour, then did a wider search where they found her bag,' DC Yates continued.

'Did they find anything interesting?'

'Crisp packets, fag ends, the usual rubbish. A big rock with blood on it – we think it might be what she was hit with. They bagged it all up. It'll take a while to sort through.' She looked back at her notebook. 'Medical exam and Early Evidence Kit is being done now that we have next of kin consent from her sister.'

'And bloods?'

'They were taken by the hospital when she first came in – they've been sent for analysis.'

'Let's have the results back as soon as we can,' Kate said, taking a swig from her mineral water and wincing at the lack of taste. The smell of coffee and bacon sandwiches filled the air and Kate cursed her latest ridiculous resolution to be healthier.

She saw Yates pause. 'What?'

Yates frowned. 'Are we sure this isn't a mugging gone wrong? I mean, there was no money, phone or credit cards found in the bag. And it was as you'd expect in a robbery, tossed in the bushes.'

'Wasn't it right at the other end of the common?' Briggs chipped in.

'Yes, but would that be so strange? Our perp attacks her at

one end, runs away searching through the bag, then chucks it when he's finished looking.' Yates continued. 'And a rock? It's hardly a premeditated weapon of choice.'

Briggs pulled up a map of the common and pointed to the entrance near one of the bordering roads.

'Gabriella was found here,' he said. 'And her bag here, by the Wildlife Centre.'

'They're a long way apart,' Kate said. She took one last look, then stood up, facing the two detectives. 'Things are far from clear at the moment, so let's be thorough. Let's keep chasing forensics, especially if they can get anything from the bag. Let's make sure the blood on the rock is the victim's. And I want the medical back as soon as we can.

'Briggs, keep going on the cameras. Find out if there's any private CCTV along the route to get a different view – anything on a house, or a cash machine, or a shop.' She turned to DC Yates. 'You and I are going to this nightclub – Heaven?' DC Briggs nodded. 'And find out what they know. Oh, and get a summary up on the whiteboard. Crime scene photos, timeline, map, all the usual stuff.'

They turned back to their files and bacon sandwiches. Kate looked at the water bottle in her hand.

'And we're going via a sodding Starbucks, okay?'

During the daytime, the nightclub Heaven looked less like paradise and more like the underworld. It was surrounded by grubby pubs and clubs, the road littered with vacant properties and *To Let* signs.

Kate and DC Yates stood outside the entrance, hands in pockets, shivering in the wind as it rushed down the street. Paint was peeling off the padlocked door, an inconspicuous bell to the right-hand side. A burly man was washing away a patch of vomit with a hosepipe, catching all the discarded fag ends and crisp packets in the process. Kate couldn't imagine standing here in a tiny dress in the heat of summer, let alone now, let alone in the dead of night. They rang the doorbell and waited before turning their attention to the bouncer as he rolled up the hosepipe.

'Excuse me?' Kate called.

The man looked across, barely giving the two women a second glance. 'Police,' Kate shouted, an instant attention-grabber. The man sighed and walked over, his broad shoulders hunched in a worn black leather jacket and tight jeans, bulging at the thighs.

'Do you recognise this woman?' Kate asked, showing him pictures – one from the CCTV and another press photo from the internet.

He nodded. 'That's Gabriella. She worked here at the end of the summer behind the bar. Still comes here for a night out most weekends.'

'And when did you see her last?' Kate asked, gesturing to DC Yates to get out her notebook.

The man shrugged, lifting his substantial shoulders barely half an inch. 'Saturday?' He thought for a moment. 'She arrived alone, about eleven thirty.'

'There was no one with her? Was that unusual?'

The bouncer laughed. 'No, not at all. She knows plenty of people here – especially the men.'

'Anyone special?' Kate said.

He paused, then shook his head in a quick movement. 'Not for me to say,' he muttered. 'You'll have to ask the boss.'

It pulled at Kate's curiosity, but she didn't want to push. She'd ask the man in charge soon enough. 'And this girl?'

Kate pulled another photo out of her pocket and showed it to him. 'Have you seen her?'

The man gave her a funny look. 'Are you having a laugh, love? What are you trying to pull?'

'It's her identical twin.'

'Really?' The bouncer smiled with a greasy leer. 'There's never been more than one of them here – I would have noticed.'

Kate quickly put the photo of Thea back in her pocket. 'Can you get your boss?'

'Yeah, sure.' He pulled a mobile out and dialled. 'Steve, some cops to see you. Yeah, at the front door.' He listened. 'It's about Gabriella.' He hung up. 'He says to bring you inside.'

He pulled the door open with a rush of warm air. Inside, the club smelt of old beer, rough spirits and cheap disinfectant. The overhead luminescent tubes were turned on, showing a long wooden bar down the left-hand side, a dance floor in the centre and a set of stairs winding up the middle of the room.

'Have you been clubbing lately?' Kate whispered to DC Yates.

She shook her head. 'Nah, I'm too tired. This job plus two kids under five doesn't leave much room for a social life.'

Kate raised her eyebrows. Two under five, crikey. She barely had the energy to take her shoes off after work, let alone look after two small people.

The bouncer beckoned them through, then pointed up the stairs to an impressive mezzanine, and followed them up. At the top he led them down a corridor to the right-hand side of the bar, a sign for the toilets overhead. The office door was at the end, and the bouncer tapped in the security code to let them inside.

He pointed to his boss, sat behind a cheap-looking desk more fitting of a council office. The man behind it stood up as they walked into the room. Tall and well built, he was dressed formally in a dark suit and purple tie, dark brown hair styled flawlessly, white teeth shining from a winter tan.

'Steve Morgan,' he said, holding out his hand. 'Owner. How can I help?'

The bouncer left, closing the door behind him and Steve gestured to the two chairs in front of the desk.

Kate forced a smile, her lips pressed together. Steve Morgan sat back down and she perched on the edge of one of the chairs, Yates hovering behind. 'Do you recognise this woman?' She showed him the same few photos and Steve nodded.

'Yep, that's definitely Gabriella. She worked here August, September time last year. I was disappointed she left – she knew how to keep the men happy, if you know what I mean,' he said, winking.

'I'm not sure I do,' Kate said slowly.

Steve Morgan thought for a second. 'She always looked good, great eye candy for a man with money. Flirty, fun – she did well on the tips. It was a pity she quit.'

'And why did she leave?' Kate asked.

'Didn't say. But I heard she was working as an escort, so perhaps she made better money that way.'

Kate nodded. 'Do you know if she was seeing anyone in particular?'

'Well, that would be telling,' Steve said, tapping the side of his nose. 'A club with this sort of reputation needs to be discreet, you know. People wouldn't like it if I went around blabbing.'

'But I'm sure a club with your reputation would do anything to help the police when a young woman has been attacked.'

'Attacked? What happened to her?' He sat forward in his chair, suddenly worried.

'Knocked unconscious Saturday night, walking home from here. It would be such a help for our investigation if you could share what you know. And your CCTV footage, of course.' Kate pointed to the camera in the corner of the room above them. 'And I noticed a few more in the club?'

Steve regained his composure and smiled, leaning back and putting his hands behind his head. 'Of course, we would be happy to oblige.' He flexed his biceps, obvious even under the suit jacket. Clearly a man who spent a substantial amount of time at the gym. Clearly a man who could easily over-power a woman. Or anyone, for that matter.

'Thank you so much. Your cooperation is very much appreciated,' Kate said, smiling as flirtatiously as she could without feeling sick. She knew as well as Steve did that he was legally required to provide the CCTV, but going through this song and dance massaged his ego enough to keep him happy.

'But it's going to take a bit of time to pull the tapes together. Not my area, you see.' Steve gave an apologetic grin and picked up a glass from the desk, taking a quick swig of the clear liquid. He winced and placed the glass back down. It said 'Mr' in big block letters on the side, and he caught her looking at it.

'Joke present from an ex-girlfriend. There's another one

that says "Mrs", for fuck's sake.' He grinned. 'That's why she's an ex.'

Kate forced a laugh. 'So who does look after the CCTV?'

'My money man. I'll give him a call, get him down here asap.' Steve pronounced 'asap' like it was a word, rather than an acronym. 'He'll drop it by the station tomorrow. And ask him about Gabriella, if you know what I'm saying.'

Kate nodded, understanding his meaning. 'And make sure you include all the cameras, all the footage from Saturday night and Sunday morning.'

'Of course,' Steve Morgan smiled, his white teeth glowing in the dim light in the office. 'You can trust me.'

Kate laughed, a flirty, tinkling giggle, but the truth was no, she didn't trust him. Who would?

She ushered Yates out of the door, keen to get as far away from Steve Morgan as possible. He walked them back to the mezzanine and pointed them towards the main entrance.

'Don't hesitate to call if you need anything else. And feel free to come by on a club night. Just make sure you're off duty,' he grinned. 'You'll have more fun that way.' Steve winked, then went back to the office.

'I don't know about you,' Yates whispered as they walked down the stairs, 'but I feel like I need a shower after talking to that guy.'

Kate smiled in agreement, then turned round. 'Just going to use the loo. Won't be a sec.'

She hurried back up the stairs, down the corridor and pushed the door open to the toilets. As she went, she made a mental note of all the CCTV cameras. One above the bar. One over the dance floor. And one above the office door, watching the corridor. She went into the toilets and sat down in a cubicle. She took in the graffiti, the ingrained dirt on the floor and, while she was washing her hands, the lipstick kisses on the mirror, obviously put there over the weekend by exuberant clientele. She wouldn't have been touching her lips to anything in this place, dirty mirrors or men alike.

Kate left the toilets and noticed the door to Steve's office was open. She could hear a one-way conversation going on inside, Steve talking in hushed tones, obviously on the phone. Kate glanced around, then listened.

'No, I don't know, why would I?' Steve was saying. 'Can you do it or not?' He paused, as the person on the other end spoke. 'It doesn't matter why, just do it, will you?' Kate could see him pacing across the small office, ducking backwards away from the door when he turned towards her,. His face was twisted in annoyance. 'She's trouble, you know she is. She was a pain in the ass when we first met her, she's been weird for the past few weeks and even more so on Saturday. You know as well as I do that we can't afford a PR nightmare right now. We need punters in the door. We don't want the shit associated with this girl bringing the club down.' He paused again, listening. 'For fuck's sake, Ryan. Just do it and stop being a whiny little pussy.'

Kate saw him end the call and she scuttled away, down the stairs to where Yates stood waiting on the empty dance floor. They hurried out of the club into the cold winter air, the bouncer still outside, smoking in the doorway. He watched them as they left.

Yates turned to Kate as they climbed back in the police car. 'Do you think we'll get that CCTV?' she asked.

'We bloody better,' Kate muttered. 'Or I'm going to arrest him for obstructing a police investigation.'

Kate put the car into gear and headed back to the station,

resolving to send the biggest, burliest uniformed copper back there first thing tomorrow morning if they didn't deliver. Police always made nightclub owners nervous, that was true, but Steve Morgan definitely had something to hide. Why the disagreement on the phone? It had seemed more than a simple request for some camera footage. Had Gabriella's association with the club led to her attack? It sounded like Heaven was struggling to make ends meet, and Kate knew that money made people do risky things. Illegal things.

She knew that CCTV was important. She just didn't know why. Yet.

5

Thea had cobwebs in her hair, dirt under her fingernails. She had started in the living room, moving furniture and belongings, checking everything inside and out. She scoured cupboards, looked on top of bookshelves; not a single nook or cranny went unexplored.

But yet, nothing. Years had passed, but she knew it had to be here. She didn't dare think that she might be wrong.

She stood up slowly, straightening out her back and wincing. She wrapped her arms around her, feeling the cold from the draughty house waft up through the floorboards, then slowly trudged up the wooden stairs to the master bedroom.

Thea stood in the doorway and shivered, looking at the four-poster bed in the middle of the room. The day was coming to an end; the light was fading and rain was peppering the window.

She felt rattled. The detective had shaken her, as much as she'd refused to show it, bringing back memories of being interviewed fifteen years ago, confused, worried and scared. But back then the police had been sympathetic. Kind to the teenagers who had lost their parents, and they hadn't pushed them hard.

Today had been different.

Her sister could be at death's door, but she felt numb. Before the argument last week, it had been nearly fifteen years since they'd last spoken. She knew her sister disapproved of her life, and in turn, she was condescending and patronising back. But being here, alone, she wondered how much she had actually known her sister. Were they really so dissimilar, even after all this time?

She walked into the bedroom, picking up the laptop left on the side and pressing it into life, then climbed under the duvet. With only the light from the screen, she sat in bed and typed into the search engine: *Gabriella Patterson*.

Within seconds the results popped up. A row of images headlined across the top, a few women she didn't recognise, obviously with the same name, then photos of the Gabriella Patterson she knew. A list of links and web pages came next, with profiles from social media and LinkedIn. She clicked on the images and took in the photos of someone looking just like her, the various looks she'd indulged in over the years. A particularly glamorous shot had Gabriella with a choppy white-blonde bob, stylish, harsh straight lines, worn with leather jeggings, high heels and a silky black top. She looked incredible, as if torn straight from the pages of a fashion magazine.

In each photo Gabriella was with a different man. Always powerful, always in classy suits and open collars, Gabriella draping off their arm. It wasn't a great way to live your life, she thought. Being paid to hang out with podgy pink-faced men.

For comparison, she opened up another window and started a new search: *Thea Patterson*. She was curious about how the world viewed them both – what trace their lives had left behind. A list of links in blue appeared on the screen, a few photos at the top. Thea's presence on social media was scarce – no Twitter or Instagram, and her Facebook page only included two photos. The best link took her to her personal website. Simple, it showed nothing more than her name and 'Photographer' on the front page. The background picture was an impressive black and white landscape, clouds billowing above with a shot of sunshine breaking through onto a single house, solitary in the middle of the countryside. Isolated, beautiful, alone.

Sighing, she discarded the laptop next to her. The introspection had made her restless, so she climbed out of bed to get some food, flicking light switches as she went to combat the dull winter gloom, running a hand over the closed doors. She paused with her fingers on the handle to their old bedroom, then opened it. The dust swirled, disturbed in the sudden gust of air.

As children, as twins, they had started out there: two tiny babies in the same cot, then two tiny cots next to each other. Two sets of everything – hats, coats, jumpers, dresses – their mother trying hard to keep them looking the same and enjoying the attention that came with it: her perfect identical daughters. But after a while it became apparent that these two little people had their own personalities, each diametrically opposite to the other. While Gabriella demanded the dresses, expressing her free will in a forceful way early on, Thea didn't care what she wore as long as it didn't stop her getting outside. Soon her mother realised that expensive frilly frocks weren't worth the bother for her tomboy daughter jumping gleefully into the nearest muddy puddle.

They would argue – about anything and everything – the fights turning physical in a second, ending as suddenly as they'd begun. But as much as they would argue, they couldn't stay apart for long: like magnets, they'd spring back into the other's vicinity without comment. Thea had never said sorry to her sister; it hadn't seemed necessary. It was as superfluous as apologising to yourself.

Eventually their parents couldn't bear the spats any longer and allocated them separate rooms in the hope of reducing the noise. But the separation didn't work. Come morning they would always be found curled up like puppies, in Gabriella's single bed.

It was funny how time had moved on, yet nothing had changed. She missed being in her sister's vicinity as keenly as if she were missing an arm. There was no doubt her twin was an integral part of her, and it had taken real effort to keep the distance between them all these years.

Resting her shoulder on the doorframe, she flicked the switch. The room was flung into light from the bare bulb, displaying the garish decoration of pinks and pastels, blue gloss skirting boards and glow-in-the-dark stars on the ceiling. It had been the same since she left all those years ago, her legacy abandoned in towers of brown boxes, inscribed with their contents in black marker pen.

She poked around in the piles. The top box was labelled *Gabriella – clothes* and she opened it. T-shirts were crumpled in with jeans and scarves and jumpers. A scrap of sequin in one corner caught her eye and she pulled at a strap, dragging it clear from the box. It was a long dress, a dress she remembered clearly from their school days. The American craze of school proms had reared its ugly head when they were eighteen. Thea had dismissed it from the beginning, but Gabriella had been surrounded by a continual throng of hormonally charged schoolboys, each hoping to be her date on the big night. Gabriella had dragged her decision out, as boxes of chocolates and bouquets of flowers arrived on their doorstep, finally choosing to go alone, with a decision that

even Thea admitted a grudging respect for. Harry had tried
to persuade Thea to go with him but she declined, preferring
to spend the night watching old Eighties movies.

And now, here was the dress. Their dad had raised an
eyebrow, but their mum had let Gabi wear it, saying that if
she looked like that, she would wear the dress all day long. It
was a tube of gold silk and sequins, barely held together by
a few strands across the back and over the shoulders. It was
full length and trailed along the ground, and she remembered
Gabi had worn a pair of gold teetering heels along with it.

She held it up in front of her, slightly creased, then, out
of curiosity, slipped out of her jeans, sweatshirt and bra and
pulled it over her head. She shook it down to the ground
and repositioned the straps, running her fingers through her
hair and fluffing it up a bit. She faced the mirror, turning
first one way, then the other.

Even she had to admit, the transformation was pretty incredible. There were a few more bumps and curves than they
had back then, but otherwise she fitted the dress perfectly.

'That's uncanny.'

She jumped at the voice behind her and turned to face
Harry, smart in his jacket and tie, scarf wrapped round his
neck.

'I remember that dress. She was quite something that
night. And here you are, looking exactly the same.'

She turned back to the mirror, impassively looking at her
reflection. Even with no make-up and translucent skin from
a winter under wraps, she looked every inch a movie star;
she could demand the attention from anyone in any room,
and all it took was a scrap of gold dress.

'What are you doing here?'

'Just finished work – I wanted to see how you were after

your run-in this morning.' He caught her eye in the mirror. 'Have you phoned any hospitals?'

'No, I got distracted.'

'I can see. Have you been trying on Gabriella's clothes all day?'

Suddenly she felt silly, standing in the cold, playing dress-up in clothes from their teenage years. She felt exposed in front of Harry, as if he had caught her standing there naked.

'Go and get some dinner downstairs and let me get changed.'

'And then we're making some phone calls.'

'Fine, just get out of my way.'

Harry turned and she could hear his heavy tread on the wooden stairs, then a tap running as he filled the kettle. Cheeks blazing, she pulled the gold dress off and tugged on her jeans and sweatshirt. 'Ridiculous,' she muttered to herself as she shut the door to the room firmly behind her, then stopped by the window in the hallway.

A large black saloon edged slowly up her driveway. She felt adrenaline flood her body and glanced down the stairs to where she could hear Harry rattling around in her kitchen. She looked back nervously. Under the canopy of the trees she saw the car door open and a man get out.

She saw a smart black coat and dark hair. She froze and in that moment he looked up, straight to the window. She couldn't breathe. She didn't dare move, her eyes locked on his. He nodded. A sudden knowing gesture, before he moved out of the protection of the trees and back to his car. The BMW reversed, then disappeared down the road, plunging the street into darkness.

She let out a long breath and pulled the curtains tight shut behind her. That was the second time she had seen him

– why was he following her? What did he want? Suddenly she appreciated the thick old walls of the house, the prison-like locks on the front door, the tall man downstairs, his presence unwittingly reassuring. Pushing down the unease, she quickly ran down to the light of the kitchen, never so pleased to see Harry in her life.

6

Harry had a permanent crouch in this house, an automatic stoop adopted as a necessity after years of banging his head on low doorframes. At six foot two he had the same problem in most places, but he had learnt it first growing up around here. Downstairs, he took off his scarf, draping it over his coat, left by Thea earlier on the newel post at the bottom of the stairs along with her others, stacked on top of each other. Harry stopped for a moment, looking at the purple velvet coat that used to belong to Thea's mum, remembering his dad's old faded green army jacket that would accompany it. He sighed, and went to the kitchen to work out what meagre pickings he could find for dinner.

As usual, the fridge was pretty much empty. He cobbled together what he could, and cooked scrambled eggs, delaying making any phone calls about Gabriella. All day at work he'd been troubled, drifting off mid-conversation with clients, absent-mindedly tapping his pen when he should have been answering emails. Should he go and visit her? Would she want him to? Something pulled him to her, and he knew there was no way he could ignore it.

He and Thea ate dinner in near silence, but as Thea tidied up the plates, he couldn't put it off any longer. There were four hospitals in their area – two NHS and two private. Harry went for NHS first, finding the right one on the second call.

'Thank you, and when are the visiting hours?' He looked at Thea, who raised her eyebrows in response. 'We're family. Yes, thank you.' He put his mobile down. 'Until eight.' He looked up at the clock, then back at Thea. 'Come on, we're going.'

He expected Thea to resist, and a small part of him wanted her to; for her to be the excuse he needed to stay away. But she sighed, and closed the dishwasher with finality.

'Let's go,' she said.

They found the hospital easily, parking Harry's car in the stuffed multi-storey, then following signs to the intensive care unit. Along a long corridor, up in a large cranky lift, then more walking until they came to an automatic door, locked with an intercom on the outside.

Harry pressed the button and pushed Thea forward.

'Thea Patterson to see Gabriella Patterson?' she said.

A loud buzz and the doors opened, releasing an oppressive, fuggy air.

The nurse at the desk looked at them both over the top of her glasses. 'Are you family?'

'Yes, I'm her sister,' she said.

'Well, obviously *you* are. But what about you?' she said, gruffly. It was late, and the nurse had obviously had enough for the day.

'I'm her brother,' Harry said instinctively, and Thea looked up quickly. The nurse indicated for them to follow her down the corridor. Closed doors to darkened rooms lined the sides, and they were shown to the last on the right.

'Has she had any visitors?' Thea asked.

'No one, no,' the nurse said pointedly, gesturing to the bed next to the window. From the door Harry could only make out the bumps under the blue blanket where Gabriella's feet were. He felt uncharacteristically mute; the smell of the hospital brought back memories of his mother: hushed conversations, sitting numb in a corridor, his father crying in the room next door.

'How is she?' Thea asked tentatively as they approached.

'I'll ask the doctor to come and see you,' the nurse sniffed and walked off, leaving them at the bedside.

Gabriella's body was closely tucked into the bed, her arms by her sides. She had a white bandage round her head and two of her fingers were strapped together. A tube protruded out of her mouth, a smaller one in her nose. An army of machines surrounded the bed.

Thea reached down to touch her, then pulled away quickly, putting her hands behind her back.

'It's odd seeing her so quiet,' Harry whispered. He stayed at a distance, unsure what to do. Seeing the twins together was always surreal, their indistinguishable features blurring the two women into one. Even given the different ways Harry felt about them, he was still hard pressed to tell them apart.

'Miss Patterson?' A voice came from behind and Harry turned, coming face to face with a slim, grey-haired man in a white coat. 'I'm Doctor Riley – I believe you would like an update on Gabriella's condition?'

Thea nodded and the doctor continued. 'As you know, she was found suffering from severe hypothermia and a traumatic injury to the back of her head. Plus a few knocks and bruises to her hands and arms. Our first priority was to assess the damage to her brain, then get her warm again.' He paused and looked up from the chart. He glanced at

Gabriella in the bed, then back to Thea. 'You do look very alike.'

'And her head?' Thea asked, keen to get the doctor moving again.

'She received a heavy blow to the back of her skull, about here,' he said, pointing to his own head, equidistant between his large ears. 'Her CT scan shows a traumatic subdural haemorrhage – bleeding on the brain – in a part called the cerebellum, controlling coordination and balance.'

'And what does this mean for her?' Harry asked.

'We currently have her under sedation while her brain stabilises. And,' he said quickly, anticipating the question, 'we won't know what impact the injury has until we start trying to wake her up. We don't know if she will be the Gabriella you knew before. Hypothermia is neuro-protective, so we are hoping it worked in our favour and limited the secondary damage to her brain. It's not getting any worse,' he added.

The room was silent apart from the repetitive beeping of her heart rate. The doctor glanced at his watch, then hung Gabriella's chart back at the end of the bed.

'We'll keep you informed if things change,' he said. 'From this point, we have to keep an eye on her. It's good you're here now.' He smiled at Thea with a fatherly air as he was called away, leaving them alone.

Harry looked around the room. It was a lonely and feature-less place to be. The overheating made Harry feel suffocated; he pulled his coat off and fidgeted from foot to foot.

'Why has no one been in to see her?' Thea asked, staring at her sister. 'I thought …' She hesitated. 'I thought Gabriella had friends.' Thea moved closer to her sister, and looked at the bandage wrapped round her head. 'When did you see her last?'

41

'Fifteen years ago, after the funeral,' Harry lied, then glanced at Thea, feeling instantly guilty. She was looking at Gabi, paying him little attention. She seemed uncomfortable and on edge, desperate to get away from the hospital ward. 'Who do you think did it?' he asked and she shrugged in response, putting a finger in her mouth and chewing on the edge of a nail.

Harry looked at the woman in the bed. They had grown up together; he'd lived next door and spent practically every waking moment of his life in their house, but early on it had mostly been Thea he'd hung around with. The absence of Gabriella from their childhood games hadn't even registered until one day he'd noticed her, almost for the first time.

He'd been eleven and the summer had been relentless. Panting and hot, Harry and Thea had balanced on the last branch of the massive oak at the end of the garden, both of them knowing the way to the top like any well-trodden staircase.

On the uppermost point of the trunk was an old bird box, wooden and worn, discarded by the occupants and the aim of their climbs. Thea had reached in and pulled out a plastic Ziploc bag. She'd opened it and tapped his arm, offering him a strip of strawberry licorice. Red and gaudy, it had a few bits of grass stuck to the end. She'd smiled and put the other piece in her mouth, chewing contentedly. He'd done the same and enjoyed the sudden sweetness, temporarily quenching his thirst.

'I'm sorry about your mum,' Thea had said, looking at him from the corner of her eye.

Harry remembered that summer, when his mum died. He remembered life tilting; not because she had gone – the truth was she hadn't been around for years, not as a mother as such – but because it was the start of his brain feeling slightly off. It buzzed constantly, conjuring up thoughts from nowhere, images he didn't want to see, feelings that made him jittery.

But as they'd sat up in the branches of that tall oak, fingers sticky and arms burning in the sun, Harry spotted Gabriella in the garden. She'd been wearing a light blue dress, her long hair braided into a complex French plait.

Thea had waved and Gabriella had looked up at them, smiling. Harry had taken a deep breath in. Somehow, even with everything that was going on, a smile from Gabriella was the only thing he needed. And it had been the only thing ever since.

'Come on,' Thea said, decisively. 'Let's go home. We know where she is, and neither of us will help her by sitting here.'

Harry nodded, following Thea. He felt an ache in the back of his throat, emotions threatening to spill into tears. Despite the distance, despite their problems, he'd always believed he'd be with Gabriella again. But now, Harry wondered, had he screwed up his last chance?

As he walked quickly away, Harry looked back to Gabi's bedside. In that moment, he would have given anything for Gabi to wake up. For him to see that smile again.

7

Kate looked up from the grainy CCTV footage and rubbed her eyes. She glanced around the office – she was the only one there, having told Yates and Briggs to go home hours earlier. Kate had wanted to stay to finish going through the extra CCTV Briggs had found, but there were hours and hours of it. Hours and hours of cheerful partygoers, drinking, smoking, a bit of illegal drug activity, some borderline pornography in darkened alleyways, but as yet no Gabriella Patterson, apart from the brief shots they had found before. Kate was beginning to wonder whether she was there at all.

They hadn't made much headway. The picture this investigation was painting of Gabriella Patterson wasn't flattering, and there was no shortage of potential suspects who crisscrossed her life, but no motives, no evidence. Along with a number of eligible bachelors Gabriella had been hanging off the arm of, there was Thea Patterson, the estranged sister, an oddball at best, but no suggestion of why she would attack her. She had received the usual call from the hospital to confirm visitors and Thea Patterson and 'brother' had made an appearance. She had done a quick search on births and deaths – they had no brother, and Kate wondered who was accompanying Thea to the hospital. She assumed he was the mysterious man who had waited for her outside the police station.

Suddenly a small figure on the tape grabbed her attention. Kate stared at the screen, then sat back in disappointment. This girl was wearing a long dark coat and boots, not the same outfit as Gabriella Patterson, not her at all.

She paused the video and rubbed her eyes. She was so tired; she couldn't concentrate any more. It was time to go. Not that there was anything to go home to.

Kate drove through the darkened streets of her neighbourhood, paying little attention to the cars around her. Once inside the house, she hung her coat on the rack and flicked her shoes towards the pile in the hallway. The automatic light had already come on in the living room; she hated coming home to a dark unwelcoming house. Dark houses shouted out 'scary person lurks here' or, more depressing and accurate, 'no one lurks here'.

Kate reached into the fridge, pulled out the bottle of white in the door and opened it, pouring a large glass. Apart from wine, there wasn't much else on offer except for the crusts of a loaf of bread and a small piece of slightly green cheddar. She cut the ends off the cheese and made a fairly respectable toastie, served with a large dab of tomato ketchup. Dinner of champions, she thought to herself grimly, and carried it through to the living room along with the glass and the bottle.

She'd lived here for nearly a year now, but in that time she'd put no effort into making the small rented house her own; it still carried the marks on the paintwork and grooves in the carpet from the last occupant. Kate told herself it didn't matter, she was hardly ever here; but the truth was she hadn't thought she would be here for long. The separation was temporary; she'd be back home soon, her proper home. Ignoring the lack of contact from him, the blocked Facebook and the short, resentful texts. Ignoring the fact she'd made no effort to change.

She ate on the sofa, the television playing out the ten o'clock news in the background, wine glass not far from her hand. She thought about Gabriella, about the club, thinking back to the last time she had been out for an evening. To a nightclub, or pub, or restaurant, or anywhere. She remembered a pretty dire hen night about two years ago – that involved some cheesy nightclub, didn't it? It certainly involved deeley-boppers and a large amount of alcohol to get through the forced fun. Dinner with friends a while back, and a Sunday lunch in a pub garden. That was a few months ago, too – Kate remembered sitting outside in the sunshine, rosé in hand, swatting away wasps. Was her life this depressing? What the hell had she been doing? She knew the answer – working. Just working.

But she loved her job. She'd always wanted to be in the police force, but for less prosaic reasons than to help people. And it wasn't about putting something back into the community – in her experience most of the community weren't fans of the police.

Above all else, it was because she hated injustice and bullying. From an early age she had wanted the world to be fair, for people to be accountable for their actions. It pissed her off when people did bad things to each other, especially in cases like Gabriella's, where it niggled in her mind until she found the solution. She didn't like the lack of headway they'd made since Sunday. There was nothing worse than an unsolved crime.

Kate made a mental note to text a few friends, but deep

down she knew this case was going to take over, like they always did, and render any arrangements void. Kate put her empty plate to the side and reached for her laptop, muting the television. She poured another glass of wine and loaded up a new CCTV file, watching a few minutes of footage: random people walking down London Road, mostly in groups, a couple of lone men. She squinted at the screen – was that her? Sure enough, the tiny figure of Gabriella Patterson was wobbling across the pavement and Kate sat up in her seat, clapping her hands together at the little bit of success. Arms wrapped around her chest, head down against the wind, Gabriella made Kate feel cold just looking at her. She was clearly the worse for wear, her legs unsteady as she made her way across the screen. Kate looked at the people around Gabi. A few gave her a long stare, a couple of men clearly flung a few remarks across the road, but nobody came close.

Kate hated to admit it, but she'd drawn parallels between her life and Gabriella's. Sure, she had a career and would rather do anything than accept a handout from a man, but she had sensed the loneliness in Gabriella's life. No one, except Thea and this 'brother', had visited her at the hospital. She had arrived at the club alone; she had left alone. Kate had often wondered: if anything happened to me, how long would it be until anyone noticed?

Depressed, Kate looked back at the CCTV and watched Gabriella totter off screen before pausing it with a sigh. She swallowed the last glug of wine, resisting the urge to open another bottle, and hauled herself up the stairs to bed; she would pick up where she left off in the morning. She shut the lights off as she went, completely unaware that on the laptop someone else had just sneaked into shot. Someone clearly interested in following Gabi, staring as she walked down the road.

Gabriella Patterson was no longer alone.

8

Rain merged with sweat as he ran. Harry's feet hit the concrete hard, step after step, his arms pumping, his breathing heavy. He ran through puddles, his feet wet and his clothes soaked, but he didn't care. The cold air bit at the back of his throat.

He'd woken on the sofa early, his mouth parched, jerked from sleep by a nightmare. He lay in the dark, his back aching from the uncomfortable position, remembering the faces, the open eyes, the explosion. The same thing, always. As he stuck his head under the kitchen tap, he saw the empty beer bottles lined up on the table, and couldn't remember falling asleep. But now he was awake again, his brain hummed with the same thoughts that had stopped him from going to bed in the first place. The best way, the only way, to get rid of them was to outrun them, pushing the physical to the limit so the mental conceded the battle.

So he ran. He threw his shorts and trainers on, and pulled open the door. He ignored the pouring rain and ran in the darkness, a few streetlights showing him the way across pavements and roads, barely any cars at this time of night. He pushed his body faster, exceeding eight- then seven-minute miles.

Seeing Thea in the gold dress today. *That* dress. The last time he had seen it, it had been Gabi wearing it. *That* night. Smiling and beautiful after the prom ... He'd been lying in bed in the early hours, listening, when he'd heard the car draw up outside the house next door. He hadn't wanted to go to the prom if he couldn't go with Thea, and of Gabi he'd not dared ask. He climbed out, his father asleep, and padded to the window in bare feet, watching Gabi return. Her hair was messy, her dress crumpled, her shoes in her hand. He'd watched as she'd stumbled up to her front door.

He'd walked down the stairs quietly, pushed trainers on his feet and gone out the back door, shoving through the hedge into the twins' garden, as he'd done a million times before. He saw her sat on the concrete steps outside her kitchen, rummaging in the bag on her lap.

'Did you have a good night?' he'd whispered from the garden, and she'd jumped.

'You surprised me!' Gabi had slurred, patting a space next to her on the step. 'Come join me, my Harry.'

He'd sat next to her, wrapping his arms round his legs, dressed only in a T-shirt and boxer shorts, suddenly aware of his lack of clothing. Gabi found what she was looking for in her bag, and put the cigarette in her mouth, lighting it with practised ease.

She had a drag, then offered it to him. He took the cigarette and drew a breath in, letting out a long plume of smoke. In the garden an owl hooted, and the wind rustled the leaves around them. He handed it back to her.

'They're all such children,' Gabi said.

'Who?' Harry asked.

'The boys in my year, such kids,' she gestured wildly with the cigarette. 'They try it on with me, all fucking bravado and swagger. They don't have a clue.'

Harry fought back the jealousy building in his chest. 'Did you ... Did they ...?'

She looked at him, and for a moment he felt lost in her stare, her eyes dark in the glow from the moon. Then she laughed. 'Fuck, no. Not with them. I want more than them.'

He hesitated. 'What do you want?'

'I want this … and this …' She prodded Harry in the chest, and ran her finger down the stubble on his jawline. He'd only been eighteen, but he knew he was bigger than he used to be; he had muscles where before he'd been scrawny and thin. She paused, her finger resting on his arm, the cigarette burning down to the filter in her other hand.

In that moment, Harry stopped wondering why he was always thinking about her. He stopped trying to analyse whether he should or shouldn't, and leaned forward and kissed her.

She responded at first, kissing him back, and he'd been lost in the feel of her lips, her tongue, the taste of the cigarette and sweetness of the last alcopop she'd drunk. Then she pulled away. She looked at him, her eyes wide, her two fingers touching her mouth, as if reflecting on what had just happened, then she stood up and ran into the house. He heard her feet on the stairs, and the slam of her bedroom door.

He stayed outside for a moment longer, looking out into the darkness of the garden. He knew even then she would always be a constant in his life. But, of course, the next day all hell broke loose. Everything happened, their family was blown apart and their simple lives changed forever.

Harry ran, pushing the memory down. His legs burned, his lungs struggling to take in enough oxygen. He didn't want this, not now. He'd been doing fine without her, thank you very much.

Harry stopped at the corner of the road, outside his flat, his chest heaving. He rested his hands on his knees and took in great gulps of air, regretting all the cigarettes he'd smoked since that day. The rain continued to fall, freezing on his hair, running down his neck. His hands and feet were numb, his muscles screaming.

He stood up and walked back up to his flat. He opened his front door and stood in the hallway, dripping onto the carpet. On the wall, next to the pile of his shoes was a large pinboard, scattered with bills to pay, notes to remember, but also bright postcards from far-flung locations. She'd sent him them from Thailand, from Australia, from all over the United States. She'd call, too – sometimes late at night, forgetting the time difference, sometimes drunk, sometimes sleepy and sober. Always from random, differing numbers. She'd tell him what she was up to. She would always say the same thing: that she missed him, but she wasn't coming back. No matter how many times he apologised.

He'd watched Gabi slowly move closer to home – from Egypt, to Greece, to Paris. And then, there she'd been, in Bournemouth, while he was away on a work trip. The last time he'd seen her, until now.

There had been other women, of course. All through his twenties he'd met women, slept with women; nice women, but nothing about them ever stuck. Something always stopped him getting too close. It was hard to form a con-nection with someone new when your heart belonged to the girl that had known you all your life.

And now she was back, and had been for a while. She'd been home but she hadn't got in touch. Not one call, not one visit. He felt the rejection like a blow, almost physically winding him every time he thought about it. She had made it clear what she thought about him now.

He needed to forget about Gabi. Perhaps this was what he needed to end his obsession for good. But something in Harry knew: this wasn't it. This wasn't how their story would end.

Tuesday

9

She could hear the rain pounding her window, the wind whipping around the house. It was dark, and Kate pushed herself up on her pillow to get a glimpse of the clock – 5.38 a.m., twenty minutes before it was due to wake her up. She felt rough: her stomach acidic and her hands shaky. That damn wine, she thought.

She raised herself up out of the warmth of her duvet and wrapped her arms around herself. It was too sodding cold and too sodding wet; she was almost tempted to go back to bed and sod them all. But she had work to do and a case to solve. The sooner she could work out what had happened to Gabriella Patterson, the sooner she could get some sleep. And a social life. Hey, maybe even a boyfriend.

Showered and dressed, she headed to the police station, her route taking her past the hospital. She hesitated, then indicated left and pulled down the side roads. They hadn't been able to track down the doctor yesterday, and it was starting to get on Kate's nerves. They needed to know more about what had happened to Gabriella.

She showed her identification as she arrived, the nurse on duty greeting her with a welcoming smile.

'Is Doctor Riley around?' Kate asked as nicely as she

could, which, given the time in the morning and the fact she hadn't yet had a coffee, wasn't very.

'I'll page him,' the nurse said.

Kate loitered round the reception desk, absent-mindedly tapping on her phone.

'How can I help?'

'Doctor Riley?' The man nodded and Kate held out her hand. 'DS Kate Munro.'

'I've been expecting you. Sorry I haven't returned your calls; it's been a manic few days.' Doctor Riley was tall and slim with thinning grey hair and long fingers. He looked tired but moved with a bright spring in his step, energetic and wiry. Kate would have put his age anywhere between forty-five and sixty – it was that hard to tell. He gestured to the small office next to the reception desk and closed the door behind them.

She got out her notebook, pen poised. 'What more can you tell me about Gabriella's injuries?' she asked.

The doctor got straight to the point. 'As you already know, Gabriella sustained serious head trauma when she was hit on Saturday night. She was knocked unconscious and suffered severe hypothermia.' He glanced at the chart in his hand. 'Now we've had a chance to properly examine her, as well as the head injuries she has a large amount of bruising on the outside of her right forearm and wrist, as well as a fractured proximal and middle phalanx on both her right ring finger and little finger.' He pointed to the middle and top of his fingers. 'Here.'

'Caused by?' Kate asked.

'That's not for me to say.'

'But if you were pushed?'

The doctor smiled. 'Don't quote me on this, but in my

experience you only get injuries like those when someone's put up a bit of a fight.' He lifted his left hand and mimed a strike down on Kate's head. Slowly, she put up her right hand to defend herself.

'Defensive injuries. Consistent with her attacker being left-handed?' Kate asked.

The doctor nodded. 'In my opinion.'

'Was there any evidence of sexual assault?'

'We did an Early Evidence Kit and full work-up as soon as you obtained consent from the sister. Your SOCO took that away yesterday with her clothes, but was she sexually assaulted? Can't say.' Kate went to say something and he stopped her. 'Even if I was pushed.' He smiled apologetically. 'These things are impossible to distinguish from medical evidence alone – there was nothing I could find that would indicate it one way or another.' His bleeper went off at his waist and Doctor Riley pulled it off to look at it. 'Sorry, I'm going to have to go. Duty calls.'

'How's she doing now?'

He paused, one hand on the door. 'Better. We're gradually reducing the sedation and hoping she'll respond positively. Time will tell,' he said cryptically, and rushed out, back into the hubbub of the main hospital.

Kate went to leave, then paused, looking down the corridor towards the room where she knew Gabriella lay. Kate herself had never been to visit, and she was curious about the girl she had seen in the photographs.

Visiting time hadn't yet kicked in, so she was surprised to see a hunched figure by the bedside.

'Can I help you?' she said. He turned and stood up, towering above her, dressed in a smart shirt and tie, the blue bringing out the sparkle in his eyes. He held out his hand and smiled.

'Harry Becker,' he said.

'Detective Sergeant Kate Munro,' she replied, shaking his hand and matching his firm grip. His name triggered a moment of recognition somewhere in her brain, but she couldn't think where from. She'd certainly never seen him before. She would have remembered that.

'You must be the copper Thea was telling me about.'

'Must I?'

'Confident, woman in charge, working on Gabriella's case, otherwise why would you be here?' He paused. 'Pretty. That's how Thea described you.' He looked at her closely. 'Sounds about right.'

Kate was caught off guard. She could feel her face becoming red, and she pulled at the collar of her shirt. 'If you say so,' she said gruffly, and turned away to look at Gabriella. 'The doctor said she was doing better?'

'Apparently so. Not that you can tell. The nurse said they want to take her for a scan today and have another look.'

'Right. And how did you get in this morning before visiting hours?'

Harry smiled again – a disarming grin that Kate could see would make women go weak at the knees. Not her though, no – certainly not her. 'I'm family. Nurses thought it would be okay to make an exception.'

'Except you're not, are you?'

He looked away and sat back down on the chair next to Gabriella. 'As good as,' he said, and turned away from Kate, dismissing her.

Kate frowned at his back. She looked at the bed where Gabriella lay mute, then marched away down the corridor.

At the end, she glanced back: Harry had turned and was watching her through the doorway. He waved, a sarcastic flick of the fingers, and she scowled in response.

'Arrogant prick,' she muttered to herself as she rushed back to the car park, her cheeks red and back sweaty.

She drove to the police station in a shitty mood, made worse by forgetting to pick up a coffee on the way out of the hospital, distracted by bloody Harry whatever his name was. She had encountered enough overconfident men in her time and was annoyed with herself for letting this one get to her.

Yates and Briggs regarded her cautiously as she threw her coat and bag down at her desk.

'Good night?' Briggs asked.

'Just been to the hospital. I managed to see the doc.'

Kate started writing on the whiteboard, listing the injuries Gabriella had sustained. *Head injury/brain damage, bruising to right arm/wrist/fractured fingers. Caused by left-handed attacker?*

Briggs watched her as she wrote. 'The nurses phoned this morning, said the brother was there again – did you see him?'

'Yes, I met him, supercilious bastard. And stop calling him the brother. They're not related.'

Briggs stood next to her in front of the board, running his finger across the wide blank space where the list of suspects should have been. The big white void made Kate feel shit. Day three and nothing concrete – it was crappy progress, by anyone's standards.

'So who is he then?' Briggs asked.

'Harry something. Began with B. Why don't you find out?' Kate barked, and then regretted it. 'Thanks, Jamie,' she added, more gently.

Briggs slouched down at the computer and typed for a bit, clicking round articles and photos as Kate watched. 'There,' she said, pointing at the screen. 'That's him.'

'Harry Becker,' Briggs read out. 'Son of Harrison Becker, currently in prison serving life for double homicide. Whoa!' He looked up at Kate. 'Did you know this?'

So that was where she recognised his name. She nodded. 'It was a massive case about fifteen years ago.'

'Do we think it's linked to our attack?' Briggs asked. He leaned closer to the screen, studying Harry's face. 'Pretty hot, if you like that sort of thing,' he said.

Yates looked up for the first time that morning and Briggs pointed to the computer. 'Hmm, not my type, too good-looking.'

'Too good-looking? Is there such a thing?' Briggs asked.

'Oh yes,' Yates and Kate replied simultaneously. 'Especially if he knows it, like this guy,' Kate added.

'Pity,' Briggs muttered. 'Perhaps I'll have him then.'

Kate looked at the blank board and thought about the list of possibles, growing by the day. Thea Patterson, Steve Morgan and now Harry Becker. They needed to do something to actually stick some evidence and motives next to these people, she thought, rather than working off speculation.

'Jamie, could you take a look at the rest of the CCTV from the street?' she asked, suddenly remembering her viewing the night before, distracted by everything that had happened at the hospital. She pulled her laptop out of her bag and typed in her password; Briggs took the computer and settled down to look.

Kate heard the phone ring and watched as Yates answered

it. She spoke for a moment, then waved the handset in Kate's direction.

'Front desk,' she called. 'A guy called Ryan Holmes is here to see you. Says he has the CCTV from the club.'

Kate raised her eyebrows. 'Tell them to put him in an interview room,' she said, eager to make the most of the opportunity. 'Let's have a little chat with Mr Holmes.'

After meeting Steve Morgan, Ryan Holmes wasn't at all what Kate had expected. He was dressed casually in jeans, trainers and a creased shirt. He pushed his glasses up on his nose as Kate and Yates came into the interview room, then stood up and offered his hand. They made their introductions and sat down opposite him.

'I'm a little surprised to be in here,' he said. He was well spoken; he matched their eye contact without hesitation.

'How well did you know Gabriella Patterson?' Kate asked.

He took a deep breath in. 'We were dating,' he said.

Yates nodded. 'We heard,' she said, and Ryan looked surprised. 'Your boss mentioned it,' she added.

'My boss? You mean Steve?' Ryan chuckled. 'He's not my boss. We own Heaven together. Equal partners.'

'And how long had you been with Gabriella?' Kate asked, keen to get back to the topic.

'Not long, about two weeks?' He took off his glasses, wiping them on his shirtsleeve. 'I've known her since she worked at the club, but it's only been the past fortnight that anything happened.'

'Tell us about her,' Kate asked, curious. There wasn't much Kate had heard about Gabriella that sounded like girlfriend material. 'What's she like? As a person? Paint us a picture.'

Ryan Holmes frowned and pushed his glasses back up

his nose. 'Gabriella's a bit of a free spirit. When she first started working for us, she was hard to get to know. She was carefree, chatty, but you always got the feeling she was playing a game. Showing the side of her she wanted you to see, nothing else. I'd see her around at the club, having fun with various guys, and I liked her, but I prefer relationships a little more, I don't know, straightforward.' He smiled. 'The party girls, well, they're more Steve's type.' He stopped and Kate waited, holding the silence to encourage him to carry on.

'So what changed?' Yates asked, when he wasn't forthcoming.

'I don't know. A few weeks ago she showed up and she seemed quieter, more introspective.' Ryan Holmes carried on, his voice considered. 'She was just...' He shrugged. 'Nicer. We had a proper conversation. We got on. I looked forward to seeing her again.'

'You slept with her?' Kate said.

Ryan's face hardened at the personal question. 'Yes,' he replied, after a pause.

'On Saturday night?'

'No. The week before.'

'Do you think you were the only person she was seeing?' Kate asked.

Ryan shook his head. 'I'm not so stupid as to think she didn't have other men around. In fact I know she did. One confronted me about her. Dark, brooding type. Said he was her husband.'

Yates started next to her and Kate gave her a look.

'What happened?'

'Not much. He came up to me outside the club, while Gabriella was still inside. Asked who I was, what I was doing with her. I told him to back off, then Frank – the bouncer – came over and that was it. Guess he wasn't up for a fight about it. Haven't seen him since.'

'And when was this?'

'About a week ago? You can probably find it on the CCTV – I've included about a week's worth for you.' He patted the package in front of him on the desk.

Kate looked to her left and saw Yates write *HUSBAND???* in big black letters on the notepad in front of her. 'So what happened Saturday night?'

'I was at the club, with Gabriella. We hung out for a bit, but then I started to feel a bit rough so I went to lie down in the office. Must have eaten something funny because next thing I know it's morning and I've spent the night on the sofa.' He looked at his hands and two red spots appeared on his cheeks.

'That's it? You just hung out a bit?' Kate said, echoing his words.

'Yes.'

'Can anyone corroborate your story? Is it on CCTV?'

'No, sorry,' he said, quickly. 'But Steve saw me, he could probably tell you.'

'And Steve? Where was he?'

'As far as I know, at the club.' Ryan looked at his watch. 'Can I go now? I've got a busy day and I wasn't expecting to get dragged into an interview room.' He got up from his chair abruptly and waited for Kate to respond.

Kate smiled and stood up. 'Yes, thank you Mr Holmes, you've been very helpful.'

'Ryan, please.' Kate shook his hand again. It was slightly sweaty.

★

Kate and Yates watched him go down the corridor, escorted out by a uniform. She weighed up the brown envelope in her hand, then opened it and peered inside. There must have been more than fifteen DVDs in there, all unlabelled, all probably containing hours of CCTV footage from the club.

'That's going to keep us busy,' Yates muttered, looking at it.

'That, and finding this elusive husband,' Kate said, shaking her head. 'How the hell did we miss that?'

'He can't have been happy his wife was having an affair.'

'No. Not at all, I would imagine. But angry enough to bash her over the head?'

'If my husband had an affair, I'd kill him,' Yates said, darkly, turning to walk back to the ops room. Kate followed her.

Plenty of people would, she thought. Plenty of people had. Jealousy and anger were a dangerous mix, and she knew many husbands attacked their wives for a lot less than sleeping around.

But had this one? And, more to the point, who the hell was he?

Thea wrestled with her duvet, twisting over to her back and staring at the ceiling in frustration. The hands on the clock pointed to the left; it was late, quarter to ten in the morning, but she felt like she hadn't had a moment of sleep.

She thought about her sister, lying in the hospital. She thought about the machines, the doctors keeping her alive. What if she died? What then? She wasn't sure she had the strength to bury another member of her family. And what if she did wake up? What if she had brain damage and she wasn't the same person she had been before? Her head whirred with the possibilities and questions, none of which she could answer. She felt guilty for forcing them to be apart all these years; she should have looked after her, she was her *twin*. Nothing should have been more important than that. Nothing, except... except...

With a cry of annoyance, she climbed out of bed, pulling her woollen cardigan over her pyjamas and stumbling down the stairs. She clicked the kettle on and put a tea bag into her mug, contemplating breakfast while her eyes itched and her body tried to persuade her to go back to bed.

Around her she could feel the house spring into life as the heating woke the walls and resurrected old smells. It had a life of its own, this house; she hated it and loved it at the same time.

She hated the cold and the draughts; she hated the gates

that banged on their hinges, the cupboard doors that fell off, the window frames where the wind rushed through. She hated the history that permeated its bones; the memories that assaulted her when she least expected it.

But she had loved it once. It was family; it was a part of her childhood. The front door creaked as it opened, releasing the smell of old wood and varnish as you went inside. The worn rugs, the bare floorboards, the beams across the low ceilings. She smiled at the memory of the secret cupboards and passageways, once an adventure playground for the twins and Harry.

This was a house of browns and blacks, dirty white and faded colours. It was a house of smashed glass and betrayal, of withheld emotion and false smiles. It was the house where she grew up and where, incomprehensibly, she was now stuck.

Three heavy knocks pulled her out of her reminiscing. She put her mug down and listened. The knocks came again, three large thuds. It wasn't Harry – he was at work, and besides, he had a key. Was it the police again? Had they worked out her lie?

She moved quietly from the kitchen, through the corridor to the front door. She peered silently out of the peephole, then reeled back. The man from yesterday was standing there: black suit, black coat, black hair. She bit her lip, trying to decide what to do.

The door was her protection. Let him in, and who knew what would happen. But leave him out there and he'd never go away. He would continue to follow her, making her constantly nervous as to what he wanted. After all, calling the police wasn't an option; the last thing she needed was more detectives sniffing around.

'Open the door,' he said, muffled through the thick oak. 'I know you're in there, Gabriella. Open the door.'

She glanced in the mirror and a meek, scruffy-haired girl looked back. She made a decision, pulled the bolts across and opened the door, squaring herself up to the man.

'I'm not Gabriella,' she said. 'I'm Thea.'

He looked at her calmly, towering over her. Light hazel eyes sat deeply below dark eyebrows, the collar of his coat pulled up to his chin.

'Don't mess with me, Gabriella, I know who you are.' He sighed. 'I haven't got the patience for this today.' He had a strong American accent, elongating vowels into a drawl.

'I'm not Gabriella, I'm her twin sister, Thea.'

'Really? This is what we're going with? You've been hiding from me for over a fortnight and this is the game you're playing?' He placed one hand squarely on the wood of the door and pushed it open. She stepped back into the hallway.

'Look at me, do I look like Gabriella?' she said, her chin jutting forward, determined.

He looked her up and down.

'You look a mess, but yes, you look like Gabriella.'

'We're identical twins. If you know her so well, she must have mentioned me.' Thea stood in front of him, all eight stone, five foot of her, compared to the six foot of him. He was slim, not stocky or muscular, but he would have overpowered her easily. He looked again. She was wearing her dirty cardigan, pyjamas and slippers, her black bobbed hair greasy and pushed back behind her ears.

He hesitated. 'If you're Thea,' he said, 'where's Gabriella?'

She could feel her heart beating, the blood rushing in her veins; doing all she could to keep her voice steady. She didn't like him being here, she wanted him to go as quickly as possible. 'She's in hospital,' she replied. 'She was attacked.'

All the wind seemed to go out of the man, and he sagged into the doorframe. 'Attacked? How, when? Is she okay?'

Thea let him into the house, and he staggered towards the living room. He collapsed onto one of the sofas, looking up at her, all his bravado gone. 'Is she okay?' he said again.

She sat down on the chair next to him. 'How do you know her?' she asked.

'She's my wife.'

Thea forced a laugh. 'And you didn't realise you were following the wrong twin? How long have you been married?'

'Three months. Has Gabriella never mentioned me?'

'We don't talk.'

'How is she, please?' He slumped back on the chair and sank into his coat, like a snail retreating into its shell.

'She's in a coma. She has some bleeding on her brain but they're waiting to see how she recovers. I'm surprised the police haven't spoken to you.'

'When was she attacked?'

'Early hours of Sunday morning. She'd been out at a club.'

He nodded. 'Take me to see her.' She hesitated. As if reading her mind, he said: 'Take me to see her and I'll leave you alone.'

She sighed. 'Let me get dressed. Stay there.' She went to go upstairs, then turned back and looked at him. 'What's your name?'

'Mortimer. Mortimer Breslin.'

Upstairs, Thea pulled a jumper and jeans on and dragged

a comb through her hair. She went back downstairs again, slowly, and paused at the bottom, composing herself.

Then she put her coat on, picking up her car keys from the table by the front door.

'Let's go,' she said, at last. 'I'll take you to the hospital.'

II

'There. You see there?' Briggs jabbed at the screen with his slim finger, leaving a greasy mark.

'Rewind it.'

Briggs pressed the button and everyone moved in reverse, before starting up again. It was the footage from the street CCTV, grainy black and white and hard to make anyone out, let alone one individual face.

'Can you see him now?'

'Just about,' Kate replied, squinting at the screen. Sure enough, a tall figure followed the tiny shape of Gabriella. 'Have we got a better shot?'

'I'll see ...' Briggs scrolled back through a list of files and loaded up a new video. Kate waited impatiently for it to start, tapping her finger on the back of his chair.

He scowled up at her. 'I can give you a shout when I've found it.'

'I'll wait,' Kate replied.

Truth was they didn't have much to go on. They had spent the morning following up on a few leads, but nothing had come to any fruition. Initial results had come back on the rock, the potential weapon, and the blood type was a match to Gabriella, but they would have to wait for more detail than that. This CCTV footage was turning out to be their only source of genuine information.

'Here, here she is,' Briggs said, pointing again. 'And there's the guy.'

Kate brushed his hand away from the screen. 'What's he doing?'

'Not a lot, but then, look …' Briggs said, gesturing to the tiny figure. He was walking behind her – fairly innocently, Kate thought – but then Gabriella stopped and glanced behind her. At that moment the man dodged out of view behind one of the parked cars down the road, only emerging as Gabriella started on her way again, tottering off the screen.

'See?' Briggs said triumphantly, putting his hands behind his head and leaning back in his chair.

'Who's that?' Yates asked, peering over their shoulders. She'd left her desk where she'd been raking through piles of evidence picked up at the scene, all neatly packed away into tiny plastic bags, red tape sealing the top. Forensics had already finished with them all, deciding crisp packets weren't worth their consideration. Their feedback: tell us when you know what you're looking for.

'Not sure,' Kate replied. 'Briggs, print out an image.' He looked up at her, eyebrow raised. 'However grainy and crap it is. You never know.' She looked at Yates, who was still hovering behind them. 'Did you find something?'

'No,' Yates said. 'But the 999 call has come in, if you want to take a listen.' Kate walked over to her desk and sat next to her. Yates clicked on the file and a hiss of static filled the air. They heard the operator connect the call, a voice ask for an ambulance, then the line went dead.

'That's it?' Kate asked.

Yates nodded. 'Afraid so. Didn't even give a location. It came from a TK so they traced the call and dispatched a first responder.'

'Play it again.'

All three of them listened to the scratchy recording. The line from the phone box had been bad to start with, and the voice was muffled.

'Definitely a man, right?' Kate said, but her voice was hesitant.

Briggs frowned. 'Maybe.'

Kate sighed and stood up. Another dead end. A few gruff words on a recording wasn't going to get them far. She looked at the empty space on the whiteboard where the suspects should have been, then back to her computer. It was still showing the image of Harry Becker and his father.

She stared at the man on the screen. Was this the guy that had been following Gabriella? Or could it be the elusive spouse?

'Briggs?' she called over. 'Can you search for the husband next, please?'

He did a mock salute and she turned back to the screen.

She continued her search, linking to articles from the photograph of Harry Becker. Click-bait headlines flashed in front of her eyes, screaming death and betrayal and graphic descriptions of the people involved in the murder of the twins' parents. Was it connected? Was a fifteen-year-old double homicide related to a woman's attack in the dead of night? It was the same people, the same families, but was it any more than the same bad luck?

Morbid curiosity niggled in her mind. The way the investigation was going at the moment, it couldn't hurt to find out a bit more about the murders.

She remembered when they'd happened; she'd been at university in Southampton at the time. People had murmured at supermarket checkouts, headlines huge and dominant, even in the national papers. Something like that, so wrapped up in scandal and passion, was bound to capture the imagination of the public. At the time she hadn't given the teenagers involved the slightest consideration. Now she wondered – how had it felt to have your calm little life changed so violently overnight? Living at home, going to school, talking to their parents over breakfast. Then it all happened – their lives obliterated, in the blink of an eye. What would that do to a person?

Kate had to know more. She downloaded the police file from the archives and started to read.

12

Mortimer insisted on bringing his own car to the hospital, so they drove in convoy, the black BMW trailing the red Micra like an unwanted shadow. Turn after turn, she watched it in her rear-view mirror, still uncertain whether she was doing the right thing. But she was committed now; what choice did she have? He waited for her as she parked, pushing her hair behind her ears and slamming the door closed.

'After you,' he muttered.

They walked down the brightly lit, sterilised corridors. Past orderlies pushing old ladies in wheelchairs, a smoking area where wrinkled men loitered in their dressing gowns, guiltily sucking on their very reason for being in hospital in the first place. She could feel his eyes on her, boring into her back, adding to her jitters. She paused in front of the lift and pressed the call button.

The lift pinged and the doors opened.

'Top floor,' she said as they got in. 'ICU.'

They stood in silence as the lift began its tortured ascent, and she chanced a look at Mortimer. Not classically good-looking, his nose was far too big for his face, and he was dark and brooding. He seemed older than her: a scattering of grey ran through his black hair, lines etched on his forehead. He was too serious. Too American. He wasn't Gabi's usual type.

The doors opened to intensive care, and Thea led the way

to the reception desk. A nurse looked up from her computer and greeted them with a smile, then gestured to the man.

'Who's this?' she asked.

'Her husband,' Thea said, and the nurse raised her eyebrows, waving them through.

Back down the overheated corridor, into the room at the end. The curtain was pulled back, the dull grey from outside barely permeating the gloom. Mortimer hesitated as they moved closer.

Gabriella lay slightly tilted in her hospital bed, her neck supported with a pillow. Both guardrails were up and the blue blanket was tucked under her arms. An IV drip was inserted into one arm and connected to a bag of clear fluid hanging next to her, the oxygen monitor clip stuck to one of the uninjured fingers on her right hand.

'Oh, Gabriella,' Mortimer said, his voice breaking. 'I'm so sorry.' He sat heavily on the chair closest to her head. 'How did this happen?' he asked, looking up at Thea. 'Was she ... Was she raped?'

'I don't know,' Thea said quickly. 'Speak to the police.'

'The police ...' Mortimer said quietly, gently stroking the top of Gabriella's hand with one of his fingers.

Thea hovered at the foot of the bed and watched him, all his attention focused on the tiny figure under the covers. 'Why had Gabriella walked out on you?'

'We had a fight,' Mortimer said, without looking away, his shoulders slumped. 'Just after New Year's. She was telling me what I was doing wrong, why I wasn't right for her, trying to push me away. It was nothing new, but usually I ignored her. It's not easy for her to get close to people.' He looked up at Thea, his face showing his regret. 'But this time I snapped. I shouted at her. I did exactly what she said I would do, and

74

she walked out.' He ran his finger up her arm, touching the tape holding the IV tube. 'She'd left her phone behind, so I couldn't call her, but I remembered what she'd said about having a twin and the old house, so I went to see if she was there. When I saw you, I thought we could make up, that I could apologise. I didn't realise you were identical.'

'Stalking someone is a funny way to apologise.'

'We have a funny sort of relationship. I know what happened in her past. That fucks a person up, I think.' He looked up quickly, realising who he was speaking to. 'I'm sorry, I mean ...' He turned his eyes away, guiltily. 'It can't have been easy for her. For you both,' he added. 'I need to make allowances for that.' They heard the squeak of shoes on the tiled floor and he glanced away from the bedside. A nurse had walked down the corridor, past the open door. He frowned. 'I'm going to find a doctor.'

She watched him as he marched out, full of purpose. She moved to sit next to her sister, in the seat Mortimer had vacated. She gently touched her hand with one finger as he had done.

She felt hot tears behind her eyes and a lump in her throat. She bit her lip, trying to stop herself crying. Was he right? She had never thought of herself in that way, as fucked up, but maybe Mortimer had seen something that she'd never wanted to admit. The murder of your parents was something no teenager should ever have to live through; it was crazy to think they could have come out the other side unscathed.

And she had lost her sister, too, that day. For so long they'd been on opposite sides of the world. While they'd been living their separate lives, she'd kept quiet that she had an identical twin. The few people she had mentioned it to had been surprised, shocked even, that there was that much distance between them.

'Can you feel her pain?' they would ask. 'Can you communicate telepathically? Did you ever swap clothes and pretend to be the other?' Predictable, boring questions, and she would laugh them off, while deep down desperately missing the sister she had grown up with.

She heard shouting in the hallway and hurriedly wiped away her tears, getting to the doorway in time to see Mortimer march away. A red-faced nurse stood next to the reception desk, her colleague gently patting her arm.

Thea looked at them quizzically as she followed Mortimer, breaking into a run to catch up with him in the corridor.

'Mortimer! Wait!' She grabbed his arm when she was alongside him, holding onto it to slow him down. 'What happened?'

He shook his head, wordlessly, his jaw clenched. Thea could feel his muscles tense. He shook her off and turned away, trying to gather his composure.

Thea came up behind him and put her hand on his back. 'What's the matter?'

'Apart from the obvious?' he barked at her. 'Apart from the fact my wife is lying unconscious in hospital and I have no idea how she got there, or even what the hell she has been doing for the past few weeks?'

Thea looked up at him, the anger clear on his face. But also something else: worry. Grief. Pain.

'They won't tell me anything,' he said, quieter this time.

'Who? The doctors?'

'They say they have no proof I am who I say I am. That the police haven't told them she has a husband and they'll only talk to her next of kin – you.'

'What do you want to know?' Thea said. 'I'll ask them, I'll tell you.'

'Why do you believe me?' Mortimer said. 'She hadn't told you about me either.'

Thea thought for a moment. 'She didn't tell me anything, ever. Having a secret husband isn't so strange for her.'

'That's just it,' Mortimer said, turning his back and walking away from her. 'Why am I such a fucking secret?'

Thea watched him go this time, his shoulders stooped as he strode down the corridor. She sighed and shook her head. Yet another person broken by Gabriella. Yet another person miserable because of her.

13

The road was empty, spots of concrete dimly highlighted by streetlights. Kate locked her car and looked out into the gloom.

She pulled her coat tightly around her, feeling the biting cold already chilling her to the bone. She shoved gloves on her hands and started to walk, her pace quick.

Southampton Common was a massive park, to the north of the main town. By day it was frequented by dog walkers, cyclists, joggers and mums with kids, taking advantage of the many paths that criss-crossed the woodland. By night, it was a different matter.

Kate had wanted to see Gabi's route for herself. The wide concrete path led her through a patch of forest, overhung with large oak trees, their branches bare, ivy covering the thick trunks. Kate noted the lack of CCTV as she walked through.

She tried to imagine what Gabriella had been thinking. Dressed in no more than a tiny dress, she'd stumbled through here, probably at about three a.m. Somewhere between here and the end of this path, she'd lost her bag. Somewhere along here she'd been attacked and left for dead.

The trees had cleared and she could see across a wide expanse of grass. The moon peered through the grey clouds, the concrete path snaking ahead. She picked up her speed, feeling very vulnerable.

That afternoon, Yates had started on the club CCTV while Briggs tracked down the mysterious husband. There were no marriages recorded in the UK system, but they'd found a wedding a few months previously in America. Gabriella Patterson and Mortimer Breslin. Married 15 October 2018, at the Loving Hearts Chapel, Las Vegas. 'Sounds like a classy place,' Briggs had muttered.

The wedding may not have been posh but his current home definitely was. He lived in a particularly nice part of town, alongside CEOs and footballers in big houses about three miles north of the common. So she'd been found in between the nightclub and his house. Had she been trying to walk there? Or perhaps trying to get to her sister's – Thea's house was in that direction too.

Either way, it was a long walk, there was no doubt about that. Even getting from the club to here must have taken Gabriella at least half an hour, and that was walking in decent shoes, not high heels.

Kate looked around her; there was nobody else in sight. She could hear cars on the road running parallel to the common, but apart from that, nothing. It had probably been the same on Saturday night. Nobody to help her if she'd called out. Nobody to come to her aid. And nobody to help Kate either, come to that.

She knew what her own husband would say. 'What the hell were you thinking?' he would shout. 'Why did you go somewhere you knew would be dangerous? It's like you're trying to get hurt.' Those were the days when he actually gave a shit about what she did. Now if she told him, he'd probably just shake his head slowly, looking at the ground.

'I can't always be worrying about you,' he'd said the last time they'd spoken. 'It's exhausting.'

And then, just like that, he'd stopped. Like he'd flicked a switch and it had gone. No more worrying. No more caring. Kate wished it was as easy for her.

Maybe her husband would be right; maybe she was being a bit silly, walking out here alone at night when her police officer self would warn any woman against doing the same. She bristled inside, suddenly annoyed. Why is it always the responsibility of a woman to censor herself, to limit where she walks and when? To keep away from dangerous spots where men might attack her? Surely it should be the job of the police force, her beloved police force, to make sure women were safe, no matter where they were. To make sure vulnerable women like Gabriella could be silly and foolish and drunk and not get attacked. Why was it Gabriella's fault, when in reality it was the fault of the person who had attacked her, and that person alone?

Kate sighed. Sometimes things were too exhausting to contemplate; society appearing too damaged to even start to try to change it. The wind whipped across the grassland, pushing her hair into her eyes and her mouth. She increased her pace, keen to get the fool's errand finished.

The trees were closing in over the path again, and Kate consulted the map in her pocket, hastily scribbled before she left the office. The crime scene should be up there, on the right, and she walked a few paces further, trying to see into the undergrowth. Off the path, the trees quickly took over, the glow from the streetlights unable to penetrate the gloom. But sure enough, flapping in the breeze, Kate could see the blue and white tape marking the edge of the crime scene, then the red of the inner cordon. These were the areas Kate knew the SOCOs would have searched thoroughly, recording and photographing every scrap of potential evidence found. But Kate knew they hadn't found much of note so far; nothing to help them pinpoint any definite suspects.

So, they had a few possibles. She ran through the names in her head, people with reason to be angry. The husband, certainly. He can't have been pleased to know his wife was with other men.

And maybe Ryan Holmes, the slighted boyfriend with a flimsy alibi and twitchy demeanour. Steve Morgan? She didn't like him, but that was no grounds for arrest. The distant identical twin. Weird, certainly, with a recent argument in their past, but was that a motive? Harry Becker. Violent past, same as Thea, but why? Why would any of these people want to attack Gabriella, and what was the proof linking them?

Kate wondered about the psychology of Gabriella's attack. In the cold, at that time of night, the offender would need to have been determined and resolute to follow her all this way. Had they planned to kill her? Had they known this was where Gabi would walk?

Or maybe Yates's theory was correct: it had been an opportune moment for a violent mugger. Maybe Gabriella had just been in the wrong place at the wrong time.

Kate ran over the actual evidence in her head, then sighed. They had blurry CCTV footage of a man following her and a muffled 999 call. Kate looked away from the crime scene towards the road, then back at her map. The phone box was up there; she'd have a quick look before she went home. They had the doctor's opinion of a left-handed attacker, and a raft of forensics they were still waiting to hear back on. Perhaps that would help. She hoped it would.

Kate retraced her steps to the path, then stopped. She felt something hard underfoot, caught in the tread of her boot and lifted it to have a look. She picked at it with her finger. It came away from the mud, and she held it in her hand, rubbing the dirt free.

It wasn't a stone as she'd assumed, but a silver button. She cleaned the muck away, holding it up to the light, noticing the intricate decoration, a purple stone in its centre. It was small, no more than a centimetre across, but it was undoubtedly pretty, and probably quite unique.

Kate looked back to the crime scene. She'd found it well outside of the cordon, so it wouldn't have been picked up by the SOCOs and probably had nothing to do with the investigation. It could have been lost this morning by someone completely unrelated. Some woman walking to work, now annoyed, a big gap on her shirt or her coat.

Kate shivered. It was too cold to be standing here deliberating. She popped it in her pocket and walked towards the road, arms swinging, trying to generate some heat in her bones.

The path came to an end by a main junction of Hill Lane. At this time of night, just past 9 p.m., it was busy, the traffic lights rotating through their signals, music blaring from the pub opposite. Kate wondered how much traffic there would have been late on Saturday night. Would anyone have noticed someone using the phone?

The box itself was boring and indistinguishable, apart from the blue and white tape marking it off. One side of the box was covered with an advert, blocking sight of the road, another pane of the door covered with the white spider webs of smashed safety glass.

Kate looked across the road at the pub. She wondered about their CCTV. Had anyone asked? The pub looked welcoming; her body needed the warmth. Her mouth already anticipated the glass of cool white wine to help her forget the day.

It wouldn't hurt to go and find out, she said to herself, and hurried across the road.

14

Thea looked up from the television when she heard the knock on the door. Three loud thuds, as before. Slow, even, deliberate.

Since she'd got home from the hospital, she'd been restless and fidgety. She'd started her search of the house again, but quickly grown bored, unable to concentrate, desperate to call Harry but knowing she couldn't. He was out at something for work; he'd said he would give any excuse to get out of it but she didn't want to be that person to him, not at the moment.

She heard the knocks again. She hesitated, then pulled herself up from the sofa.

Mortimer was standing in the doorway, one shoulder resting on the frame, his body at a slant. He peered at her, his eyes half closed, and held up the bottle of wine in his hand.

'I brought this,' he slurred, and Thea sighed.

'You'd better come in,' she said.

She managed to steer him to the sofa at the edge of the living room, and took the bottle of wine out of his grip. He smiled lopsidedly at her.

'You look so much like her,' he said, his accent dry and lazy.

'That's the whole point about identical twins,' she said in a monotone. 'We look alike.'

'Yes, but still.' Mortimer paused. 'I don't normally drink.'

'No kidding,' Thea said, looking at the label on the bottle of red. It was a Castelli Martinozzi and a good year at that. She went to the kitchen and got two wine glasses, opening the bottle and pouring two generous measures. She walked back into the living room and handed one to Mortimer, sitting down next to him on the sofa, pulling her legs up underneath her.

'You even sit the same,' Mortimer muttered, taking a sip of the wine.

Thea didn't say anything, just put the glass to her lips. The wine was smooth on her tongue and she appreciated the distraction, enjoying the rich flavours. She watched him. He was dressed in the same clothes as earlier – black shirt, black jeans, black coat now discarded on the arm of the sofa – but his hair was messy, his shirt creased. His body had a loose air to it, like everything wasn't screwed on straight.

'I'm sorry I was rude to you at the hospital,' Mortimer said. 'It wasn't your fault. It's just your sister is so ...'

He stopped, holding himself back.

'Infuriating? Difficult?' she said.

'Both of those.' He laughed softly to himself. He seemed calmer now. 'We're married, but nobody knows the slightest thing about me. I haven't met any of her friends.' He pointed a wobbly finger at Thea. 'Her family.'

'How long have you been together?' Thea took a big mouthful of wine, suddenly more in the mood to binge than savour. But she was enjoying sitting here; she liked his company. Despite his drunkenness, and she suspected he hadn't had much to get himself in this state, she felt reassured by his presence.

'We met six months ago, been married for three. It was a

spur of the moment thing. We were away in Vegas and she thought it would be funny to get married. She was drunk and beautiful and I thought, why not? Life would never be dull married to Gabriella.'

'That's true,' Thea muttered.

'She made me see things differently,' Mortimer carried on, seeming to want someone to talk to as much as Thea welcomed the distraction. 'Gabi came along and she made me laugh. Marrying her felt right. Even though it was so unlike anything I had ever done in my life. It was good to do something so insane, so spontaneous. I looked at her, and thought, why not? What could possibly go wrong?'

He stopped and looked at his glass of wine.

'What if...' He looked at Thea, and his stare was unwavering, his eyes solemn. 'What if she doesn't wake up?'

Thea shook her head, staving off the wave of panic she'd been barely keeping at bay herself. 'She'll be fine, she always is.'

Mortimer nodded slowly. 'I feel so stupid. I shouldn't have let her leave. I should have tried harder to track her down. I just thought she needed space, and she'd come back to me. But then I found out about her and this guy...'

Thea stopped him. 'What guy?'

'This Holmes guy. Part of that club in town. She and him were together. I saw them, last Saturday night, leaving the club.'

Thea frowned. 'Really?'

'Yeah, they walked somewhere, must have been to his place. I was so fucking angry.' He shook his head. 'Fuck,' he said quietly. 'What a fucking mess.'

Thea took another mouthful of wine, looking down at the glass, surprised to see it empty. She could already feel the alcohol going to her head, hitting her empty stomach and making her dizzy. She reached over and took his hand. It felt soft and comforting.

'It's not your fault,' she said. She looked down, his long fingers entwined with hers. 'Gabriella, she ...' Thea paused. 'She does what she likes. She's selfish, she's inconsiderate, she acts on impulse. She doesn't always think straight. But she loves you, I'm sure of it.'

She looked up quickly. Mortimer was still staring at their interlocked fingers, his thumb stroking the top of her hand, his hair falling over his face. He looked sad and wounded and beautiful.

'She wouldn't have married you if she didn't love you.'

He looked up at her and their eyes met. Their faces were barely inches apart. Then, without thinking, she leaned forward and touched her lips to his.

Mortimer jumped back, as if electrocuted. 'Shit!' he said. 'Shit. I'm so sorry. I shouldn't be here, I'm so sorry.'

He picked up his coat and ran from the room, pulling open the front door and disappearing into the night. Thea touched her fingers gently to her lips.

She'd missed that. She'd missed kissing a man who loved her. But this man didn't love her; he loved the woman lying unconscious in hospital. And now she'd made everything worse. So much worse.

Wednesday

15

'I can see why she married him,' Briggs muttered. Kate frowned but said nothing, silently agreeing with his judgement.

Rain was battering the tiny Skoda, the wipers struggling to keep up with the deluge. They'd been unable to find the place at first, cruising slowly down the empty streets, tall hedges lining the road, each house hidden behind gates and long driveways. None of them had numbers, only names, so they had to squint through the rain at each one, eventually finding Mortimer Breslin's residence at the end of a cul-de-sac.

Kate looked up at the house. It was two floors, and immaculately maintained: the plaster was crisp and white, the driveway charcoal tarmac. Perfectly trimmed shrubs lined the outside of the property. Their car was the only one on the driveway; the house seemed empty and dark.

'Why do we know so little about him?' Kate asked, and Briggs tapped at the ancient laptop, connected into the network via his mobile phone.

'There's nothing much on the PNC. Just that he lives here and has a black BMW 5 series registered in his name.' He pressed a few more keys, then looked over at Kate. 'Oh, but look at this.'

She shuffled over in her seat as he turned the screen around to face her. 'Red light jump?' she replied. 'Bassett Avenue, nineteenth of January, eleven oh five p.m.' Kate looked up at Briggs with a smile. 'So he was in the area that night,' she said and he nodded. 'Come on, let's see if he's in.'

They pushed the car doors open then ran to the house, the two of them cramped under the porch trying to keep out of the rain. Kate rang the bell and they heard it echo down the hallway.

When there was no answer, Kate left Briggs by the door and pressed her nose up against the glass of the nearest window. It was obviously the living room, with dark brown sofas, a modern-looking coffee table and a massive television on the wall.

'What can you see?' Briggs asked, joining her at the window. He peered inside. 'It doesn't look like anyone actually lives here,' he said, wiping the rain from the window and looking again.

Kate felt a drop of water find its way under the hood of her coat and trickle down her neck. She turned and stalked back to the car, shutting the door with more force than was necessary. This was the first decent lead, and they couldn't find the guy. She picked her phone out of her pocket and dialled, watching Briggs continue his nose around the house.

'Boss?' Yates said as she answered the phone. 'Have you got him?'

'Nobody here. Did you find anything on the pub CCTV?' Kate asked, hoping for another connection to Mortimer Breslin.

Kate had dropped by the office first thing to pick up Briggs and set Yates to work on the file as soon as she could. The landlord had been more than accommodating the night before, dashing off to find the right bit of footage and emailing it to Kate while she sat at the bar, free glass of Sauv Blanc in her hand.

'Yes, but…' Yates sounded reluctant and Kate sighed. 'It's hard to make much out. The camera's pointing the wrong way, and it's old, the quality is terrible.'

'Can you see anyone or not?'

'Not really. There's a bloke in shot, and it could be the same man from before. It's hard to tell for sure.' Yates paused. 'But…'

'What?' Kate snapped, irritated.

'I went back to the club CCTV and I think I've got something.'

Kate waited, trying to quell her excitement.

'It's the overhead camera from the main bar,' Yates continued. 'Ryan Holmes is there, and he's with Gabriella. And they're fighting.'

'Physically?' Kate asked as the car door opened and Briggs threw himself back inside, showering Kate with water from his coat.

'Mainly just shouting. But yes. Neither of them are happy.'

Briggs gestured to Kate, showing her the screen from his phone. It was the daily update from the hospital, but today's was more interesting than usual.

Kate went back to the call. 'Rachel, we're going to head to the hospital, the husband's there.' Briggs started the engine and reversed the Skoda out of the driveway at speed. 'Keep going with the club CCTV. I want more on Ryan Holmes before we interview him again.' She hung up the phone before Yates could complain. Kate knew she'd be cross-eyed from staring at the screen already, the pile of DVDs from Heaven hardly dented.

Kate strapped herself in as Briggs hurtled towards the hospital. She felt some of the jigsaw pieces starting to appear. She couldn't narrow it down just yet, but she knew one of them could be the break they needed.

16

Harry knew he shouldn't be there. He was late for work, his boss had already left him a shitty voicemail and something inside him was telling him to stay away. But there he was, back at the hospital. And as Harry rounded the corner into the ward, he realised his gut reaction had been correct.

The man sitting at her bedside stood up as Harry approached, and held out his hand.

'Mortimer Breslin,' he said. 'And you must be Harry.' The man was almost his height, but had something about him that Harry had been trying to emulate his entire life. His confidence was natural, his posture relaxed.

Harry shook his hand, nodding.

'I've heard all about you,' Mortimer said, and Harry laughed nervously.

'That can't be good,' he replied.

'The neighbour, right? You grew up together. Gabi talked about you all the time.'

'She did?' There was an awkward pause between the two men. 'I'm sorry,' Harry said. 'But I don't know who you are at all.'

The man shook his head, embarrassed. 'No, not many people do, it seems. I'm her husband.'

Even before he said the words, deep down Harry had known. He felt the blood drain out of his face, his limbs heavy. He smiled and went through the proper things he was supposed to say, then he turned and started to walk away.

'Don't you want to see Gabi?' Mortimer called after him.

'No, I'm sorry, I'm late for work, I have to go,' he said, and ran out of the stifling room, out to the corridor and into the cold air. He felt the rain on his face, his hair soaked in seconds, but he didn't care. He had to get out of there. Away from Gabi, away from her *husband*.

Suddenly it was all so clear. It was over. She was *married*. He stopped in a narrow alleyway between two hospital buildings, his breathing shallow, his heart racing. He lit a cigarette with fumbling fingers, taking a long drag of soothing nicotine. The rejection was absolute; all the ridiculous daydreams he'd had about the two of them had been nothing more than fiction. Maybe it had all been wishful thinking, and she'd just been waiting for a tall handsome American to come along. And there he was. All black hair and piercing eyes, friendly and nice, even when his wife was lying in a coma in hospital.

Harry felt his body sag. The anger started to build. He turned and rammed his fist at the brick wall, punching it with all his might. The pain started in his hand, spreading from his knuckles to his fingers to his wrist, but it felt good. It felt good to have something physical to focus on, when the mental shit was suddenly all-consuming.

'Fuck, fuck, fuck,' he shouted and hit the wall again, punching until he was forced to stop, cradling his smashed right hand in his left, and gently resting his forehead against the rough brickwork. He looked at his shaking hand as the pain took over: shredded skin, broken knuckles. Blood ran down his wrist, mixing with the rain. He was a mess. A barely functioning wreck. How stupid could he be to believe someone like Gabriella had wanted to be with him. What an idiot.

'Fuck,' he said again quietly, and sank to the ground.

17

The nurses pointed him out to Kate when they arrived. She watched him from across the room. She recognised his dress and his posture – there was no doubt to her he was the man who had followed Thea from the police station on Monday.

She started walking down the ward. He was sat next to the bed, a copy of the *Financial Times* in front of him. As Kate got closer, she realised he was reading it out loud.

'Does Gabriella like the *FT*?' she asked when they were next to him. Mortimer stopped and turned in his chair.

'No,' he replied. 'Does anyone? But it's all I have.'

'DS Munro and DC Briggs,' Kate said, showing her ID badge. Briggs did the same and he nodded at the introductions.

'Mortimer Breslin,' he said, making no effort to get up.

'You're American?' Kate asked. 'Where from?'

'Tremont, New York.'

'Nice place?'

'Not really.'

They looked at each other in silence.

'Mr Breslin,' Kate started. 'We'd like to speak to you about the night your wife was attacked.'

'I thought you might.' He folded the pages of the *FT*, stood up and gestured for them to follow him. Out of the room he stopped in the corridor, his arms crossed.

'Down at the station, if you would be so kind.'

'Are you arresting me?'

Kate hesitated. They could place him near the common earlier that night, but that wasn't exactly solid evidence. She might have a feeling about this guy, but she didn't want him to know it.

'Not at this point, no,' she replied, and she heard Briggs make a dissatisfied huff behind her.

'Then I would like to stay close to my wife.'

Kate nodded, and they moved to a quieter part of the corridor, away from the other rooms, next to the nurses' station, currently unoccupied. She could hear faint chatter from the kitchen around the corner: people talking, making tea.

'Where were you last Saturday night, the twelfth?' she began.

Mortimer frowned, obviously considering his answer. 'I ate dinner at home, and then went to a nightclub in town.'

'And why did you go there?'

'I was following my wife. I wanted to see her.'

'And did you?'

'No.' His answers were polite, but unhelpful, making Kate work to gather any information from him.

'Did you talk to anyone that night?'

'Yes, the guy she was with. I believe he owns the club.'

'Why did you speak to him?'

'He seemed ... close, with Gabriella.'

'What made you think that?' Kate asked.

'I saw them earlier that night. He had his arm round her, they were laughing,' he frowned, his jaw clenching. 'They were kissing.'

'That must have made you angry.'

Mortimer stared at Kate without answering and she could

see the intensity in his eyes. Yes, he'd been angry, there was no doubt about that. He still was.

'And what happened?' she pushed.

Mortimer ran his hand through his hair. He looked tired, his skin sallow.

'The bouncer warned me off. I went back and sat in my car. I waited for a while and then I saw both of them come out and walk down the road. I didn't follow them,' he added, quickly. 'I went home, went to bed. I haven't seen her since.'

'And where were you this Saturday night? The nineteenth?'

'Home. Alone. I watched television then went to bed at about midnight.' His reply was smooth, without hesitation. He was slick, this one.

Kate took a measured breath in. 'Why are you lying to us, Mr Breslin?' she asked, slowly.

Mortimer didn't say anything. Just looked at her with those calm hazel eyes.

'We have your BMW on camera, jumping a red light north of the common,' Kate continued. 'So we know you weren't having a peaceful night in with Netflix. I'll ask you again, Mr Breslin. Where were you on Saturday night?'

Mortimer crossed his arms in front of him. 'Yes, I went to the club. I parked outside, I waited for about an hour, but I didn't see anyone. Not Gabriella, not that man, nobody. I felt stupid, sitting there in the cold, so I changed my mind and went home. That's all.'

'What time was this?' Kate asked.

'Just after eleven.'

'You expect us to believe you went home, and that was it?' Kate continued. 'That you didn't repeat your trick from the week before and have it out with her?'

Mortimer shook his head slowly. 'No. I didn't.'

'Except this time, you went too far. You were mad with her for cheating on you, and your anger got out of hand. You attacked her and left her for dead, cold and alone on the common.' Despite her words, Kate's voice was quiet and slow. Briggs took a step towards the man, trying to intimidate him. She watched Mortimer closely: he didn't budge, his feet firmly planted on the floor, his shoulders square.

'No,' he repeated, speaking carefully, his words measured. 'I didn't. I sat outside the club until about eleven, then left alone. But on Monday I changed my mind and went to the house to try and speak to her again. I followed her a few times – at least, the person I thought was her – until I realised it was her identical twin. Thea brought me here, and that's when I found out. Until yesterday, I had no idea Gabriella was in hospital.'

Kate noticed his cheeks had flushed; he seemed uncomfortable. He was definitely hiding something. Maybe he wasn't so unbreakable after all.

'It must have made you pretty furious? Seeing your wife with another man?' Briggs chipped in, pushing the same point to try and get a response.

'Yes, it made me angry. As I said, I had words with the guy the week before, but it got me nowhere.' Mortimer met Briggs's gaze. His voice was level and calm. 'Being angry has never helped solve a problem, has it, Detective Constable Briggs?'

'You felt Gabriella leaving you was a problem to be solved, did you, Mr Breslin? That's very clinical.'

Kate nudged Briggs with her foot, warning him to back off. She wanted to go away, do some more digging. Then, when they had something solid, they would arrest him properly, do a search, find something and make it stick. She didn't want to unnerve him too much now.

Mortimer sighed. 'I want to help anyway I can, I do. But this is not it. I am not the person you are looking for, however badly you want that to be the case.' He took a step away from them and picked up a pen from the nurses' station. Kate watched him write his phone number on a corner of the *FT*, rip it off and pass it to her.

'Phone me, if you want to talk in a more civilised way. Now, I'd like to get back to my wife.'

Kate watched him leave, going back into the room and closing the door behind him. She liked him for this; there was something about him. His apparent complete control of his emotions. The way he had followed his wife, tracking her down, like she was property he couldn't let go. Men like that can't hold it together forever, she thought; sometimes they snap.

'Well, he's an interesting fish,' Briggs said under his breath. 'He was there that night, and I don't believe for a second he just changed his mind and went home.'

'Not only that,' Kate said, turning the piece of paper over in her fingers. 'Didn't you see when he wrote down his number? He's left-handed.'

18

Thea saw them standing in the corridor when she arrived, their backs to her as they spoke. She could see Mortimer was annoyed, his posture defensive: hands on his waist, his shoulders back.

When she'd woken that morning, she'd gone downstairs and seen the empty bottle of wine. She'd looked at the two glasses, then picked up the phone. But what would she say? I'm sorry? She wasn't sure there were words to make the situation any better.

She'd had breakfast, drunk a cup of tea. She'd continued her search, scouring the kitchen, emptying cupboards, ticking a few more places off her mental list, then sat on the sofa, impatient. She was fed up of feeling so guilty. She could do something nice: go and visit her twin, take some grapes or flowers – isn't that what you're supposed to do? If you were a normal family?

So Thea had arrived, and crept into the room while Mortimer and the police were in conversation. She sat in the chair next to her sister, and looked at her.

She saw the bandage round her forehead, the bruises on her arms, the tubes, the wires. She reached over and took her sister's hand, gently wrapping her fingers round her twin's. She stared at them entwined together, looking so similar. She missed her; so much, she felt an ache in the middle of her chest, stopping her breathing. It almost hurt, being so close to her sister but not being able to speak to her.

She saw her eyelids flicker. She felt a finger move.

'I didn't see you come in.'

A voice behind her but she didn't turn. 'I'm sorry, Mort,' she said, not able to look at him.

Suddenly a cacophony of alarms sounded at the bedside, and she heard feet rushing down the corridor. She jumped from the bed as two nurses ran in, closely followed by a doctor.

She backed away, watching as the nurses and the doctor crowded the bedside, talking in rushed tones, all medical terminology and stethoscopes and concern. Mortimer looked at her, his eyes wide, scared for his wife.

She couldn't wait and see what happened. It was all too much. She took one last look, then turned and ran. Away from the lies, the regret, the guilt.

She should have known better, she told herself as she fled. Secrets had a habit of coming to the surface. No matter how far down you buried them.

19

The call came through the overhead speaker in the car, jolting Kate to attention with a blast of adrenaline. She and Briggs were on their way back to the station as Yates's voice shouted out, loud and sudden.

'Sarge? Go back. Gabriella Patterson. Nurse said something's happened.'

Kate swore. Briggs turned the car round in the middle of the road, ignoring the horns around them, and floored it back the way they'd come.

They parked the car in a disabled bay and ran into the hospital. When they arrived on the ward, Mortimer was standing in the doorway, watching a flock of white coats at Gabriella's bed, his hand over his mouth.

'What's happened?' Kate asked, catching her breath.

'I don't know,' he said. 'I went back in. Thea was there.' He paused, gathering his words. 'Then a whole load of alarms went off.'

Kate looked over. Doctor Riley was leaning over the bed, a melee of nurses and equipment around him.

'What did you do?' Briggs said, moving behind them, blocking the exit. 'Did you try and kill her off? Finish what you'd started?'

'What? No!' Mortimer replied. 'Look at her!' He pointed

towards the bed. 'She's not dying! She moved her fingers. I'm sure she opened her eyes. She's waking up.'

The three of them watched as the medical team worked. After a while the curtains were drawn around the bed, blocking their view. Kate fidgeted as time ticked by. Waiting to speak to her, waiting to know more. An hour passed. Eventually the curtain was pulled back and Doctor Riley moved away. He said a few words to the nurse, then came over, flanked by the trailing white cape of enthusiastic trainees.

'Good news – she's awake, but she's groggy,' Doctor Riley said. 'We made the decision to take her entirely off sedation first thing this morning and it looks like it's paid off. She's responded well and we've extubated her to make her more comfortable.'

'What set off the alarms?' Briggs asked.

'She woke and found herself on the machines. It can be distressing for anyone. She's going to be confused for a few days, but initial tests are good. She seems pretty lucid, all things considered.'

Mortimer thanked the doctor, then rushed over to Gabriella's bedside. Kate and Briggs watched him as he sat down and gently took her hand.

'Has she said who attacked her?' Kate asked the doctor.

'No, I'm sorry, and she probably won't be able to at this point. We'll do some more tests later today, but to warn you, it's likely she'll have some retrograde amnesia from the head injury.'

'Can we talk to her?'

'For a moment. She's still healing, so don't be surprised if she falls asleep. Five minutes,' he said, and the group bustled away.

Kate walked over to the bedside, Briggs close behind. The bed had been raised, so Gabriella was now half sitting, pillows propping her up. The white bandage was still wrapped around her head and she had her eyes closed.

Mortimer was next to her, his face in his hands.

'Do you mind if we have some time with Gabriella?' Kate asked.

He nodded and backed away from the bedside. Kate noticed he was more subdued than he had been, his confidence faded. 'I'll go and get a coffee.' Mortimer hesitated. 'I'm not sure what she remembers. She says she doesn't know who I am.' He frowned, took one last look and then left, striding down the ward. Briggs's eyes followed him.

'Gabriella?' Kate sat down on the chair next to the bed. 'Gabriella? I'm DS Kate Munro, this is DC Jamie Briggs. We're with the Hampshire Police.' Gabriella opened her eyes slowly. 'We've been investigating your attack,' Kate continued. 'Do you mind speaking to us for a moment?'

Gabriella nodded, a barely perceptible movement.

'I don't remember much,' she said, her voice hoarse. 'I was at that nightclub. The music was loud.'

'Who were you there with?'

'Um,' Gabriella was silent for a moment. 'No, no I can't... They said I was found on the common. Why would I have been there?' She looked at Kate, confused.

'What else can you recall?'

'I was at the club. I felt terrible, unsteady.' She winced. 'But that's it, it's all a blank fuzz. I don't remember leaving.'

'That's okay, Gabriella, try and get some rest.' Kate could see the nurse hovering at the doorway. 'We'll come back and see you another day. And if you remember anything else, get the nurse to call us.'

Briggs closed his notebook and they both turned to leave.

'Wait,' Gabriella said.

Kate turned back.

'Stop calling me Gabriella.'

Kate leaned in closer. 'What do you mean?'

The girl looked at her, suddenly awake, suddenly very conscious. 'I'm not Gabriella,' she said, her dark eyes fixed on Kate. 'I'm Thea.'

Part 2

20

'Didn't anyone check?' Kate paced across the office. 'Didn't anyone actually confirm that the twin lying in the hospital bed was the right one?'

'We took fingerprints, but there was nothing in the system,' Briggs said, staring into his coffee cup. 'And then we found her bag on Sunday, and the driving licence matched up.' He shrugged. 'The uniforms picked up Thea Patterson from her house and she came with us without a word, so what were we supposed to do?'

'They look the same,' Yates added, miserably.

'They're identical bloody twins!' Kate shouted. 'Of course they look the same!'

'But they have the same colour hair,' Briggs pleaded. 'The same haircut, the same ...'

'Body shape,' Yates added, and Briggs gave her a grateful look.

'And what the hell was Thea – Gabriella – Patterson playing at?' Kate added, looking at the photo stuck on the board. 'Why was she at Thea's house? She was obviously lying to us all along, laughing in our faces.'

'We'll interview her again.'

'Yes, we bloody will. And find out all you can about Thea Patterson.' They both nodded, and looked at Kate expectantly. She walked to the whiteboard and picked up a pen.

'Let's start from the beginning – what do we know? And what do we know for certain?'

Hours ticked by and the night closed in. Alone in the office again, Kate rested her bum on the edge of the desk and knocked her pen against her forehead. In front of her the whiteboard was decorated with rows of faces and names, a long black line with dates and times scrawled along the top.

After hours with Briggs and Yates, wiping it all clean and starting over, it seemed they were no further forward. Where before they were looking at suspects for one attack and one victim, now the intended recipient of the attack could be either woman, effectively doubling their suspect pool. Not that adding Thea as the victim actually raised many new names. Her client list came up empty of suspicion, and she didn't seem to have many others in her life outside those they had already identified.

Thea waking up had distracted them, but they needed to keep going. With renewed focus, they had taken a look at the CCTV from the club, the three of them crowding round Yates's screen.

The footage was dark and grainy, but Kate could clearly make out the bar they had been standing in a few days ago, only this time it was full of beautiful people: dancing, flirting, all with drinks in their hands.

'She's talking to Ryan Holmes, here ...' Yates had said, gesturing towards the shorter guy with glasses, in a shirt and jeans. He was holding a glass and frowning as the woman they had all assumed to be Gabriella waved her hands wildly at him. He said a few words – if only this tape had audio, Kate had thought – and then scowled again as 'Gabriella' gestured, clearly angry, clearly drunk. He said something else, then she leaned forward and went for him, slapping him squarely across the face, knocking his glasses to the floor.

'Fuck!' Briggs had said. 'That would piss me off.'

Ryan Holmes stayed completely still, then bent down and picked up his glasses, rubbing his face with his right hand. A larger, well-built guy appeared at his side and spoke to him – Steve Morgan. Gabriella (Thea, they had to stop calling her by the wrong name, Kate thought) had stormed out of shot.

Motive, evidently, but what had the argument been about? They'd have to get Ryan Holmes back in here again, and ask him a few more detailed questions.

She picked up the marker pen and wrote *Interview Ryan Holmes* on the board, then considered the rest of the 'to do' list. They needed to chase forensics for anything found on Thea's clothes, as well as the fingerprint evidence from the bag. Plus the EEK and blood work. They weren't going to be well liked by the lab once they'd finished nagging.

And what about Mortimer Breslin? They knew he'd been in the area; they had the ticket for jumping a red light nearby. But what else was there? Could he be the voice on the 999 call or the shadowy figure on the CCTV, following who he assumed to be his wife? Kate liked him as a suspect, so they had stuck his photo on the board next to Ryan Holmes. And then, for completeness, Briggs had added Steve Morgan and Harry Becker, with question marks underneath.

'They're not suspects,' Kate had argued. 'We have nothing against them. No motive, no evidence.'

'I prefer this to the empty space,' Briggs had said, and she had to agree with him.

Meanwhile, Yates had been pushing her random assailant theory. Kate still wasn't convinced, but for the benefit of team engagement she had written *Mugger?* under the suspect list.

And now Briggs and Yates had gone home, leaving Kate staring at the board. She swore, then threw the pen across the room in frustration. It hit the far wall and rolled under a chair. They were supposed to be finding evidence and leads and doing good solid police work, she thought, not standing in an empty room hurling stationery.

Her phone beeped next to her and she picked it up, reading the screen and cursing. She typed a quick reply then threw her coat on, pushing her hand in the pocket and coming into contact with something hard and metal. Kate pulled it out and turned it over in her hand, looking at the shiny silver and purple button she remembered picking up the night before on the common. Distracted by thoughts of CCTV from the pub, she'd forgotten to put it in an evidence bag; she'd forgotten to do anything that maintained the continuity of exhibits. Oh well. It probably wasn't relevant anyway. She threw it into the pot of paperclips on her desk without a second thought and ran out of the office, car keys in her hand.

21

Gabriella was exhausted. She sat hunched at the kitchen table, Thea's kitchen table, cradling a mug of tea.

She'd driven back from the hospital in a blur, barely making it through the door before collapsing in a heap in the bed. She'd feared the worst – her sister was dying, she'd never wake up – and Gabi was alone. Alone and trapped as a person she didn't want to be, in a house she wanted nothing to do with. She'd covered herself with the duvet and sobbed, shouted, wrestled with the unfairness of the universe, until she'd fallen into a disjointed sleep.

When she woke, hours later, she felt groggy and numb, but strong enough to phone the hospital. So when they told her that her sister was in recovery, she didn't know what to think. 'Recovering, how?' Gabriella had asked, confused, feeling a flood of relief as they explained. She was alive! Thea was still ill, with chunks of her memory missing, but she was alive.

But Gabi knew the reprieve was short-lived. Thea had woken up. Everyone knew who she was. Gabi's head ached from the stress of the past few days but she knew there was more to come. She had lied to the police; she was nervous at what she would have to face. Who she would have to face.

She looked round Thea's kitchen; she wouldn't miss being back here. Every turn brought up memories she would rather forget: her mum washing paintbrushes in the sink, flicking blue or red tinted water on the white splashback. Her dad, tired after a day at work, telling Gabi to get changed, that skirt didn't even cover her bum.

Sometimes the grief of her parents' death would hit her like an avalanche. Even relaxing on a perfect sandy beach in a far-flung location, a tiny snippet would break through and she'd end up bent double, struggling to breathe, the loss knocking all the wind out of her. Sometimes a smell – summer barbecues, freshly cut grass – sometimes a voice, carried on the air. Her parents had been far less than perfect, but they'd been stability, at least. It blindsided her, even now.

She didn't know how Thea felt about it all. She assumed she must have been equally as distraught but Thea had been a blank canvas, almost devoid of reaction. It never ceased to amaze Gabriella how the twins had turned out so differently – how the same experience of childhood and the same genetic make-up had produced such different people. Perhaps one neuron in the brain fired slightly differently. Perhaps a few cells can change perception of a person and a place.

Gabi heard the front door slam open and heavy footsteps march through the house. She'd been waiting for this, the part she dreaded the most.

He appeared in the kitchen door, ducking instinctively under the low beams. Today he was dressed casually, in blue jeans and a navy jumper, the collar of a checked shirt poking out the top. He stopped dead when he saw her.

'How could you, Gabriella? What was the bloody point?'

'Hi Harry,' she said, forcing her voice to stay calm. 'Would you like a cup of tea?'

'Cut the crap, Gabi, what the hell were you thinking? Was this a game to you?'

She shook her head. 'I didn't start this. This was Thea's fault — pretending to be me.' She thought back. It seemed like a lifetime ago now. 'I knew she was up to something, so I let myself in. I still had a key. Then the police turned up and I thought, what the hell? Why not?'

'Why not? Why not?' Harry shouted. 'Because it was mean, because it was deceitful. Because you might hurt the people you ...' He stopped, the unsaid word hanging in the room. 'How long did you think it could go on for? What did you think would happen?'

'I don't know, I didn't think.' Gabi turned away and filled the kettle at the sink, just so that she could have something to occupy her hands. She couldn't tell him the truth: that Thea being in hospital gave her access to the house. Gave her an opportunity to search — to find the one thing that would release them all from the deception that had plagued her all this time.

'You even lied to me, Gabriella.' Harry collapsed at the kitchen table, the fight knocked out of him. He ran his hands through his hair, a characteristic Gabi recognised from their childhood, and she caught sight of the white bandage encasing his right hand. 'We all grew up here,' Harry continued. 'It was always the three of us, nothing was stronger than that bond — you, me and Thea. I believed in that, and we lived through the worst possible time in our lives together. And yet you can do something like this.'

The kettle clicked off and she poured the boiling water into a mug. She'd been assimilating into being Thea, and had consequently abandoned her usual espresso habit in favour of Thea's endless cups of tea. It had been nice to have a change. Gabi pulled out a chair and sat down next to him.

'I'm sorry,' she said softly.

He looked at her. She forced herself to look up, to meet his blue eyes with hers. There had always been something about making eye contact with Harry she'd found difficult. He didn't look away, ever, and his gaze felt intimate, like he could see every thought she'd ever tried to hide.

'What did you do to your hand? Are you still having problems with it?' she asked and he looked at it, almost surprised.

'It's nothing, I fell over running.' He moved it under the table, out of sight. 'How long have you been home?' he asked, changing the subject.

'Six months,' she admitted, cupping her hands round the mug. 'Since August.'

'Since ...' Harry stopped and shook his head.

They stayed silent for a moment, Harry looking down, Gabi staring into her mug.

'How can you stand to be here, to come here every day?' she asked quietly.

He sighed and looked at her. 'I don't think about it. I block it out. It's Thea's house, nothing more. It's not ...' Harry stopped himself. 'I don't think about it,' he repeated.

'I can't bear it. I hate being here.' She paused. 'I'm sorry I didn't tell you I was home. But being back brought up a whole load of memories I didn't know how to deal with. So I pushed them away, I ignored them. And I ignored you.'

Harry shook his head, avoiding her gaze.

'And I was scared. I didn't know what you wanted from me.'

He looked up quickly. 'Don't put this on me, Gabi. You know exactly how I felt about you.'

'But it's too much, Harry. There's so much shit that gets in the way. I didn't know what to do with it all.'

'But you don't even try, Gabi.'

Silence enveloped the room. Gabi felt the weight of it, judging her, judging her lies.

'And now you're married.' He looked at her and she felt his hurt. She knew she should have been the one to tell him, but once again she'd fallen short of doing the right thing.

'Did you ever care about me?' he asked, staring at the table.

Gabi opened her mouth, but she didn't know what to say. There wasn't anything that could make it better.

Harry shook his head, his mouth a hard line. 'I don't know why I fucking bother.' He stood up and picked up his coat. 'I should just forget all about you. Fall in love with someone who deserves it for a change.'

She felt the sting of his dismissal. 'Perhaps you should. We've never been more than friends, Harry, I don't owe you anything,' she shouted at his back as he walked towards the door. She regretted it the moment the words were out of her mouth.

He stopped in his tracks and looked back at her. 'I'm sorry you feel that way, Gabriella,' Harry said, and stormed out of the room.

Gabi heard the front door slam, and a car screech out of the driveway in a shower of gravel.

She put her head in her hands and closed her eyes tight. She wouldn't allow herself to think of that time, those brief moments with Harry. That was gone, and had been over before it had even started. The whole thing had been ridiculous, she told herself.

She was alone, again. It was better this way. It would always be better this way.

22

Thea woke. The pressure of the blanket held her firmly to the bed, and for a moment she struggled to place where she was. She was hot, and her skin felt itchy.

She lay propped up in bed. A sharp knocking pain echoed in her head as she stared at the ceiling. A small patch of brown had spread across from the wall and she studied it, struggling to pull her eyesight into focus. She felt a bit sick. She could smell bleach, and a faint aroma of baked potatoes. She heard voices in the corridor outside, then the rustle of someone shifting in the seat next to her bed.

She turned her head slowly to see a man sitting there. He was dressed all in black, with straight dark hair and light brown eyes. His face was rather long, but even so Thea thought he was kind of handsome.

'Mortimer Breslin. I'm your sister's husband.' His accent was unmistakably American: drawn out, the syllables slightly slurred.

'I didn't know my sister had a husband.' Her voice was scratchy, her throat sore. She looked at her wrist where a needle punctured a vein, and she scratched around the site, wincing at the sting.

'Not many people did, apparently.'

Thea nodded, unsurprised by her sister's secrecy.

'How are you feeling?'

'Horrible. My head hurts, my arm aches and my mouth

feels funny.' She gestured towards the jug of water on the table, and Mortimer passed her a cup. She took a sip, the water cooling her tongue, washing away the fuzz in her mouth. 'Thank you,' she muttered.

'I shouldn't be here,' Mortimer said. 'I should be trying to find Gabriella, but I haven't worked out what to say to her yet. I'm not sure yelling will help.' He smiled apologetically.

'How did you meet?' Thea asked, leaning back on the pillow. She didn't really care but was glad of the company, someone being here with her. His accent made him sound languid and relaxed; she closed her eyes as he spoke.

'Some awful charity fundraiser. I was regretting being there, barely tolerating all the ego and bluster. Too many people with something to prove, you know?'

Thea didn't know, that world was alien to her, but his deep voice was soothing and she hoped he'd carry on.

'And then there she was. She was wearing this amazing red dress and her hair was messy. In a room full of Botox and plastic surgery, she was real. She was refreshing; I'd never met anyone like her before.'

He stopped, and Thea opened her eyes and looked at him.

'She lied to me,' he said. He looked miserable, his dark hair falling over his face as he studied the floor.

'She does that,' Thea said.

'She was so convincing.'

'We were always good at being each other. Sometimes it's easier to be someone else.'

Mortimer sighed and sat up straight. 'I should go. It was good to meet you, Thea.' He smoothed his shirt down and adjusted the collar, symbolically pulling himself back together. 'When you see your sister, please tell her to come home. I won't shout. I just want to see her. Properly, this time.'

Thea watched him go. She liked his assumption her sister would visit, that the bond between twins was unshakeable. She clung onto that hope, because after what she'd been doing, she wasn't so sure.

Earlier, the doctors had descended en masse, the man in charge surrounded by a flock of keen white coats. The older one had prodded and poked, then flashed a penlight up to her face and looked in her eyes. He said she would have a headache for a while (*No kidding!* she thought), but everything was looking promising for a full recovery.

If only her ego could be repaired in the same way.

She remembered going out to that club, dressed in a ridiculous outfit, make-up slapped all over her face. She'd been there two weeks before, originally to see Gabriella: she knew Gabi went, and thought she could take her by surprise. Thought they could talk. But then they'd assumed she was Gabi, and she felt a dizzying rush of popularity. People wanted to be with her. She had a taste of what it was like to be her sister, and she enjoyed it.

It was like a drug. She didn't have to worry about small talk, the introductions she'd always been so bad at, because Gabriella had done it all for her. It was addictive, being admired. And a bit of alcohol had eased things along nicely.

And then she met Ryan, and she liked him, so she kept on going. He seemed to like her, too. They spent the next Saturday at the club together, then he invited her home. She spent the night with him; it was new, it was exciting.

She remembered seeing Ryan again that Saturday. But she'd drunk too much, too quickly, and ended up feeling dizzy and unsure. She winced in embarrassment at the

memory – what the hell had she been thinking? She remembered the beginning of the night, but that was it.

Thea felt sick. He would know now who she actually was.
He would never speak to her again, and she didn't blame
him. Thea had hated the deception and the lies, something
she couldn't stand in others.

Aged twelve, she'd come home from school early, ill, and
chanced on her mother and Harrison together. At first she
hadn't known what she was seeing; Thea had sat through
embarrassing sex education classes, but what they were doing
hadn't seemed romantic or special or any of the things she'd
been told about. It seemed harsh and uncomfortable; why
would they want to do *that*? And she'd crept away, a part of
her instinctively knowing she had to keep it to herself.

Over the years, she'd thought about telling Harry and
Gabriella so many times, but like the situation she'd got
herself into with Ryan, she'd been afraid of the repercussions.
It was too late now. For both her and Ryan, and her parents
and Harrison. Much, much too late.

And like then, the lies had consequences. She'd wandered
into Gabriella's life, and look what happened. She'd woken
up here, head banging, messy and ill.

Thea felt a wave of dread creep across her, making her legs
twitchy and her stomach churn. Who had attacked her? Had
they thought she was Gabriella? Or was it something she
herself had done? She wished she could remember, anything
at all, just to make the uncertainty go away.

She had felt this way before – all those years ago, watching
her mother betray her father. She had known something bad
was going to happen then, and she hadn't been wrong. She
knew it then, and knew it now.

And she was terrified.

23

The man was perched on a stool by the bar, turning the pint in his hand round and round. Kate saw him the moment she pushed open the door, moving from the chilling night wind to the smug and suffocating bodies inside.

She knew why her husband had chosen this place, and why he was sat where he was. Less opportunity for a long drawn-out conversation, people around to prevent her making a scene. Plus alcohol all around them: a pathetic test. He didn't look up as she came over, not acknowledging her until she placed a hand on his shoulder and pulled out a stool to sit next to him.

Kate gasped her apologies, and he nodded.

'I wouldn't expect anything different,' he said and pushed a brown envelope towards her. She put a hand on it but didn't open it; she knew what it was.

'Are we going to talk about it?' she said, and he shook his head.

'I think we've done enough talking,' he replied, and when he looked at her, she saw he was tired and stressed.

She knew his face almost better than her own. Kate had met Sam at university, when their ambitions and drinking habits had been aligned. After graduation it seemed natural they would get married, her an insignificant uniform and Sam up and coming in marketing. They both worked long hours; it didn't matter that they socialised with different people, that she rolled home drunk in the early hours. It didn't matter that he discovered yoga and the gym, while she moved on to harder and more toxic spirits. They were together, they would work it out, it didn't matter.

Until it did. He wanted her to stop drinking; she denied she had a problem. He worked longer hours, travelled, mentioned different work colleagues, female names. She got jealous, they argued. She drank some more. Not a big deal, just to forget a hard day, to have some fun with colleagues, or to help her get to sleep.

Kate looked at him now – had they changed so much? They were both older, greyer, more lined. She had tried to cut back for him, stopped trying to be one of the lads, but she always failed. So, angry at his ultimatums, she'd moved out for a break that turned into a permanent solution. And now, here they were: the paperwork and the awkward silence.

'I miss you,' she said quietly.

'Kate, please.'

'I'm sorry, I'm not going to kick up a fuss. But I don't want this.' She tapped the brown envelope in front of her.

'I'm sorry, but I do,' Sam said. 'You know what I said.'

'So why ask me to meet you here?' Kate said, angrily gesturing round the room.

'I was hoping you'd tell me no. I was hoping you'd tell me you had got help, that meeting in a bar wasn't a good idea for you.'

Kate looked at him, tears pricking behind her eyes. 'I don't need help,' she whispered.

He paused, turning away and looking at his pint. It was almost finished, probably bought when he had arrived on time, and drunk furiously while the minutes ticked by. 'You know it isn't just about the drinking,' he said, picking up his glass and studying it carefully.

'So what is it about?' she asked.

He sighed. 'I'm not going over this again, Kate. It's over, we're over.'

She looked away from him; she didn't want Sam to see the tears start to run down her cheeks. She angrily brushed them away. So this was it, then. He'd moved on, probably got himself someone else to occupy his time. She should do the same. She picked up the envelope and opened it, pulling out the thick white paper and flicking through the pages. Some legal wording on one, some numbers on another. Their whole marriage distilled into a monetary value.

'You don't have to look at it now,' Sam said, 'but I think you'll find it's more than generous. Just sign it and send it back.' He looked at her, then swallowed the last dregs of his pint. 'Do it this time, please?'

He got up from the bar stool and put his coat on, pulling a scarf round his neck. Kate couldn't look at him. She couldn't watch him leave; she didn't want to make a scene. To be that woman sobbing alone on a bar stool. She felt him pause next to her.

'Look after yourself,' he said, and left.

Kate took a juddering breath in, and let it out slowly. She picked up the papers again. Sure enough, little sticky yellow tabs marked the places she would need to sign.

The barman appeared and placed a shot of something in front of her, and she waved it away.

'I didn't order that,' she said.

'You didn't, he did.' The barman gestured to a figure at the other end of the bar. He smiled and slowly waved, and Kate recognised him within seconds.

She knew him because she had been staring at his face on her whiteboard not twenty minutes before. One of the prime suspects in the attack and attempted murder of a vulnerable young woman. Someone she shouldn't be accepting drinks from. Not now, not ever.

Kate looked towards the door to the bar. This was bad, very bad indeed. She knew what she should do. She should push it away, stand up and go home. Drink some water, eat a well-balanced healthy dinner with avocado or quinoa or something, and go to bed, alone. But Sam's words echoed in her head. She felt the rejection, the jealousy. She felt lonely and discarded. She picked up the envelope and stuffed it in her bag, standing up and looking back at the door.

Kate downed the shot and gestured to the barman.

'Two more, please,' she said.

Thursday

24

The noise was loud and pulsing. It jerked Kate into life and she fumbled to turn her alarm off, her brain foggy with the familiar blur, her mouth stripped of all moisture. She lay in bed for a moment, eyes adjusting to the dim light that trickled in through the window. She was at home, that was something, at least. But even in darkness, she knew she wasn't alone: she could hear the steady in and out of his breathing, sense the presence of another person in her bed.

He hadn't woken, so she carefully extracted herself from the duvet, one hand resting on her thumping forehead. She tiptoed across the bedroom, picking up some clothes left on the side and opened the door, wincing at the slightest creak. Just before she closed it, she allowed herself to look back at the slumbering man. She could only see a toned arm and a mess of hair amid the jumble of bed covers. She winced at the memory.

As she scalded herself in the boiling hot shower, she thought back to the evening before. She remembered him sitting beside her at the bar, ordering glass after glass of expensive wine. She remembered them talking: her frosty at first, cutting him off mid-sentence, distracting him from talking about the case, about Thea or Gabriella. He had moved on and talked about other things, about her, what she did, what she liked – who was that man that she had been talking to? She forgot her previous impression of him and let her inhibitions go, lubricated by yet another bottle of wine. Oh, and she had talked. She shuddered and covered her face with her hands, remembering a long rant about her marriage, her soon-to-be ex-husband; her tongue loosened by the alcohol.

She climbed out of the shower and wrapped a towel around herself. She ran one hand across the mirror, wiping away the steam and taking in her pale face, the bags under her eyes.

Oh shit, and then what? The night stuttered and skipped. Blank spots and snapshots where memories should be. She went to go home. She knew she shouldn't be with him, so she took herself out of the bar. But then he left too, and somehow, outside, they were kissing. His lips on hers, soft, tasting of wine and vodka. She missed it, the kissing; the company of a man. A man in her bed. They took a cab, back here, back to do things that would ruin her career and her reputation if people found out. What a spectacularly stupid thing to do.

The phone next to her started vibrating and Kate picked it up. She grunted a greeting.

'Sarge? Are you on your way? I'm waiting for you at the hospital,' Briggs barked down the phone.

'Just leaving the house,' Kate lied, hastily throwing on her clothes. She gulped a pint of water, washing down paracetamol and retching as her stomach rebelled from the onslaught of the night before. She groaned and leaned on the kitchen counter, her brain woozy, willing the nausea to subside. It was going to be a long day.

As she tiptoed towards the front door, she glanced back to the bedroom. She shut her eyes and shook her head. He would be gone by the time she got back and she would pretend it had never happened. It certainly wouldn't happen again. She picked up her bag, and the brown envelope from the night before fell to the floor. Kate picked it up and looked at the legal document within.

Last night, however stupid, had obviously marked some sort of watershed in her subconscious mind. She flicked through the little yellow tabs.

The pages were signed.

25

Thea was stirring her cornflakes dejectedly when she saw the police officers arrive. Half of her dreaded the questioning, while the other half was desperate to have someone to talk to.

She'd had another visit from the doctors that morning; they'd taken the awful nasogastric tube out, but her appetite wasn't up to much. The grey-haired one was optimistic about her progress. 'But it'll be a few weeks before you can go home,' he had said. 'And that's only if you have someone who can keep an eye on you.' Harry probably wouldn't mind; she was longing to get out of here, to peace and quiet without the constant bothering.

The police officers hovered at her bedside. She remembered them from before, but her memory was hazy, and she'd forgotten their names. The woman seemed to be in charge and waited quietly for Thea's attention.

'We're here to ask a few questions,' she said.

Thea pointed to the seat next to the bed.

The woman officer sat down, moving carefully as if she was the one who was ill, not Thea. The bloke stayed standing, shifting his weight from foot to foot, seemingly eager to get going.

'What were you doing at the nightclub that evening?' the man said.

The woman gave him a look and gestured for him to sit down next to her.

'What my impatient colleague means to say is...' She gave him another stare. 'We know you were at Heaven that night, and we know you were pretending to be your sister, Gabriella.'

Thea didn't say anything.

'We are curious as to why.'

'Why does it matter?'

'It matters because we would like to find the person who attacked you. And it makes a difference whether they thought they were attacking you, or whether they were after your sister.'

Thea's head was hurting again and she lay back on her pillow, putting her hand on her forehead. It was cool and helped the throbbing.

The woman leaned forward. 'We won't be long, but we would appreciate the insight.'

Thea looked at her. She didn't look old, but seemed tired, her smart grey suit creased and her eyes bloodshot. Thea knew she wasn't at her best, but this woman could clearly do with a good night's sleep.

'Detective...?'

'Kate. DS Munro, but please call me Kate.'

'Kate.' Thea took a deep, juddering breath out. 'It wasn't the only time I'd been. I mean, as Gabi. The first time I just wanted to see Gabriella and I knew she used to work there.' Thea paused and looked out of the window. A line of grey cloud lingered over what little daylight there was; a few birds settled nonchalantly on a telegraph pole. 'It was an innocent mistake. They thought I was her, and then... I just wanted to see what it was like.'

'What what was like?' the man asked.

Thea looked at them. 'What having friends, male friends,

any sort of friends, was like. Being *popular.*' She spat the last word out. 'What being Gabi was like. And then I just ...' She paused. 'I just kept on going.'

'And how do you know Ryan Holmes?' Kate asked.

'He's ...' Thea stopped. 'He owns the club.'

'And that's all?'

'I thought there might be something else. But I guess not, not now.'

'And why were you arguing that night?'

Thea shook her head. 'I don't remember an argument.' She winced, the pain in her head making her feel dizzy. 'It's all a big blank. I remember turning up, having a cocktail. I didn't like it, so Ryan took it off me. After that, nothing.' She looked at the detectives. 'I'm sorry.'

'Was there anyone there that night who worried you? Who you were wary of?'

Thea thought back and frowned. 'No.'

'And you can't remember the attack?' The man again, getting another look from DS Munro.

'No, nothing at all.'

She put her head back on the pillow. Outside, it had started to rain, the sky torn and ominous. She didn't want to say anything else.

The police officers took their cue and left. The room was quiet again, except for the murmur of nurses in the corridor outside. She pushed her breakfast away from her.

The truth was, she had remembered something. A flicker of memory. A smell, a feeling. It made her embarrassed; the shame burned inside her. But it was nothing she wanted to share with the police. She just wanted to forget. And she wanted to get out of this place, as quickly as she could.

26

Gabi's search continued.

After Harry had left the day before, Gabi had started on the disused study, channelling her fractured emotions into something productive. She'd lifted up large white sheets, throwing years of grey dust into the air and causing her to sneeze. But she'd come up empty-handed, and as night closed in, she'd trudged up the stairs to the four-poster bed, collapsing without dinner or even cleaning her teeth.

She'd woken that morning in that big bed, alone, feeling fragile and unsure. Every moment she spent in that house she could feel the memories swirling around her, mocking her attempt to get away. The smells were the same; the way the light fell through the dirty windows, lighting up specks of dust in the air; it was all so familiar, yet surreal, like a long-forgotten dream.

She could leave; she had other places to live, after all.

Her tiny rented flat on the other side of town was magnolia and soulless. She'd had it for six months but had barely been there, living out of Mortimer's almost the moment after she'd met him. And oh, Mortimer. Poor Mortimer. She knew she needed to make amends there, too. She'd lied without thinking; it had been mean, unforgivable, to fool him in that way. He didn't deserve that. She didn't deserve him.

She should have told him, when he'd shown up at Thea's door on Tuesday. She should have told him everything. About why she'd come home. About what had really happened all those years ago. But to do that would have meant trusting him and saying sorry. It would have meant accepting some sort of responsibility for the mess she continued to make of her life.

Mortimer was different. He looked at her in a way she hadn't felt before: a small smile as she talked, his eyes locked on hers. He was quiet when other men bombarded her with words; he was still when she was jittery. And now she'd fucked it up.

She felt the anger take hold of her and she rolled over in the bed, screaming face down into the pillow. She screamed out of frustration and rage and pure bloody hatred of all the people around her who had made her life this way. Of Thea, of her parents, and Harrison, still rotting in prison.

Gabi rolled over onto her back and stared at the ceiling. She had to get out of there. It was making her crazy. Do what you came here for, then leave, she told herself.

She took a hot shower, cleaned her teeth and put on clothes that belonged to her, rather than Thea's misshapen wardrobe.

She had breakfast. She made a cup of coffee and carried it to the back of the house where she hadn't yet begun to search, to the small studio her mother had used for her art. Art was a generous word – the works she produced could only be described as junk, naive sculptures at best. Wood and metal stuck together with nails and glue, approximating people and shapes and animals; crude and immature despite years of art school. Nobody bought them, and Gabi could see Thea had cleared them out, to a destiny she could only guess at.

She blew dust from her finger, then caught a glimpse of a

large cloth covering something at the end of the room. She pulled a corner of it and there stood three huge boxes, their ends taped shut. On the side, in black marker pen, were the words *Photo Albums*.

Curiosity tugged at her and Gabi opened the top of the closest, selecting an album at random. She sat on the floor, cross-legged, and opened the pages, turning them over one by one.

This first showed laughing toddlers, fashion from the Eighties, colour-faded. Two identical babies, dressed the same, their smiles the same, their podgy hands and chubby arms matching. She could see why her mother got adoring stares – they looked picture-book gorgeous: dark shocks of hair, black eyes, full red mouths and rosy cheeks. And their mother was stunning, too. Long curly hair, dark eyelashes, fashionable flowing dresses and high-heeled boots, pushing a Silver Cross pram, two babies inside.

She flipped the pages again, looking for a shot of their father, eventually coming across one of him holding them both, grinning to the camera. His face was thinner than she remembered, his hair thicker. And he looked in love; they both did. Gabi struggled to remember the last time she had seen her parents happy together.

She put the album down and pulled out another. They were older, maybe four or five. First day of school, in matching red uniforms. Already their differences starting to show: Thea scowling, her hair coming out of one plait; Gabi playing up for the camera, a big smile, face thrust forward.

The photos progressed; they grew older, and here was Harry. She smiled at the image of the ten-year-old boy – long legs, long arms, knobbly knees. Trousers a bit too short, T-shirts needing a wash. In boyhood, Harry wasn't so different to the man she now knew, but adulthood had been kind to his long limbs. He filled out, became tall and handsome, building a carefully constructed confidence over the gawkiness. But somehow the awkwardness resurfaced when she least expected it. Poked out from the arrogant charade and disarmed her.

Gabi remembered their childhood, but the bits and pieces seemed skewed now. She remembered them always together, the three of them. Sometimes she'd go round with other friends; she'd push Thea and Harry away, wanting her individuality. But they'd always be there when she returned, waiting for her.

She flicked over another page and took in the photos. All of them older now. One of her mother sitting alone in the garden – she remembered Thea had taken that one – then a close-up of her mum and Harrison. She studied the photo. They looked like a couple: Harrison looking down into her mother's eyes, their arms locked around each other. Gabi frowned. She remembered her devoted love for her mother, and then the shattering realisation that her idol was flawed. It was all here, captured in Polaroid so she could see for herself.

She closed the book and stood up, placing the albums back in the boxes. But as she moved them, another book fell into view. She hadn't noticed it before, wedged down the side of the box, and now falling flat. It was a basic notebook, bought from the local supermarket, with lined pages and two holes punched down the left-hand side of the spiral binding. It looked worn, as if someone had turned its pages a thousand times. It was thicker than it should have been, and scraps of newspaper stuck out of the sides. She rested it on the cupboard next to her and opened it up, then gasped, her hand over her mouth.

Every page screamed murder. Every page declared infidelity and bloodshed and deception. Every page showed a photo of their parents. She turned them one by one, horrified but unable to look away. Her mother, looking young and beautiful. An old photo, taken long before it happened. Her father, old and haggard. And finally, Harry's father, Harrison himself, being taken away in handcuffs, looking behind him to the house.

House of horrors, a headline declared. After the murders Gabi hadn't wanted to stay here, and that had been fine. By that point they were eighteen, all of them ready to leave the nest. But of course she was the only one to go. She'd run, and hadn't been home in fifteen years.

The newspaper articles continued, documenting Harrison's trial, the guilty plea, the sentencing. *The lover's revenge*, they screamed in black and white. Even now Gabi couldn't look at a photo of Harrison's face without seeing the kind, sad man she remembered visiting their house for so many years. Sometimes he'd come round and their mother wouldn't be there, so he'd pause, then make supper for the girls and Harry. He would sit at the old wooden table, a mug of tea never far away, and listen to them all chatter and argue. Egg mayonnaise sandwiches with cress, Gabi remembered. She found it hard to reconcile that man with the cold-blooded killer the newspapers claimed he was.

She heard a key in the lock, and quickly closed the notebook, pushing it under a pile of albums. She heard heavy footsteps and looked up, guiltily. The door to the studio was open and she saw Harry walk past, then stop and turn back as he noticed her.

'I thought you had given up on this game,' he said, his face dark.

'I had, I have. I just wondered about something. What are you doing here?'

'Thea wants some spare clothes. Pyjamas and stuff.'

'She's feeling better?'

'Mmm.' Harry bent down and picked up one of the albums, the one covering the notebook. 'What's this?' he asked, flicking through the pages.

She watched in silence, the album balanced on one hand, Harry skimming pages with the other. His forehead furrowed as he caught a glimpse of his father. He looked up at her.

'Why were you looking at these?' he asked, but before she could answer he saw the notebook. 'What's that?'

When Gabi didn't reply he picked it up and opened it, turning the pages. His face remained expressionless.

'Is this yours?'

'No,' Gabi replied. 'It must be Thea's.'

He paused, his eyes stopping at the photo of his father.

'Do you visit him at all?' Gabi asked, tentatively.

Harry didn't reply, taking so long that Gabi wondered if he had heard her. Then: 'No.' He hesitated again. 'He wrote to me for a long time, one letter a week. I didn't ever open them, then I started writing 'Return to Sender' and putting them back in the post box. He stopped after a while.'

'You know he's...' Gabi started.

'Dying. Yes. I know.' Harry shook his head, his mouth clamped shut, his forehead bent to the floor. He stood very still, and Gabi could see the tension in his jaw.

'He had an affair with your mother,' Harry said quietly, closing the notebook decisively and dropping it to the ground. He looked at her, his blue eyes narrowed. 'He destroyed this family long before the shooting. He did that without a thought to me, or you, or Thea. So no, I don't think about him, the same as he didn't think about what would happen to me.' He kicked the book with the toe of his shoe. 'I have all the family I need – same as I ever did. My dad's dead to me. I am not going to go through this again.'

With a waft of his coat, he strode out of the room. 'Now come and help me tidy up this house,' he shouted from the kitchen. 'You've left it in a fucking mess.'

Gabi stood up and brushed the dust from her jeans. She picked up the photo album and replaced it in the box, sealing the lid shut again. The notebook lay where Harry had dropped it, fallen open to the last page, the headline screaming out in black block capitals.

GUN NEVER FOUND, it said.

27

The police were back at the house, and the woman was blunt from the get-go.

'Gabriella Patterson?' she asked, and Gabi nodded.

'How do we know?' the woman continued.

'Well, since my sister is in the hospital, you'll have to assume I'm telling the truth.'

'Can we come in?'

In line with Harry's demands, Gabi had been tidying the house, hanging Thea's shapeless black sweatshirts and torn jeans back in the wardrobe, throwing whatever seemed dirty in the washing machine. She had heard Harry downstairs, and the sound of an ancient hoover jumping into life.

Gabi held the door open reluctantly, and the police officers pushed past her. In the kitchen the vacuum cleaner was now silent. She showed them into the living room, and the one she remembered from the interview, DS Munro, sat down on the sofa while the other one hovered next to the front door. Gabi perched opposite her, waiting.

'Why did you lie, Gabriella?'

Gabi forced a smile. 'I'm sorry, but I needed some breathing space. You gave me an opportunity.'

'You mislead us, you delay our investigation by nearly a week so you could have a holiday? You realise it's an offence to waste police time? I could arrest you right now.'

'Don't you ever fancy a break, DS Munro? Wouldn't

you take the chance to hide from your own life, see how the world views you from the outside?' Gabi met her gaze, determined not to be intimidated on her own turf. They had fucked up, these police officers, and they knew it. She would be damned if they were going to make out it was her fault.

The detective shook her head, resigned. 'So where were you the night Thea was attacked?' she asked.

'I was at home.'

'At home with your husband, or at your flat?'

'At my flat.'

'Did you know your sister was pretending to be you? Going to nightclubs, sleeping with your boyfriends?'

'I assume you're talking about Ryan Holmes.' Gabi stopped, taking a moment to still herself, knowing the detective was desperate for a reaction. 'He's never been my boyfriend. And I didn't know, no. Not until you knocked on the door.' She was lying again, but she didn't like the police sniffing around. Something about it made her sneaky.

'And what do you think your husband feels about Mr Holmes?'

'He doesn't know anything about Ryan.'

'He does, Gabriella,' the detective said with a small smile. 'And he thought Ryan was with you. Do you think it made him angry? Angry enough to try and kill you?'

'Mortimer's not like that.'

'No? Are you sure? You haven't known him for long. We know he was in the area that night. We know he was following the person he thought was you. Men do strange things sometimes, Gabriella. When someone they love pushes them to the edge.'

Gabi cleared her throat, tears threatening behind her eyes. The guilt of what she had put Mortimer through nagged at her; she felt shit enough without these blundering detectives reminding her. She shook her head, refusing to say any more.

DS Munro paused. 'Why are you still here, Gabi?'

'I was just leaving. We were tidying up, ready for when Thea comes home.'

'We?' The detective stopped abruptly as Harry moved into the doorway from the kitchen. He dried his hands on a tea towel then put it over his shoulder, leaning against the doorframe. He was stooping slightly, a mocking smile on his lips. Gabi recognised the stance from their teenage years; his perfected façade of coolness and poise, designed to throw off the most confident of women.

The detective cleared her throat and looked away quickly. 'Do you mind if we look around?'

'Yes, I do,' Gabi said. 'As you said, this isn't my house – I'm not comfortable with you snooping. I think it's time you left.'

The detective nodded and, with one last glance towards Harry, went back into the hallway, her colleague opening the front door. Once outside, DS Munro turned and held out her hand, offering a small white business card.

'My contact details, in case you ever want to talk,' she said. Gabi took it, then watched them leave, closing the door behind them.

'You should be pleased they didn't arrest you,' Harry said. He moved to the window and peered through, watching their grubby Skoda pull out of the driveway. 'Try not to piss them off next time.'

'I'm hoping there won't be a next time,' she replied.

'You should know better than that by now, Gabriella.' Harry pushed past, picking up his coat and opening the front door. He looked back at her. 'With our history, there's always a next time.'

Gabi watched him go, climbing into his blue estate. She knew he was right. The police were never far away, especially now. Gabriella stared at the card in her hand, embossed with the logo of the Hampshire Constabulary. Despite herself, Gabriella was beginning to have a grudging respect for DS Munro. She was determined and perceptive; all the more reason to keep her at arm's length, Gabi thought, ripping the card into four small pieces.

She peered into the corridors of the house; it was getting dark and the dim light threw unfamiliar shadows across the walls. She was sick of being here. This game was over; she'd had enough. And there was someone else she needed to talk to.

Gabriella walked out into the cold winter's air, pulling the front door closed behind her. She didn't look back; she wouldn't. But at the same time as she stepped away from her childhood home, she stacked the four pieces of ripped white card into a pile. Then carefully pushed them into the back pocket of her jeans.

28

The taxi drove away. Gabriella slowly walked up the driveway. A black BMW was neatly parked on the left, perfectly
parallel to the front door.

None of the lights were on, but Gabi could see a dim
glow at one of the front windows. She knew where he
would be, and what he would be wearing. Her husband
had a quiet life: minimal, both in activities and possessions.
In their last argument she'd told him it was boring, but in
truth she liked the predictability. She was tired of surprises.

She let herself in as quietly as she could, closing the front
door with a perfectly designed click behind her. She slipped
her boots off, leaving them in the middle of the massive
hallway, walking in her socked feet towards the kitchen.

He looked up as she opened the door, his shoulders sag-
ging when he saw her. He was sat at the kitchen table, laptop
open and papers scattered around him, hair a mess and glasses
perched on his nose. This and the fact he was dressed in his
trademark black made him look like a wise crow. It made
her smile.

'Hi Mort,' Gabi said.

'So it is you,' he replied. He reached up and took his
glasses off, deliberately closing his laptop and laying the
glasses on top. 'You called me that, at the hospital. Only you
call me Mort.'

Gabi walked over to the fridge and pulled out a bottle of

white. With her back to him, she opened it and poured a fishbowl-sized glass. She took a sip.

She turned round and he was watching her, waiting. He seemed calm, so fucking calm. She wanted him to shout, to scream at her, to make her feel something other than guilty. Especially when she had such a lot to feel guilty for.

Gabi took a seat in front of him at the table.

'I'm sorry,' she said.

He paused. 'For walking out the other week, for pushing me away? For pretending to be your sister? Or for kissing me on Tuesday night?' He shook his head. 'You made me think I'd cheated on you, Gabi. With your twin, of all people. How do you think that made me feel?'

'I know. I'm sorry.' Gabi took a deep breath. 'For all of that. But mostly for the last few days. It was unforgivable, I'm sorry.'

Mortimer sighed and put his hands flat on the lid of his computer. His wedding ring shone in the overhead light. 'What do you want, Gabi?'

'What do you mean?'

He looked at her. 'You walked out. You pretended to be someone else so you didn't have to talk to me. Nobody knows who I am. You don't seem to want to be married, period. But yet you're here in my house, our house, today.' He rubbed his eyes. 'So, what do you want?'

Gabi sagged in her seat. What did she want? She had no idea, not really. But she was tired of being alone, tired of pushing back from the people who seemed to love her, to spend time in the company of people who didn't. She was scared of what had happened with Thea. But she couldn't say any of that. She felt hot, embarrassed tears on her cheeks, and covered her face with her hands, letting her shoulders rise and fall with her sobs. This wasn't what she did; this weakness, this wasn't her. But she couldn't help it. The disguise fell, and he was there with her. She felt Mortimer's arms round her and rested her head on his chest, feeling reassured by him pulling her in.

After a while, he slowly pulled her to her feet, then cupped her face in his hands. With his thumbs he gently wiped the tears from her cheeks, then kissed her softly. She let him guide her upstairs to their bedroom, where he took off her jumper, her jeans. She undid his shirt, all the time feeling his eyes on her, his lips on her face, her neck, her body. He pulled her onto the bed and she lay back, relaxing for the first time in what seemed like months. It was time to let go, she told herself. It was time to stop running.

The initial flash woke Gabi, and she lay in bed for a moment, waiting to see what would happen next. She could hear the rain pelting the window, the wind rushing round the walls.

She saw it again, lighting up the room for an instant, and in an automatic reaction started counting. After five, the rumble came, a shockingly loud break through the silent night, starting quietly, then growing into a huge bang, shaking the whole house.

She remembered at age eight or nine, lying in bed with Thea. They were both terrified of the storm, so they would play a game.

'Ask me a question,' Thea would say. 'Then I have to tell you the answer as soon as the thunder strikes. And it has to be the truth, or the lightning will get you. Make it a hard one.'

Gabi would think for a moment. 'Who's your favourite, Mum or Dad?'

'Dad,' Thea blurted out as the crack echoed round the house.

A new flash: 'My most annoying habit?' Gabi giggled.

'Biting your nails,' Thea laughed as they heard the thunder. Then the storm didn't seem as scary any more.

Gabi got out of bed, leaving Mortimer, and pulled one of his jumpers over her head. She walked into the hallway and stood at the window, looking out into the soaking landscape, waiting for the next bang. The lightning lit up the trees, followed instantly by thunder, enough to rattle the windows. She jumped, then laughed at her own skittishness.

'It's beautiful, isn't it,' came a voice behind her.

She didn't turn around. She took in his body heat as he stood against her, his arms round her middle.

Another flash lit up the sky, the lightning bolt snaking to the ground in the near distance. The crack came seconds later.

'It's getting further away,' she said, pulling the sleeves from the jumper over her chilly hands. Her legs and feet were bare, and she could feel the cold night air starting to seep under the jumper.

Mortimer pulled her in tighter and she leaned into him.

'I didn't cheat on you, Mort. You know that, right? It wasn't me.'

'I realised that,' he whispered into her hair. He rested his mouth against the back of her neck, and she could feel the gentle rise and fall of his breathing.

'We could leave, you know,' he said, his voice deep and quiet. 'We can go anywhere you want, just say the word.'

She didn't turn around; she didn't dare look at him and risk him seeing the uncertainty on her face. 'But you have a life here, you have a home.'

'It's only a house,' he replied. 'They're only things.' He paused as another lightning bolt lit up the sky.

She turned to face him, and put her nose against his. It was cold. She kissed him. Shadows from the window cast Mortimer's face into odd angles. 'Come to bed,' he said, pulling her away from the window.

She climbed under the duvet, leaving the jumper on and curling her knees into her chest. Mortimer lay next to her, on his front, his face turned towards her. In the darkness, she could only make out a few of his features: his eyes looking at her, his hair messy and falling over his face.

He reached out and smoothed a strand of her hair behind her ear.

'You know I'd do anything for you, don't you,' he said, his voice little more than a whisper.

She nodded. 'I know.'

Mortimer's breathing slowed as he fell back to sleep. She rolled over onto her back, warm now, but wanting to keep the jumper on. It smelt of him – of his skin, of freshly ground coffee – and it reassured her.

Everyone left her, everyone. Only her twin sister had been a constant, but that hadn't been true for a very long time. Her parents had left her, Harry was angry; people were transient and not to be relied upon. The police had said Mortimer had been there, yet he'd acted like he'd known nothing about Thea's attack. Was he lying? Had he seen something that night?

She closed her eyes, hearing the thunder recede into the distance, getting quieter until she could no longer make out the noise above the rain. But before the storm disappeared, she asked herself a question: should she trust him?

Perhaps he wouldn't leave her; perhaps he was telling the

truth. Perhaps Mortimer was exactly who he said he was. He muttered in his sleep and rolled onto his other side. She wanted to move next to him, to curl her body round his, but in the darkness something stopped her.

The lightning may already have flashed, but she knew the thunder was still to come.

Friday

29

'Thank you for coming back in to see us, Mr Holmes,' Kate said, closing the door to the interview room.

'I'm not sure I had much choice in the matter,' Ryan muttered.

Yates rattled through the formal warnings, Ryan shaking his head at the mention of legal counsel. Kate watched him while he signed the paperwork at the bottom – right-handed. But that wasn't necessarily a deal breaker, she told herself.

And he did look nervous. He crossed and uncrossed his legs under the table, then knitted his fingers together in front of him. A visible sheen of perspiration was forming across his forehead.

'We appreciate you bringing in the CCTV from the club,' Kate began. 'We've been looking through the many disks you gave us – you were very thorough.' Yates huffed next to her, only too aware of the wasted hours she had spent watching them, Briggs left in the office to continue working through the pile. Kate went on: 'But we found something we wanted your opinion on.'

Yates pulled the laptop out next to her and pressed play. Ryan stayed silent, squinting through his glasses.

'I'm not sure what I'm looking at,' he said.

'I'll describe it,' Kate said. 'For the benefit of the video and Mr Holmes, the laptop is showing the upstairs bar in the nightclub, Heaven. Would you agree?'

Ryan nodded. 'And here ...' said Kate, jabbing at the screen, 'here's you, and here's Miss Patterson. You seem to be arguing. And now ...' The three of them watched the slap play out in grainy black and white. 'Why did Miss Patterson hit you, Mr Holmes?'

Ryan took his glasses off and placed them on the table in front of him.

'It's last Saturday, nineteenth of January.'

'I remember.'

'So what was the argument about?'

Ryan sighed and leaned back in his chair. 'Gabriella had been acting weird, and I was sick of it. She'd been at the club that Tuesday night and she'd been the life and soul of the party – bubbly, friendly, fun – but she'd practically ignored me. Hadn't even acknowledged what had happened the Saturday before.' Kate noticed his cheeks colouring slightly, but stayed quiet, waiting for him to carry on. 'Then she came back on the Saturday night ...'

'The night of the attack?' Kate asked, and Ryan nodded.

'Yes, the nineteenth, and she was quieter again. More ...' he shrugged. 'Herself. So I mentioned Tuesday night and asked her what was wrong. Told her every time I saw her she was like a different person, and that's when she slapped me. Said something about me wanting her to be someone else, I don't know, I couldn't make it out.'

'And then she left?'

'She stormed off. I didn't see her after that as I started to feel odd and went to lie down. As I said the other day,' he added, pointedly.

'And that's where you were for the rest of the night?' Kate asked.

'Yes.'

'Asleep?'

'Yes.'

'Where nobody saw you? Where no one can vouch for you? Awfully convenient, don't you think?'

'Not really,' Ryan said, his face serious. 'Given you've pulled me back here today.'

'And this,' Kate rewound the file again, and pointed to the grainy figure in the dress on the screen. 'Is this the person you know as Gabriella?'

Ryan put his glasses back on, then nodded. 'Yes.'

Kate drummed her fingers on the table for a moment, pretending to think. 'Because, Mr Holmes, we now know this isn't Gabriella. And we think you knew that too.'

Ryan sat up straight in his seat. She felt his blue eyes lock on hers.

'What on earth are you talking about?'

'This is Thea Patterson, her twin sister.'

He looked at the screen, then back at Kate. 'So the woman in the hospital...'

'Is Thea, yes.'

'So where is Gabriella?' Ryan asked.

'Roaming Southampton, as healthy as can be,' Kate said. 'That was probably the real Gabriella on Tuesday night.' She noticed a blush starting to creep up his neck, his cheeks turning red. He was still mute, looking at the laptop screen, his mouth open. 'But you knew that, Mr Holmes. You realised what was going on that night, and you confronted Thea about it. She slapped you, and you were angry. Furious, even. Thea and her sister had been playing you for a fool, swapping round, both pretending to be Gabriella.' Kate paused, watching his expression. 'So you followed her when she left the club, all the way to the common, where you hit her over the head. Isn't that right?'

Ryan looked at her. He shook his head. 'No, not at all. I didn't know. I hadn't realised.' He put both hands over his face, pushing his fingers under his glasses, then taking them off and putting them on the table. He looked up at the ceiling. 'Oh, fuck. What a fucking idiot,' he said, more to himself than to them.

He shook his head again. 'I didn't know,' he said.

Half an hour later, Yates and Kate hadn't got any further so they'd terminated the interview, letting him go. He hadn't said anything else of use; he hadn't changed his story.

'I honestly don't think he knew,' Yates said, pushing open the door to the office where Briggs sat, bleary-eyed, still glued to the CCTV footage. 'Did you see his face when he realised they were two different people?'

'He looked mortified,' Kate agreed.

'So what now?' Yates asked, sitting back behind her computer. 'Should we get Harry Becker in for questioning?'

Kate frowned. 'And ask him what?' She picked up the silver button abandoned among the paperclips on her desk and rolled it around in her hand. 'We'd just be fishing. No, let's wait. We need something more before we get him in here.'

Briggs looked up from his screen, interrupting their conversation. 'The chief called. Wants to see you,' he said.

Kate winced. 'That can't be good,' she muttered. 'Did you manage to get an answer out of forensics?'

'Today. Or next week,' Briggs said, and Kate swore under

her breath as she started up the stairs to the detective chief inspector's office.

Bloody vague as usual. Bloody forensics. They could do with something coming back from them soon. As much as she didn't want to admit it, she did believe Ryan Holmes when he said he hadn't known about the twins' deception. Kate wondered who actually *had* known.

She'd seen herself how convincing the twins had been. When they'd met Gabriella the day before, she had looked different: more groomed, better put together. She stood up straight, while as Thea, she had cowered. It was as if Gabi had consciously tried to mimic her sister in the police station. It hadn't been a simple case of mistaken identity; while she was Thea, she had assumed her persona.

As Kate approached the DCI's office, the door opened and the man himself swung out into the corridor. DCI Jennings looked over his glasses at her. He was short and round, with stubby, fat fingers and a bald head with two tufts of hair sticking out either side. He had his coat in one hand and his phone in the other, clearly on the way home.

'I can come back tomorrow ...' she started, but he stopped and beckoned her to the side of the corridor.

'Ah, DC Munro, just the girl. No, no, let's talk now.' The chief inspector was sweating through his shirt and Kate swallowed down the condescension. 'I've had to do a bit of rebalancing in the department, regarding the Patterson case.'

'Rebalancing, sir?' Kate asked.

'Yes, moving things around. I assume you heard about the burglary last night, the house of one of our prominent councillors?'

Kate nodded; she already didn't like where this was going.

'I've asked forensics to prioritise the evidence there,' Jennings said. 'So there'll be a little delay on your GBH for the time being.' He patted her arm with a sweaty hand.

'We're investigating it as an attempted murder.' Kate paused, measuring her words carefully. 'A young woman was attacked, left for dead, sir. We have a duty to do everything we can to get this guy off the streets.'

'Yes, yes, carry on, do your stuff.' The chief pulled a face and waved his chubby hand in the air. 'You'll just have to be a bit creative with what you have until we get this burglary sorted.'

Kate watched him bumble off down the corridor, round body rolling on top of two little cone-shaped legs. She couldn't imagine the last time her DCI had been on the front line, let alone completed the bleep fitness test.

'For fuck's sake,' she muttered under her breath. Be a bit creative? What the fuck did that mean?

She knew exactly what was going on. Some poor little rich guy had been broken into and pulled a few strings with his powerful mates to get it looked at sooner. Meanwhile, their guy went free. It made her want to scream with frustration, rage at the injustices in the system. But whatever she did, she knew nothing was going to change today.

She sighed and made her way back to the ops room. Jennings may be done for the day, but for her there was work to do.

As she walked her phone beeped in her pocket and she pulled it out. A text from an unfamiliar number. She glanced down the now-empty corridor, feeling her cheeks redden.

What a night! Let's do it again. Xx

She put the phone away quickly, cringing but feeling something else. An undercurrent of excitement.

Kate didn't remember giving him her number, but she knew she should go back with a curt *No, thank you* and put an end to this stupidity. But something stopped her. That sudden jolt. A kick of expectation.

Despite the risk, she left the text there, a part of her wanting to feel the thrill again.

30

Thea heard footsteps behind her on the gravel, but didn't turn. They were delicate, considered, slow. She knew who they belonged to.

'They said you'd gone home.'

Thea turned to her sister. She took in her nose, her eyes, her chin. The face she saw every day in the mirror. But today, Gabriella looked different. Younger. She had minimal make-up on and her hair was natural, the wind pushing it around her face. Thea saw Gabi's reticence, her worry; it matched her own trepidation.

Thea looked up at the house. The sky was a dull concrete grey; drizzle clung to her coat. She shifted the small bag of belongings in her hand.

The doctors had been adamant she couldn't leave the hospital. She was seriously ill; she'd only just woken up from a coma. But she signed the forms and walked away, determined to escape. She had been stuck in the hospital too long, where monitors beeped and nurses chatted as they walked down the corridor. Where it was never quiet. She needed the quiet.

But now she was here, she wasn't sure. She did feel awful: her head rattled, her arm and her fingers ached; she could barely stand. The house watched her, quiet and overbearing. She knew what to expect when she turned the handle and let herself in: the smell of damp, the cold, the draughts. For the first time, she yearned for something sleek and modern, a place nondescript and unemotional to lay her head.

But her sister was here. Gabriella was back home, where she belonged.

Thea went first, walking into the gloom then up the stairs to her bedroom. Gabriella followed her, hesitant and silent. Thea's headache was back, and her skin was itching under the bandage as her stitches adjusted from the cold to the warmth inside. She looked at her bed – the crumpled duvet, the pillows askew. It was a welcome sight and she climbed in, her feet, in their muddy boots, poking out the side.

She closed her eyes and heard Gabi's footsteps. She felt Gabi pull the boots from her feet and drop them on the floor. Then the bed moved and her sister climbed in next to her.

She felt Gabi's breathing calm and slow. Thea listened to her sister, and dropped off to sleep.

When Thea woke the sky was dark. She looked over in the bed at her twin. Gabi was already awake, staring at the ceiling.

'Harry said you stayed here,' Thea said, and Gabi looked over quickly.

'Yes.'

'You said you never wanted to come here again. You said you couldn't bear it.'

'It's been a long time.' Gabi hesitated. 'What do you re-member from that night? Do you know who attacked you?'

Thea felt Gabi's eyes on her. She knew she looked dread-ful. Dark bags under her eyes, her hair matted, the bandage round her head stained and bloody.

'I remember going to the club, I remember speaking to

Ryan but after that, not much.' Thea pulled the duvet up to her chin, reluctant to leave the warmth of the bed. 'I'm not used to drinking. I think the alcohol went to my head.'

Gabi took a deep breath in, and let it out slowly. 'And how long have you been pretending to be me?' she asked.

Thea stared at the ceiling, silent.

'How long, Thea? It's been at least a week, because Mortimer says he followed me to the club last Saturday and I know I wasn't there.'

Thea sighed. 'A few weeks,' she said quietly. 'I first went to try and talk to you and then they thought I was you, and ...'

'You nicked my driving licence!' Gabi said, incredulously.

'You dropped it on Wednesday. I was going to give it back ...' Thea said, but Gabi interrupted her.

'That's why the police thought you were me, you know? And they're blaming *me* for the deceit.' Gabi stopped and thought for a moment. 'And what about Ryan? Have you been sleeping with him?'

'Once. That Saturday night,' Thea replied.

'Thea!' Gabi cried out.

'I wanted to feel a little bit what you felt,' Thea said quietly. 'I wanted to feel special and wanted. And desired.'

Gabi sighed. 'That's not how I feel.'

'I know that now,' Thea said. She paused, and slowly pulled herself up to sit. 'They said nobody came to visit you in the hospital, nobody except Harry and Mortimer.'

Gabi turned round quickly. 'Don't you go feeling sorry for me. Your life isn't so perfect ...'

'I never said it was ...'

'I've stayed here these past few days, in this house. Your life isn't exactly a whirlwind of joy and happiness. Nobody ever comes here. Nobody ever calls you. What do you do all day?' Gabi shouted, jumping out of the bed.

'I don't need people around me all the time, hanging off my every word. I do all right for myself.' Thea threw the duvet off and stood up on the bare floorboards, turning on the overhead light. Her legs felt uncertain and wobbly; the sudden movement made her head pound. 'You left me. I was never scared when we were growing up because I always knew I had you. Even when we fought, we always had each other,' Thea said defiantly, facing her sister, feeling the anger from fifteen years ago return. 'And then you left and I had to work out how to survive without you. And I did. I have a successful business – I make a living for myself rather than cadging off desperate men.'

Gabi prodded a finger in her direction. 'You hide. That's what you do, you hide. In this cold, run-down house that should have been demolished years ago. At least I get out there and experience life.'

'And all the mind-altering substances you can get your hands on, right?' Thea picked up some clothes from the floor, then turned to face Gabi again. 'Why did you come back? Everything was fine with you on the other side of the world.'

'Harrison's dying!' Gabi shouted. She turned towards her sister, taking a deep, shuddering breath in, letting it out slowly. 'I saw a newspaper article. It said he'd been denied compassionate release because of the violent nature of the murders,' she said, softly. 'Harry's dad will be dead, and he'll never forgive himself. Harrison will be gone and we'll never be able to put this right.'

Thea paused. 'Is that such a bad thing?' she asked.

Gabi stared at her, her mouth open, then went to walk past her, trying to get to the door. Thea blocked her.

'Let me through, Thea.' Gabi went to push her out of the way, but Thea was surprisingly strong. 'Let me past.'

'Leave it alone, Gabi,' Thea said, then stopped, making the connection in her head. 'Is that why you stayed here? You were looking for the gun?'

Gabi shook her head and shoved her sister out of the way.

'You couldn't find it, could you?' Thea shouted at Gabriella's back as she clattered down the stairs. 'What were you planning on doing with it? Giving it to the police? Telling them what happened? There's no reason why you have to do this. The right person is in jail. What difference would it make?'

Gabi's footsteps stopped. Thea heard her sister pause, catching her breath.

'You know, that's what scares me the most,' Gabi said from the floor below, her voice breaking. 'That you don't seem to care about this at all.'

Thea heard the front door slam and looked out of the window, watching Gabriella, cradling her thumping head.

That damn gun. They should have got rid of it years ago. Thea cursed ever finding it in the first place. It had been that same summer: the summer of their A levels, the end of the affair, the summer of the murders. Thea remembered the tedium, the baking sunshine, lying in the garden with Harry, surrounded by discarded textbooks.

'I'm bored,' Harry said, drawing the word out into a long sigh of syllables. He pulled himself up and looked to the back of the garden. 'What do you suppose is in those sheds?' he asked.

He stood up, pushing his battered trainers back on. He held his hand out to Thea.

'Let's go see,' Harry said.

The inside of the shed was lit by a dim shaft of grey light from the one grimy window on the far wall. After pulling the lock away from the rotten wood with ease, Harry bowed his head and stepped inside, his trainers crunching on old dried leaves. Thea followed him, ducking low, feeling the delicate strands of cobwebs across her face.

'There's nothing in here but old tools and paint.' Thea poked at the lid of one of the pots and it opened easily, revealing a dried-up sphere of bright blue. 'Let's go.'

'In a moment,' Harry said from a corner of the shed. 'There's something here.' He pushed a rickety basket out of his way and crouched down next to a small black cupboard. 'I think it's a safe.'

'Really?' Thea craned her neck to take a better look. Sure enough, a small black metal safe, complete with a silver dial, had been left in a far corner of the shed. It was rusty and covered in mud, abandoned on the floor.

'What have you found?'

Both of them jumped as a figure appeared, blocking out the light and casting a shadow across the dust. Gabriella stood in the doorway, long dark hair tumbling around her shoulders, wearing a light yellow sundress that barely covered her bum.

Harry stood up and brushed his hands off. 'It's no good, it's locked.'

Gabi leaned over and looked at it, then turned and moved some tools around next to her. 'Try this,' she said, offering a rusty black crowbar from the depths of the shed.

Harry took it and weighed it up in his hands. He put it into a hole in the door of the safe, then pushed all his strength against it. His shorts fell low on his hips; Thea could see Gabi looking at the muscles of his back as he tensed against the crowbar. The safe creaked, then gave way with a loud grating of metal.

The three of them crowded round the tiny door, pushing each other in the confines of the shed, trying to see what was inside. Harry reached into the safe and pulled out a small rattling box, and something else wrapped in a dirty cloth. As he unwrapped it, they all drew back.

'Shit,' Harry said, as he took it out of the piece of material.

They looked at each other in the dim light, their mouths open. 'Put it back, quickly,' Thea said, backing up, but Gabi reached over and took it out of Harry's hands.

The gun was small and black, with a short muzzle and a textured black handle. Gabi turned it over, then held it how she had seen in films, her hand round the grip, her finger over the trigger.

'Is it real?' Thea whispered.

'It looks it,' Gabi replied, her voice soft and breathy, wheeling it round so it pointed at Thea.

'Fuck, don't point it at us,' Harry shouted. 'Put it down, Gabi, we don't know if it's loaded.' Gabi lowered the muzzle to the floor and Harry let out a big whoosh of air. 'Who does it belong to? Your parents?'

'Who knows,' Gabi said, her eyes locked on the gun. 'What's in the box?'

Harry turned it over in his hand and opened up the cardboard. 'Bullets. Must be about twenty in there.'

He rattled it in front of Gabi. She looked, then held the gun up again, pointing it away from them towards the back of the shed. 'It's heavier than I thought it would be,' she said, weighing it up with her hand. 'It's kind of nice.'

Suddenly the shed erupted with a roar and Gabi screamed.

Smoke rose from the floor, making the light turn grey. The smell of burning filled Thea's lungs.

Her ears were ringing as she ran out of the shed, closely followed by Harry. They stood, blinking in the sunlight as Gabi emerged behind them, covered in dust, her face a mask of shock.

'Fuck, Gabi, what did you do?' Harry stood, his hands on his knees, bent double, getting his breath back.

Gabi started laughing. Small at first, then growing until she couldn't contain her hysterics, tears running down her face. Then Harry joined in, collapsing onto the grass, his body shaking.

Thea remembered their father hadn't been quite so amused. He'd appeared behind them, shocked into anger, ranting at their smirking faces. He'd taken it away and sent them back into the house – to their revision, to watch television, anything as long as they stayed out of trouble.

And the gun had been forgotten, until that fateful day.

In a moment of curiosity years ago, Thea had looked into it; apparently it was a common occurrence to find vintage guns abandoned in old houses. Kept after the war and left behind as veterans died. But what if her dad hadn't taken it back into the house? What if he'd taken it to a police station straight away, like he intended? Would her parents still be alive? How different their futures might have been.

Thea watched her sister run down her driveway into the darkness. She pushed her hand up against the glass, as if reaching out to her twin.

'Leave the past alone, Gabi,' Thea said. 'Leave it alone.'

31

Kate started expensive – a nice New Zealand Sauvignon Blanc. After all, nobody orders that when they're planning to get drunk, do they? This was a wine to be savoured. She cradled the glass in both hands, feeling the cold before she took a sip. It was nice. It wouldn't be a crime to have more than one of these. Even though she wouldn't. Of course not.

She took a stool at the bar, the exact same one from which her husband had presented her with the divorce papers. She knew she was nursing her depression, feeding it with more morsels of failure, but she couldn't stop. The misery was addictive, and gave her a convenient excuse to have that first glass of wine. Her insides churned with the events of the day; with frustration, annoyance.

It was Friday night, and she had nowhere to go. She was pissed off. Her social life was a disaster, her career heading that way too. Everything they did on the case was a dead end. The CCTV was long and tedious, street footage was grainy and inconclusive, and they still hadn't found anything else to link either Mortimer Breslin or Ryan Holmes conclusively to the attack.

And to top it off, there was the conversation with DCI Jennings, making her fume inside. 'Arsehole,' she muttered under her breath. Why hadn't she stood up to him? Why hadn't she said no? She wouldn't sit around and wait for his golf buddy's burglary to be solved; they needed those results and they needed them now.

Because those retorts hadn't occurred to her until half an hour later. Because it had taken her that long to overcome the ingrained compliance she had towards men in charge. She took another gulp of her wine. Pathetic, she told herself.

The bar started to fill up. People were leaving work, ready to have a few drinks before heading back to their loved ones. Her elbow was jostled, and she spilled her wine.

She felt the absence of people around her, of warmth and friendship. Of people that gave a shit about her and her life. She was lonely, no doubt about that. Tears pricked behind her eyes again, and she took a deep breath, looking up at the ceiling to keep them at bay.

More people arrived. The door opened and closed, wafts of cold air chilling her toes. More laughter, more fun. This was a bad idea. She'd had nights begin like this before. Usually with other people around her, but always ending the same way. Staring in the mirror with half-closed eyes and a puffy face. Memories missing; playing detective on her own life; trying to reassemble the evening from receipts and hand stamps and texts on her mobile phone. Counting the bruises on her legs.

She needed to stop this now. She downed the last dregs of her second glass of wine and picked up her coat.

'That's a pity, I hoped you would stay.'

He appeared at her elbow, a welcome sight for her addled brain.

'I've not had a great day, I'm not good company.'

'Would it help to talk about it?'

Kate paused. 'You know I can't. Not with you.'

'Don't talk then, let's just drink. Misery loves company.'

'What have you got to be miserable about?'

He laughed and sat down on the bar stool next to her, gesturing to the barman to come over.

Kate looked at her empty glass. She'd have another one – how could she resist? Especially when she knew, deep down, he was the reason she'd come here in the first place.

He lay back in the bed, pulling the white cover over his bare chest. Kate lay on the pillow next to him, staring at the ceiling, the spinning starting to abate. She knew it had been the wrong thing to do, but the wine relaxed her. Silenced the voices in her head, telling her she wasn't good enough, that nobody loved her. Sterilised by alcohol. And she'd only had four, maybe five glasses at most, although she hadn't finished that last one so it didn't count.

In the growing darkness she watched him out of the corner of her eye as he stretched. He was different to Sam: lean while Sam was stocky, overconfident where Sam was shy. She liked the change, something new to explore.

'I'd kill for a cigarette,' he said. 'Do you want one?'

He offered her the packet with his good hand and she pulled one out of the box, the dry tobacco smell following the cigarette to her lips. They'd gone to his flat this time – it was closer, round the corner from the bar.

He reached over her and opened the window, pushing his naked torso next to her in the process. She resisted the urge to lick it.

He flicked the lighter to a flame and lit her cigarette. She caught his face in the sudden brightness, seeing him from a different angle, almost as a different person. He lay back next to her and blew a long plume of smoke towards the window. The cold air blew in from outside, moving the curtains around her. She could hear people talking on the street below and a police car siren; she wondered what the emergency was. Kate took her own long breath in and felt the ache in her lungs, a burn on the back of her throat.

'What happened on the case today?' he asked.

'You know I can't tell you,' she replied.

He raised himself up on his elbow and took a drag on his cigarette. The tip glowed red in the darkness.

'I'm a suspect,' he said, matter-of-fact.

Kate glanced over. Even in the dim light she could see him looking at her, trying to read her face. 'I am,' he carried on. 'You think I did it.'

'We can't rule anyone out at this stage,' she said.

'But you can sleep with them? That's considered okay?'

'Of course not,' Kate snapped.

'Yet here you are.'

Kate stubbed the cigarette out in the ashtray on the windowsill.

'Kate, wait. Please.' He looked at her, no longer the cocky man in the bar. The vulnerability showed in his face. 'I didn't do it.' He pulled himself up in the bed, the cigarette between his lips, and placed a hand on her arm as she bent to pick up her shirt. 'I didn't attack her, I swear.'

She paused and looked at him, his blue eyes trained on hers.

'You believe me, don't you?'

And she did. In that moment, Kate believed he was telling the truth. He wasn't a suspect; he couldn't possibly have tried to kill Thea Patterson. He wasn't someone who could attack a young woman in the dead of night. A cold-blooded would-be murderer.

Because otherwise she, Detective Sergeant Kate Munro, was making the biggest mistake of her life. Of her career. At that moment, drunk. And lying naked in bed with Harry Becker.

Saturday

32

It was early, just past seven, shards of light edging into the dawn. Thea had been awake for about an hour, her headache forcing her out of bed to find painkillers. She was standing in the kitchen, pushing pills out of their blister packs, when she heard a light tap at the door.

She listened and waited, then heard it again – almost tentative.

She looked down at her clothes: messy T-shirt, tracksuit trousers, slippers. She moved down the corridor and peered out of the small window in the door to have a look at who was there. Her normal bravado at living alone had faded – the attack had made her cautious.

Ryan Holmes was standing on her doorstep. Half of her wanted to run away, hide back in her bedroom, while the other half was curious. What was he doing here? He must know now, surely, about what she had done. Thea took a deep breath and opened the door.

'I'm sorry, I didn't mean to disturb you,' he said. 'It's just I was passing and I saw the light was on, so I knew you were up.' Outside the rain had started to pour, coming down in torrents and gushing from the broken guttering on the right-hand side of the porch. Thea saw what other people must think about her house: it was run-down, falling apart.

Much like her, she thought, with a sting of embarrassment. 'I went to the hospital yesterday, but they said you'd checked yourself out.'

'It's okay,' Thea said, too aware of her unwashed hair, her messy clothes. She looked at Ryan, taking in his smart shirt, hair wet, showing the lines of a comb where he must have just used it. He had specks of rain on his glasses.

'How are you?' He offered a bunch of flowers to her, a pretty mix of yellow and white, out of place in the dull grey of the weather. 'I brought these. I didn't know what you would like.'

Thea took them from him, pulling her cardigan around her. 'How do you know where I live?'

'Google,' he said, apologetically. 'Are you ...' He stopped, studying her face. 'I mean, are you Thea?'

She smiled. 'Yes, I'm Thea.' She shivered, the cold creeping under her clothes. She opened the door wider. 'Would you like to come in?'

Ryan stepped into the house, diligently wiping his feet on the doormat. Thea turned and headed down the corridor to the kitchen. He followed her, taking his glasses and rubbing the rain off on his sleeve.

She filled up a glass vase and placed the flowers in it, still with her back to Ryan. She was cringing inside, knowing what she had done, what they had done, while she was pretending to be Gabi. She regretted answering the door now; she should have kept quiet. But here he was, in her kitchen.

'How are you?' Ryan asked again, hovering uncertainly in the middle of the room. 'Does it hurt?' He gestured to the manky bandage on her forehead.

'Yes. A lot.'

He smiled. 'I'm Ryan,' he said. 'It's nice to meet you. Properly, I mean.'

'I'm sorry,' Thea blurted out. 'I shouldn't have ...' She couldn't finish her sentence; she didn't know what to say.

'It's just ...' He paused. He looked nervous. 'I need to know – was it just a game? What you and Gabriella were doing?'

'No, no it wasn't. Gabi didn't even know – it was all my fault. I meant what I said ... before. I liked you.'

'It's okay,' he said. 'I mean, it's not okay, and I was angry, but then ...' He stopped, and Thea sensed his uncertainty. 'I only slept with you, that one time. I wanted you to know that. Gabriella and I, we never ...'

'Okay,' Thea said.

They stood in silence for a moment. Thea fidgeted, crossing her arms across her chest, then uncrossing them.

'Well, I just ...'

'Do you want a cup of tea?'

They both spoke at the same time. Ryan smiled.

'Yes, a cup of tea would be good, thank you,' he replied.

Thea busied herself with the kettle, with cups and tea bags, anything to avoid looking directly at him. She couldn't work out why he had told her that, but nonetheless it made her feel different. Like she was special to him or something. It was nice.

Ryan pulled out a chair from the kitchen table and sat down, taking off his coat and his scarf and laying them next to him.

'Are you on your way to work?' she asked, putting the cup of tea down. 'I guess Saturday is one of the busiest days of the week, if you own a nightclub.' She gabbled, inwardly cringing at her effort at small talk. 'I hope I'm not making you late.'

'No, it's fine. I can get there whenever.' He paused, and took a sip of his tea. 'And you're a photographer?'

Thea raised her eyebrows. 'Google,' Ryan said again, and Thea nodded. 'Are these yours?'

He stood up, mug in hand, and walked to the black and whites framed on the wall. He paused next to one of Thea's favourites, an informal shot, sneaked one day in town. A small blonde girl with ringlets had been looking at her, peeking backwards over her dad's shoulder and smiling. She didn't know them; she hadn't intended to capture a photo but instinct took over. Just as she raised the camera the sun lit them from behind, creating a halo of light around the little girl. An angel in her father's arms.

'I love this one,' Ryan said, not looking away from the photo. 'There's just something about it that catches your eye.'

Thea came up and stood behind him. He wasn't tall, and she came up to his shoulder. 'I always wonder about that little girl,' she said. 'She's probably about seven or eight now. I hope she's as loved as she seems to be here.'

Ryan turned and his face was close to hers. She could see a small patch of stubble he had missed just under his chin; she could smell his shampoo, and a trace of mint toothpaste. He reached up and took off his glasses. He paused, as if to say something, then stopped.

He cleared his throat. 'I should go,' Ryan said, and Thea stepped away from him as he put his empty mug by the sink and picked up his coat and scarf. She followed him to the door and he opened it to the cold morning, the rain having abated to a mild depressing drizzle.

Ryan turned back as he stepped over the threshold.

'Would you like to go out sometime?' he asked. 'On a

normal date, you know, to a restaurant, rather than a night-club.'

Thea nodded. 'I'd like that.'

He passed her his phone and she inputted her number. 'See you soon, Thea.'

Thea watched as he made his way to his car. It was an old green Renault Clio and she was surprised – she had expected something flashier. As he reversed, he looked back at her and waved. She waved back, then closed the door.

She took the leftovers of her cup of tea back to bed, picking up the packet of pills on the way. From her bed she could see out of her window to the bare trees and grey sky beyond as daylight started to grow, throwing strange shadows on the white ceiling.

She thought about Ryan, running their exchange through her head, internally wincing at how she must have looked to him. Simple exchanges, making small talk, had never come easily to her. Silence was much more straightforward, but she knew other people found it awkward. Found *her* awkward.

She then remembered how he was that night, and frowned. She felt a niggle, something forgotten from the knock on her head, but now coming back to the surface. She remembered an argument, shouting and – oh my God – she had slapped him. She put her hands over her face, feeling a flush of embarrassment. And there was something else. What happened after that?

The uncertainty made her fearful. What if they tried again? There was no way she could defend herself at the moment, her body broken, every inch of her painful and weak. She shouldn't have let Ryan into the house; she needed to be more careful. After all, it could have been him. How did she know? It could have been anyone.

She knew there was more, and something inside her aching head knew it was important. But she could only remember parts, hidden deep below recovering neurons. Snippets in the grey, like the shadows on the ceiling.

33

Gabi woke to a bright room. Daylight sneaked in through the curtains and she looked around, disorientated for a second, an empty pillow next to her. She could hear tinny voices from downstairs. She glanced at the clock – it was just past 9 a.m.

She remembered leaving Thea's. Running out of the door into the dark night, phoning Mortimer to come and pick her up. She remembered him bringing her back here, going to bed, her head churning, him worried but silent. It had been fifteen years – fifteen years of running, just so she didn't have to think about what had happened that day. She'd held onto the secret for so long it had become ingrained, but now it was starting to consume her, eating her from the inside out.

Gabi had been at Waterloo Station when she'd seen the article: Harrison's face, preserved in time, looking out of a newspaper at WHSmith. She was oblivious to the people bustling around her, reading how he had barely months to live and would die in prison. *FINAL JUSTICE*, the headline screamed, but she knew it wasn't. None of this was fair. Without thinking, she took the next train to Southampton.

But once she arrived, it hadn't been that easy. It had been August, and the heatwave reminded her of that ill-fated summer. Of lying in the grass, bare feet dirty, hands sticky from ice lollies. Of Harry. The intoxicating, clean smell of him after a shower. The tan lines at the bottom of his back. The way he looked at her after they kissed, like he was seeing her for the first time. She couldn't, she just couldn't. So she pushed it away, got a job at the nightclub, had a life. And met Mortimer.

Gabi climbed out of bed and opened the wardrobe. Some of her clothes had been left from before, so she pulled out a pair of skinny jeans and a jumper and put them on.

She padded downstairs in her bare feet, feeling the underfloor heating. The house was warm, and she could smell coffee and toast.

Mortimer was still a mystery to her. He had moved to England after university and adopted a myriad of British habits to complement his American ones. He loved strong coffee and freshly baked bread, always starting the day with toast and butter and marmalade.

He didn't understand why hot and cold taps were separate, or why there were switches on electric sockets. He loved electric kettles. When they first met, Gabi had to explain to Mortimer what kippers were, and he found it funny that the strips of toast that came with soft-boiled eggs were called soldiers.

His house reflected the way he dressed. Where he wore mostly black – black jeans, black T-shirts, black jackets, a black coat, with the exception of a white shirt for work – his house was decorated in only white, with bare oak floors and doors, fawn carpets, oak furniture and a brown leather sofa. When she asked what he liked about her, he said she brought colour into his life.

As she walked through to the kitchen, she could see him at the kitchen table, cup of coffee by his side and an empty plate covered in toast crumbs. He had the radio on in the background, the laptop open, and Gabi knew he would be on one of the many newspaper sites he liked to read: a mixture of *The Times*, the *Guardian* and the red tops, although he said he tried not to linger on those. He'd studied politics at Harvard, and Gabi knew he was some sort of adviser for the government. Any more than that baffled her. He worked from home for the most part, occasionally taking a train to Westminster or a plane to a far-flung summit. He lived there, in the north of Southampton, for nothing more than practicality: close to the train lines and airports and with more reasonable house prices than London.

She stood in the kitchen doorway for a moment, watching him. His hair was messy from sleep, and he was wearing a black T-shirt and jeans. He had his glasses on and his feet were bare. Without averting his eyes from his screen, he picked up the mug and took a sip, then placed it back down on the table.

He glanced up and saw her.

'Sleep well?' he asked, smiling.

'Yes, thank you. I needed it,' she said. His smile was the best part about him. Everything about Mortimer was straight – the way he stood, even his hair, without a single kink. But when he smiled, in that gentle, subtle, almost hesitant way, things curved. Lines appeared round his eyes, wrinkles across his forehead; he relaxed. She liked it. She liked him.

Being around Mortimer made her feel calm; something about his stillness soothed her and took away the constant humming in her head. She liked that this house was nothing like the home she had grown up in. She liked that he was nothing like her parents had been.

Gabi poured herself a mug of coffee from the pot. It was strong and hot.

He looked at her, peering over the top of his glasses. 'Do you want to do something today? Together?' he asked.

She nodded, then sat down next to him at the table and fiddled with her mug. She needed to ask him something: the question she had asked herself as the thunderstorm raged round the house. She took a deep breath, and bit her lip.

'Could I stay here, again?' she asked. 'Would you mind?'

'This is your home, Gabi.'

'Can you help me move my stuff in? Go and get the rest of my clothes from my flat?'

Mortimer smiled. 'Of course.' He leaned over and kissed her gently on the lips. She felt the prickle of his stubble, the smell of fresh coffee and taste of marmalade. 'When do you want to do it?' he asked. 'This weekend?'

'That would be good.' But Gabi knew she had another conversation to have. 'I need to see Thea first.'

Thea answered the door and walked wordlessly ahead of her to the kitchen.

'Are you here to go through my cupboards again?' Thea asked sardonically, passing her a mug of coffee. Gabi already felt slightly on edge from the morning's injection of caffeine with Mortimer, but took the mug anyway, just to have something to hold onto.

Gabi saw the flowers on the table and looked at Thea.

'They're nothing,' Thea said, her face flushing. Gabi raised her eyebrows. 'They're from Ryan,' she muttered.

'You've seen him? Does he ...'

'Know? Yes, he knows. And he still wants to see me again,' Thea said. 'You can't keep all the men, Gabriella,' she snapped.

Gabi sensed an edge of triumph from her sister, that Ryan had chosen her over Gabi, but she stayed silent, biting back a retort. Gabi wasn't interested in Ryan, he'd been no more than a friend, but there was an unwritten rule that identical twins don't mess around with each other's men, however casual. Gabi took a deep breath, trying to quell the anger. She was surprised Ryan didn't feel the same.

'We need to talk,' Gabi started, but Thea cut her off.

'What more is there to discuss, Gabriella? You've made your view perfectly clear, and I've said no. Same as I did last Wednesday.' Thea was calm, sitting down carefully at the table.

Gabi stayed standing by the kitchen counter. 'The police know we were arguing.'

'And?' Thea asked.

Gabriella hesitated. 'I lied, again. But this has to stop, Thea.'

'Why, Gabriella?' Thea said, quietly, meeting her sister's gaze. 'The dead would stay dead, the guilty would stay in prison. Telling the police what really happened wouldn't change a thing. And besides,' she added, slowly, 'you're just as guilty as anyone. You started the whole mess.'

Gabi shook her head. 'That's not the same.'

'Tell yourself what you like, Gabi,' Thea replied. 'But you told Dad about the affair. Without that? Well ...' Thea picked up her packet of pills, twirling them around the fingers on her left hand, her good hand. She stopped and looked up at Gabi. 'Who knows what might have happened.'

Gabriella took a step back from the table. She looked into her sister's eyes and saw her resolve. She had forgotten how cold Thea could be. There was no understanding, no emotion. And was she right? Was Gabi as guilty as everyone else?

*

It had been another long tedious summer's day and the three of them had been in the garden, exams finished, bored and restless. They'd heard their parents arguing, carried on the air, sharp bullet points interspersed with ominous silence. And they'd been arguing about Harry.

'He's always here, eating our food, disappearing off with the girls. Why can't he hang out with boys for a change?' Robert had been saying. 'Don't roll your eyes at me, Maddy. You know it's strange.'

'He likes them, they like him, they're friends. What does it matter?' her mother had replied.

'It matters because he's a teenage boy and I have a duty to protect my daughters. Were you aware he slept here last night? Again? In their room?'

Gabriella had been angry, she remembered that. Angry that her father was making judgements about Harry's behaviour, when it had been her mother and Harrison in the wrong.

She'd stormed into the kitchen, hot temper driving her actions.

'There's nothing going on between us and Harry. We're doing nothing wrong,' Gabi had shouted. 'Unlike you,' she'd added, looking at her mother.

Madeleine had stared at Gabi, her eyes narrowed. Her mother had known what Gabi was going to say. And there was nothing she could do to stop it.

'She's been cheating on you, for years,' Gabi had said and that had been it. The beginning of the end. Thea was right. She may not have held the gun, but she had lit the fuse that started it all.

*

Thea glared at her from the other end of the kitchen.

'I knew. I kept it quiet,' Thea said. 'And you had to blunder in and blow it all out of the water. If you're looking for blame, Gabriella, you don't have to look far.'

A slam diverted their attention and both women looked to the front door as loud footsteps marched through the house.

'Thea? What the hell?' Harry stood in the doorway, his face flushed from the cold outside. He looked from one twin to the other, his gaze eventually settling on Thea sitting at the kitchen table. 'I've just come from the hospital and they said you'd left. Against medical advice?'

'I couldn't stand it there,' Thea said. 'I just wanted to be home.'

'You're sick! Three days ago you were in a coma.' Harry looked to Gabi. 'Tell her, won't you? She should be in hospital.'

Gabi blinked back the tears, hiding her emotions from her argument with Thea. 'I can't make her do anything she doesn't want to do,' she muttered.

'Oh, you two!' Harry threw his arms up, and slumped into a chair at the table. 'You're impossible.' He looked at Thea next to him and sighed. 'Just promise me that if you start to feel worse, you'll call a doctor.'

She nodded and Gabi offered him a mug of coffee.

'So, are you two talking again?' he asked, taking it from Gabi as he joined Thea at the table.

'Arguing,' Thea said, with a nervous glance to Gabi.

'So nothing's really changed,' Harry smiled.

It had been fifteen years since they'd all sat together in this way. Fifteen years, gone in an instant, yet nothing felt different. Gabi felt like a teenager. Still just as unsure, as much as she tried to pretend otherwise. Still just as scared. She swallowed it all down, hiding it from Harry.

Harry and Thea sat together on the far side of the table, shoulders almost touching. Thea had her camera in front of her, and was idly fiddling with the shutter. Harry looked the same, but somehow ... what? Gabi looked at him, trying to make out what had changed. His face had lost the softness he had as a teenager, replaced with a few more lines. He seemed stronger. Older. He caught her looking at him, then reached into his back pocket and pulled out a packet of cigarettes and a lighter. He took one out of the box and moved to the far side of the kitchen, opening the back door, leaning in the doorway. A cold breeze rushed in as he lit the cigarette, bending his face down to the flame.

'Harry, come on. You need to quit,' Gabi chastised him.

'You can hardly complain. It's your fault I have the habit in the first place.' He took a deep drag in, blowing it outwards into the winter's day.

'I gave up years ago.'

'Every Sunday morning you'd bully me into having one of your fags. And now look at me.' He brandished the lit cigarette at Gabi and laughed.

Gabi smiled. Nights in the garden, just the three of them, a large bottle of White Lightning smuggled from the off-licence, the owner fooled by Harry's height into assuming he was over eighteen, years before he actually was. She'd turn down invites to go out with friends, pretending her parents wouldn't let her, when secretly she wanted to spend time with Harry and Thea, just them, alone. She felt most comfortable then. No pretence, no worries about seeming cool. She'd wear one of Harry's old hoodies and bury her nose in the fabric. She didn't know what it was then, but she knew now it was the beginning of something between them.

They'd go to bed when they were tired and groggy, Harry sleeping on the sofa on the other side of their bedroom, sometimes in the living room. Gabi would wake him, wordlessly offering him a mug of coffee and a cigarette, and they'd sit on the kitchen steps and smoke. That was their moment, before Thea emerged.

Thea had been watching Gabi and Harry's banter through the viewfinder of her camera, but now put it down and looked at them both.

'It's all I've ever wanted,' Thea said. 'The three of us, together. I've missed this.'

'Why didn't the two of you go to university, as we planned?' Gabi asked. 'All those years ago. You could have done, without me.'

She saw Harry glance at Thea and a look pass between them.

'It wouldn't have been the same,' Thea said.

Gabi nodded, then noticed Thea's grey pallor, the black bags under her eyes. 'Are you okay? Do you need to lie down?'

Thea stood up, wobbling slightly. 'I think I'll have a little nap,' she muttered. She pointed at Gabi. 'You,' she said. 'Stay away from my stuff.'

'Here.' Harry stubbed his cigarette out in the plant pot by the door, then closed it behind him, going to her side and pulling her arm around his neck. Gabi watched them go, hearing Thea protest that she didn't need help, she was fine, followed by Harry's deep dulcet tones as they went up the stairs.

Gabi stood up, putting her coffee cup in the sink. She

stayed there for a moment, remembering what it had been like, the three of them. It could be that way again. Perhaps Thea was right. She was still her twin. They had shared a womb together, and then barely left each other's side for the next eighteen years. It was more than just shared DNA; there was a connection she couldn't deny.

'What's going on between the two of you?' She heard his voice behind her, and turned to face Harry as he came to join her in the kitchen. He leaned across her, helping himself to another mug of coffee. 'She told me I had to kick you out of the house. What are you arguing about?'

Gabi feigned nonchalance. 'It's nothing, normal twin stuff. Is Thea in bed?'

'Practically asleep the moment she climbed in,' he said.

They stood against the kitchen counter, side by side as he drank his coffee. Harry leaned against her gently. 'Are you staying in Southampton this time?' he asked. 'You're not going travelling again?'

'I think so.'

'Because I missed it, too. When you left, it felt like a piece of us was missing.' Harry's phone beeped in his pocket and he pulled it out, looking at it and hiding the screen from Gabi.

'Who's that?' she asked.

'A friend,' he said, putting the mug down. 'I have to go.'

'To see the friend?'

Harry looked down at her. 'You don't get to be jealous, Gabi. Not now. Not now you're married.' He tapped her left hand, noting the new wedding ring.

Gabi nodded. 'I know,' she said. She reached over and grabbed a pen and paper off the counter top, writing down

Mortimer's address. 'But if you need anything, I'm staying there. And that's my number.'

He leaned down, took the paper and kissed her on the cheek. 'Come on, let's go,' he said.

'What about Thea?'

'I'll come by and check on her later.'

Gabi followed him through the house, making no argument. She had no wish to stay. She pulled the door shut behind them and watched Harry leave. Gabi looked down at the new ring on her finger, picked up from her drawer that morning, discarded in anger weeks before. It felt odd and uncomfortable but the right thing to do – a symbol of her commitment to Mortimer.

She knew she had no right to these feelings towards Harry. She should feel happy for him, that he had someone to care for him in the way she couldn't. But it didn't stop the slow burn of envy. The regret, the part inside of her that wanted to scream, *he's mine, leave him be*.

Thea was right, she couldn't keep them all. But it didn't stop her wanting to.

Sunday

34

Kate wiped the steam away from the mirror. Her face was slightly pink from the shower, her eyes bloodshot. She looked as awful as she felt; her mind full of feathers, her stomach queasy. 'What are you doing today?' Kate shouted from the bathroom.

'I'm busy,' she heard Harry call back.

'What with? Can I come too?' She hated herself for asking, for being so embarrassingly needy, but she couldn't hold back. She was enjoying it too much; another night spent wrapped round Harry, immersed in cigarette smoke and an inebriated haze.

Her head hurt, and she opened the bathroom cabinet. She pulled out a packet of aspirin, and in doing so another bottle of pills fell into the sink. She swore under her breath and picked them up.

The bottle was half-empty, and she looked at the label. *Paroxetine*, it said, *take one pill once a day*.

'You don't want to come,' she heard Harry shout, and she hastily put the pill bottle away.

Kate took the aspirin, bending her head down for water from the tap, then went back into the bedroom, where Harry was in bed, sitting up on the pillows. 'Where are you going?' she asked.

He reached for the packet of cigarettes on the bedside table and shook out the last one. 'I'm going to visit my mother,' he mumbled as he lit it.

'Your mother?' Kate asked. 'I thought she was dead,' she added, gently.

Harry took a deep drag from the cigarette. He blew out a plume of smoke, then offered it to Kate.

'She is,' he said.

Kate looked up at the massive iron gates, the high stone wall. Measures she was more used to seeing to keep people in rendered unnecessary here. She looked at Harry – his face was blank. She took his hand but he didn't respond, his fingers staying limp as they walked through the gates to the graveyard.

It was another depressing winter's day, drizzle gently falling around them, settling on her coat, in her hair. It crept under her sleeves and down her collar and she shivered. She was starting to regret coming along; she could have been tucked up in bed with a newspaper and cup of tea, but no. Despite the damage this could do to her career, despite the fact he hadn't said a word since they'd arrived at the car park – here she was.

For Kate, this was no more than the latest in a long line of bad ideas. She was starting to get used to the constant sinking feeling; it was at least congruent with the way her face looked when she saw herself in the mirror: grey, tired, beaten.

They came to the end of one of the rows and stopped, Harry turning to face the grave, his mouth serious. He hadn't brought flowers. He hadn't made an effort for the occasion, wearing jeans and trainers, his coat layered over the top.

It was a simple stone, nothing elaborate about the carvings. No angels, no cross, no wiggly borders or embellishments. *Ellen Marie Becker*, it said. *1960–1997. Wife and Mother.*

'How often do you come here?' Kate asked.

'Last Sunday of the month,' Harry said, still staring at the grave. 'My dad used to do the same.' He bent down and touched the words on the stone. 'Ironic, really.'

'What is?'

'That being a wife and mother is what she'll be remembered for. When she wasn't good at being either.'

This was a side of Harry Kate hadn't seen before. Normally he exuded an air of overconfidence: he stood straight; he didn't seem to care what the world thought of him. But today he seemed unsure. Softer somehow.

He stayed crouched next to the grave, his hand resting on the stone. Kate wasn't sure what to do. Despite what they'd been up to in bed, she'd still only known him for less than a week. She hesitated, not sure whether to give him space, or wrap her arms round him. If it were her, what would she want? She didn't know, but then her parents were alive and well in Devon, rather than locked away in prison and buried in the ground. Her own experience didn't equate.

'Can you give me a moment alone, please,' he said without looking up, his voice hoarse, answering the silent question for her.

Kate turned quickly and headed for the gate. When she reached the stone archway, she looked back. Harry was knelt next to the grave, his face in his hands, his shoulders shaking.

Kate waited by the car, pulling her coat tighter round her as the drizzle evolved into full-blown rain. Her head was thumping; she was desperate for something to eat, her hands shaking from the onslaught of wine from last night. Just as she was considering looking for proper shelter, she saw Harry coming towards her, his head bowed, the collar on his coat pulled up. He didn't apologise as he opened the car and they both climbed in.

They drove in silence, taking a different turn towards the centre of town, Harry's eyes firmly fixed on the road, his face stern.

He parked the car and walked resolutely away, not waiting for Kate to catch up. She scurried after him, coming to stop at the door to a pub. Unlike the bar where they had first met, this place was old-fashioned. There were no sleek chrome lines here; just worn-out velour sofas, a roaring log fire and tattered old tables. Harry walked straight to the bar, where the bartender nodded at him and reached for a bottle of whisky, pouring Harry a generous shot. He'd obviously been here before. The barman looked at Kate and she held up her fingers.

'Two,' she said, and he poured her the same.

Harry downed his whisky as a pint of beer appeared in front of him. Kate took her cue and tossed hers back, then asked for a large glass of white. She didn't care what she got any more. House would do the trick.

They took their drinks and sat down at a table on the other side of the room.

'Are you okay?' Kate finally said, gently. He glanced up quickly, as if remembering she was there. He shrugged, and rubbed the side of his nose with his finger, screwing up his face.

'Sorry, you shouldn't have come today. I'm never great company.'

'It's fine.' Kate wanted to give him a hug, anything to

take away the look of misery on his face, but she sensed it wouldn't be welcome. She put a hand on his arm instead. 'What happened to your mum?'

He didn't reply at first, picking at the frayed edge of the bandage on his hand. 'She was ill as long as I can remember,' he said eventually, taking a large gulp from his pint, then placing it back on the table, staring at it intently. 'When I was little, she was always different to the other mums. She was sad most of the time and didn't come out of her bedroom, and sometimes when she talked, she didn't make sense. She'd just say random patterns of words, like word association games. If she was coherent, she wouldn't be able to get to the end of the sentence, just stop halfway through. She said they were sucking the thoughts out of her mind.'

'They?' Kate asked. 'Who were "they"?'

Harry didn't look at her, hunched over the table and moving his pint glass around in front of him. 'She said she was a puppet, that the machines were controlling her. That was her delusion.' He shook his head. 'As a little kid I didn't understand. She always looked confused and sad. I thought it was because of me.' He laughed, a short sharp noise. 'Eventually it got so bad that she tried to kill herself, and Dad had to hospitalise her.' Harry glanced at Kate for the first time. 'She got out, she seemed happier, but then ...' His voice tapered off and Harry took another swig, pulling the pint closer to him. Kate took a sip of her wine.

'I found her.' He shrugged to himself, the sides of his mouth turned down. 'She'd obviously realised slitting your wrists didn't do the job, so she ...' He paused. 'I found her, hanging there, in the bedroom. It worked that time.'

'How old were you?' Kate asked, her voice coming out in little more than a whisper. She felt guilty; while she wanted to be there for Harry, a large part of her was relishing the additional details about the case. Was she really this callous? Taking advantage of his emotional state to find out more about a suspect?

'Eleven,' Harry said, and Kate gasped. 'It's okay. I mean, it wasn't, obviously, but I had Thea and Gabriella, and Dad seemed happier. For years. Then it all changed. Gabi told Robert about the affair, they all started shouting. A week later everyone was dead, the police were there and Dad was being taken away.' He looked at Kate. 'Have you read the file?' he asked, and she nodded.

Harry took a long swig from his pint, then rested it back on the table, staring into it.

'Fucked up, isn't it?' He looked at her properly for the first time since they'd left the graveyard. 'Sorry, I didn't mean for things to get so serious. But there we are.'

'It's fine,' Kate said. 'Really, it's fine, Harry.'

'Except it's not, is it?' he said.

They finished their drinks in silence. Harry went outside for a cigarette and in his absence Kate picked up her phone and stared at the empty screen. It was the weekend, but nobody had contacted her; since the separation things had got a bit tricky. Friends had taken sides, and not with her. Dinner parties were awkward without a plus one. Was that what Harry was now?

Is that what this was? she wondered. A relationship? It was ridiculous to even think that way, given how they had met, but wasn't this what a relationship was? Mutual support, sharing their lives? But this was nothing like she'd had with Sam. The two of them had always been a partnership, solid and supportive, while with Harry she felt uneven and wrong-footed. She missed Sam. She hadn't heard anything, despite having deliberately not sent the divorce paperwork back.

She was hoping Sam would call her and they could talk. But she knew they were beyond that. It hadn't just been about the drinking, that was true. Early in their relationship, Sam had said he'd admired her determination. But later, that wasn't a good thing. They'd argue and she was right, that was it, end of story, no matter what he said, no matter who got hurt. The last argument Kate remembered was over one of Sam's work colleagues. A female work colleague. They'd gone on a business trip together, and he'd mentioned her, of course he had, he'd spent the week with her, but Kate couldn't accept they were no more than friends. She's married, Sam had said, she's not interested in me and, more to the point, I'm not interested in her. But Kate didn't believe him. She knew she was right, and that was all there was to it. She'd searched his belongings, checked his emails, broken every single rule of trust between them and for what? She'd found nothing, and he'd not bothered to argue any more.

Harry swept back into the bar in a fug of cigarette smoke and drizzle. He sat back down at the table, and downed the whisky in one.

'Do you want another drink?' Kate asked.

He nodded, taking a final swig from his pint. 'Why not? But it's my round, take this.' He reached into his pocket awkwardly with his left hand and swore. 'Bugger this thing,' he muttered, poking at the bandage on his right. Kate looked at it. Running accident, he'd said, but it looked to her like the sort of injury you got from being in a fight. She'd seen enough men with their fists broken; she knew what happened when you punched someone.

Harry pulled out an assortment of change and screwed-up notes, dumping them on the table in front of him. He stirred them with his finger then pulled out a crumpled twenty, passing it to her.

She got up to go to the bar when a flash of purple caught her eye. She reached over and picked it up.

'What's this?'

He took it and hurriedly put it back in his pocket. 'It's nothing. Just a button. I found it at Thea's, it got jammed in the hoover last week.'

'Can I see it?' she asked, forcing herself to sound relaxed.

Harry looked at Kate. 'Why?'

She shook her head. 'It's pretty, that's all,' she said, and he dug around in his pocket again, passing it to her reluctantly.

She picked it up between her finger and thumb and looked at it in the dim light of the pub. It was the same one, she was sure of it, same as the one she had found on the common. Bright silver, with a purple stone in the centre. Harry watched her closely, then held out his hand. 'I need to give it back to Thea,' he said.

Kate's brain was jumping with excitement but she didn't want to give anything away. She couldn't take it now; if it was vital to the case it needed to be found on him, while on proper police business. Seizing it while getting drunk in a pub after spending the night in bed with the suspect was hardly going to stand up in court.

Kate handed it back grudgingly. Harry gave her a funny look and put it back in his pocket.

She hesitated, then picked up her coat. Harry looked up, his face confused. 'I'm sorry, I have to go.' She waved her mobile at him, by way of an excuse. 'Work,' she muttered, then ran out of the pub.

After all, she was telling the truth: she was heading to the station. She had to check now, while the memory of the button was fresh in her mind. She didn't know what was going on, but whatever it was couldn't wait until tomorrow.

35

Thea dreamt of hospitals and white sheets, of rainy nights and cold pavements. She struggled to stay asleep, her body wanting to get away from the unknown demons, but her mind desperately needing the rest. When she eventually fully woke, daylight pouring in through the curtains, she couldn't remember the dream – it fell like sand out of her grasp, an unconnected collection of images and feelings, all confusing.

Her head was pounding and she reached over to her bedside table, fumbling with the pills and the glass of water. She swallowed them down then lay back on the pillow, wincing. Not for the first time she regretted leaving the hospital and the sweet surrender of knowing someone was looking after you, however busy and noisy the nurses were.

But now she knew what Gabriella was up to, she knew she had to be here. She couldn't have her sister digging around in her house unchecked, undertaking some sort of crusade.

Thea rolled over in the bed and groaned. Where was Harry when she needed him? She picked up her mobile and turned it on – a few text messages flashed into view.

Gone to see Mum, the first one said. *Will be by later. Call if you need me. Hx*

Then another. *Pissed gone home need zzzz. See you tomoz. Hx*

Typical, she thought, turning her phone off again in

frustration. Nothing from Gabi. Feeling sorry for herself, a tear escaped and ran down the side of her face. She wiped it away angrily. Why couldn't Gabi be here, by her side, like she'd always been?

As teenagers, the three of them would have done anything for each other. Thea remembered them walking home after school, probably no more than thirteen or fourteen, the usual bullies trailing them, taking the piss.

When Harry's mum had died, they were the ones that sniggered in class. There were the boys who called them freaky clones, who nicknamed them the Grady twins, after the ghosts in *The Shining*. But that day they were taking it a step further, the one at the front miming hanging himself, his hand pulling up an imaginary rope, his head to one side, tongue lolling out of his mouth.

Harry's eyes had narrowed.

'Ignore them,' Gabi had whispered, trying to pull them along, until Thea felt the first stone hit her. She turned, then the second hit her forehead, hard. She'd felt the sting, and a trickle run down to her nose. She'd touched it and looked at the blood on her hand, surprised.

That had been enough for Gabi. With a cry, she'd launched herself at the group of boys, kicking and screaming, landing a punch square on the side of the ringleader's head, flattening his ear. The boy had howled in pain and the others had tried to pull Gabi off him.

But then Harry was there, and he was substantially bigger than the twins. He pulled the ringleader away from Gabi and focused a blow square on his nose. The boy ran away crying, clutching his face, blood pouring from between his fingers, the others not far behind.

Thea raised her hand to her forehead at the memory,

running her finger down the faint silver scar she knew was there, hidden in her hairline. Their parents hadn't cared when they got home, their uniforms torn and bloody. Their mother had been more concerned about what the PTA mums would say than the wounds on her daughters, but the three of them had felt safe knowing they could take on anything, anyone, together.

Thea wished it was the same now. She'd been ecstatic when Gabi had got in contact to say she was home. They could be a family again – the three of them – but then Gabi had kept her distance. Once, she knew exactly what her sister was thinking, but now she didn't understand her in the slightest.

Thea felt herself fade, her mind hazy as the painkillers kicked in. When she was better she'd fix this, she thought as she sank back into nothingness. She had to. Because the alternative wasn't a future she could bear at all.

36

Kate sprinted out of the taxi and into the police station, ignoring the curious stares from her colleagues.

She skidded into the chair next to her desk and dug around in the pot of paperclips on her desk. There it was – the silver button. She placed it on the desk in front of her. There was no doubt in her mind it was the same as the one Harry had, the one he claimed to have found at Thea's.

Kate squinted at it. She wished there wasn't quite so much alcohol coursing round her bloodstream. It hadn't just been seeing its pair that had jogged her memory; she had seen it somewhere else before. But where? She stared at the whiteboard, and the stern faces of Ryan Holmes, Steve Morgan and Mortimer Breslin looked back, along with Harry Becker. *Harry Becker.* What the hell was going on there?

He'd looked confused when she'd sprinted out of the pub, but she hadn't had a call or text since. She assumed he was still there, drinking himself into oblivion. Thinking about him caused her stomach to flutter, although she wasn't sure whether it was the fear at being found out or something else. There was something about Harry that she couldn't put her finger on. The physique and the cool blue eyes and the hands and the – oh – she felt her cheeks turning red just thinking about it. But there was something else, too. The traumatic past, the damaged soul. It was too much of a cliché for Kate to admit, but some part of her wanted to look after him, to be the woman that fixed him. Oh, for fuck's sake. Emily Davison hadn't thrown herself under a horse for this shit.

She remembered their conversation in the pub, talking about his mum and the murders, and pulled the case file back up on the screen. Finding no more insight in the black and white images, she typed *Harrison Becker Robert Madeleine Patterson* into Google. While the murders had been committed in the early days of the internet, someone had obviously gone to the trouble of uploading information since. She clicked on the images tab and looked through the photos of Gabriella and Thea's mother.

Madeleine Patterson was clearly beautiful, the sort of woman to turn heads in the street. Dark hair in disarray, big lips, big breasts. A casual messiness to her appearance that suggested an easy-going attitude to life, and probably sex. Long flowing skirts, bare feet, bright colours, gorgeous dresses any vintage shop would pay a fortune for nowadays.

Kate picked up the button and held it in her hand, rolling it around in her fingers. As she did so, a photo appeared on the screen. Madeleine, her arm awkwardly around Robert, standing in their garden. She looked amazing, wearing knee-high brown boots, a short skirt, a black roll neck jumper and a coat over the ensemble. A purple coat. With silver buttons.

She clicked the zoom button and squinted at the screen. 'Fuck me,' she muttered under her breath.

There was no doubt in her mind. The button used to belong on a purple coat, owned by Madeleine Patterson. She looked at the one in her hand, the one found on the common. Miles away from Thea Patterson's house, but close to where she'd been attacked. The same button. But what did this mean? Could it be that the double murders fifteen years ago were linked to the attack on Thea Patterson?

Kate grabbed a pen and started to scribble theories on the notepad in front of her. *Did Thea know something?* she wrote. *Did Gabi? Was there something about the murders that someone wanted to cover up? Is Harrison Becker innocent???*

Kate gasped and looked at the words on the page. She underlined the name *Harrison Becker* three times, then picked up the phone, scrolling through numbers in her contacts list, looking for the one she needed. It was time to call in a favour, she thought as she dialled. There was someone she needed to talk to. Someone who held the key to this whole sorry mess.

Monday

37

The boxes arrived. Stack by stack of old case files were deposited in the office, wheeled in by grumpy men with trolleys. When the last one was unloaded, Kate stood back and looked at them, Briggs and Yates behind her.

'Well, that's my week gone,' Briggs muttered.

Kate turned to give him a look, and caught the eye of DCI Jennings standing in the doorway. He beckoned her into the corridor with his forefinger.

'What's this?' he asked, pointing towards the boxes. 'This is a closed, convicted case, Kate. Someone's in prison for this.'

She plastered a smile on her face. 'I know, but something tells me it's connected to this girl's attack. You told me to be creative,' she grinned. She didn't dare mention the button, sitting in her desk drawer. A piece of evidence, an unrecorded exhibit that she knew she couldn't use in any court case. But they would need something tangible to link the two cases if her hunch was correct – and Kate hoped these archives held the key.

'It was nearly fifteen years ago.'

'It was their parents, sir. Either they're unlucky or the two crimes are connected.'

Jennings looked back at the boxes. 'Fine. Do your digging. But this is it – paperwork only. For God's sake, don't unearth something that challenges the conviction. Everyone knew who did it, he confessed, and it was wrapped up in a matter of hours. People got promoted on the back of this, if you know what I mean.' He looked back at Kate, his stale coffee breath in her face. 'Don't make me look bad.'

She nodded and he shuffled away, back to his office.

In the operations room, Briggs and Yates had started prodding round the boxes, opening lids and tentatively poking at the paperwork inside. Kate came back into the room, picked up her bottle of water and took a large swig. She frowned.

'Jamie, go and get some coffees, on me. Large, double shot.'

Briggs took the money cheerfully and headed off down the corridor.

Kate looked at Yates. 'Search for anything odd, any loose ends that don't make sense. Let's crack on – we have a case to review.'

Hours later, they were all still in the office, surrounded by paper and photos and brown files. An array of coffee cups littered the tables, with sandwich cartons and chocolate wrappers in between. Kate sat on the floor, her shoes discarded, two files on her lap, while Yates and Briggs reclined on chairs. Outside the sky was dim, the fluorescent lights hurting her eyes.

She leaned back and stretched her hands in the air.

'What do we have?' she asked, for what seemed like the hundredth time.

Briggs tapped his hand on one of the piles of paper. 'Same as we had at the beginning – a cast-iron conviction.'

'Except for the missing gun,' Yates added.

Kate pointed a finger at Yates. 'Yes, that. Where did it go? How did he have time to hide it? It couldn't have gone far.'

'Police searched the house and the garden. Metal detectors, dogs, the lot.' Yates waved the search report and Kate gestured to her to throw it over. It headed her way with a flutter of pages.

'Those poor kids,' Yates continued. 'They were barely eighteen and their parents got shot. I can't imagine what that does to an adult, let alone a teenager.'

'At least they didn't see it,' Kate said. 'They were in the garden when it happened. They couldn't even get in; everything was locked when Armed Response showed up. See?' She pointed to the report in her hand. 'They had to bash down the doors.'

Kate looked up at the row of photos on the board, at Harry Becker, then Gabriella. What does that do to a person? Does it make them more likely to do something similar later on?

She heard an email ping in her inbox, and pulled herself up on aching legs. She opened it and smiled, picking up her coat.

Briggs and Yates looked at her expectantly, both keen to get out of the office.

'You two stay here, I won't be long,' Kate said, receiving groans in response. 'But go back to the Patterson attack. Chase up forensics – it's worth a try – and finish off that CCTV. See if the tech department can't clean up the images from the street cameras.'

'Where are you going?' Briggs asked.

Kate tapped the side of her nose, deliberately annoying. She knew she probably shouldn't be going, and didn't want to get the other two caught in any fallout from above. She'd noticed the name written at the bottom of many of the reports: DC Jennings. She knew exactly who had been promoted as a result of Harrison Becker's conviction.

'I'll let you know when I get back,' Kate said. 'Just keep your fingers crossed.'

She grabbed her car keys and rushed out of the police station. It was going to be an interesting day.

38

Kate tapped her fingers on the steering wheel of her car, running through questions in her head. She had one shot at this. She wanted to get it right.

The building in front of her was smart red brick, with rows of identical rectangular windows. She looked back at the white security gates, slowly lifting and closing as visitors showed their identification and drove inside. A large official sign stood at the entrance: HMP Winchester.

Looking through the case files that morning, they had a lot of evidence to convict Harrison Becker, including an admission of guilt. But Kate had her reservations. Once Harrison had confessed, it seemed the investigation had stopped. Jennings and the team had their man; nothing else mattered. But the loose ends bothered Kate. Where had the gun gone?

She climbed out of the car and smoothed down her jacket. She took a deep breath and started walking.

She had been here many times before, always in an official capacity, but this was the first time she had gone under her own steam. When her email had pinged, she'd found the approved Prisoner Production Form she had applied for last night. Quick work, a favour called in by the warden, a man whose son's drug habits had eventually led to a visit to rehab rather than a custodial sentence, an action recommended by a certain DS Munro.

Kate made her way to the visitors' centre, through the metal detector, past the intimidating dogs, handing her personal property in along the way. She showed her official police identification and authorisation, signing her name on the form.

She'd been allocated a private room, and the prison officer stopped at the door, pointing towards the man sat facing her.

She walked over, taking in the grey hair, the stooped posture. As she came closer, he looked up at her and she saw the resemblance. He had the same frame, tall and slim, but he was skinny where Harry had muscle. His hair was shorter, greyer. But when he looked at her his eyes were the same dazzling blue.

He held out a hand as Kate sat down. 'Harrison Becker,' he said. 'But you know that.'

'DS Kate Munro,' she said. 'How are you?'

She'd been warned by the warden that Harrison was not well and now she was here, she could see the ravages of the illness clearly on his body. His bones protruded, cheeks hollow. He held himself gently, as if every movement brought him pain.

'Not great,' he said. 'Cancer. Not got long to go.'

'I'm sorry,' Kate said.

'Not your fault.' He shrugged. 'How can I help you? It's not often I get visitors.'

She paused. 'Someone you know was attacked a week ago. Thea Patterson.'

'One of the twins? Is she okay?' He stopped, a half-smile on his face. 'I assume I'm not a suspect?'

She smiled in return. 'No. And she's fine, well on the road to recovery. We've been investigating, and—'

'And you wondered if two violent incidents fifteen years apart are related?' Harrison cut in.

Kate nodded. Fifteen years in prison had obviously not dulled his intellect. 'I wanted to talk to you about that day. Could you tell me what happened?'

He furrowed his brow. 'I assume you've read the file.'

'Yes …'

'So you've read my statement.'

'Yes, but …'

'What more is there to say?'

'What did you do with the gun?'

He sighed. 'As I said to your colleagues at the time, I don't know what happened to it. We were arguing, about lots of things, and I fetched the gun.' Harrison shook his head. 'I don't remember why. To show Maddy, I think. To prove that Robert wasn't such a good guy, because he hadn't turned it in to the police station.' He leaned forward onto the table and rubbed his eyes. 'I don't know what happened. I had the gun in my hand and I shot Robert and Maddy. I must have slipped and fallen. Next thing I know I'm on my front, my hands behind me with someone pressing their knee into my back. If the police couldn't find the gun, then I have no idea where it went.'

She looked at him. It was hard to remain objective when Harry's dad looked so much like him. It was like seeing Harry in another twenty years, except where life hadn't been kind. 'Why did you do it?'

Harrison took a sip from the plastic cup of dark brown liquid in front of him. He winced. 'Robert knew about me and Maddy, about the affair, and he was angry, shouting. He wanted them to leave, to sell the house and get away. I …' He stared down into his coffee. 'It had been nearly eight years.

All that time sneaking around, pretending. I wanted to be with the woman I loved, but when Madeleine agreed with Robert? I had this strange feeling come over me.'

'You were angry?'

'Furious. But it was different to that. It was like I wasn't even thinking any more – emotion completely overtook me. I had the gun ...' He paused. He looked up at Kate, his eyes bloodshot. 'Look, what exactly are you after, DS Munro? This is all done with. I'm in here, probably for the rest of my life. However short that may be. What else do you need to know?'

'Where were the twins? Where was Harry?' Kate asked.

'They were in the garden,' he said quickly.

Kate looked at the man in front of her, barely more than a shell, searching his face for any signs of a lie. But his eye contact was constant, his body language open. 'That's all,' she said. 'Thank you for seeing me.' Kate closed her notebook.

Harrison grabbed her arm, stopping her. 'Have you met my boy? How is he?'

'Harry's good. Do you want to see him?'

He let go of Kate and shook his head. 'I don't expect him to forgive me. I don't expect to ever forgive myself. Just knowing he's doing well is enough.' He looked down at the table. 'It scared me. I never knew I was capable of such a thing. And yet, here I am.'

'Thank you, Mr Becker,' Kate said, and stood up to leave. Harrison stayed, his head bowed, not moving.

Outside, it had started to rain. Kate made no attempt to avoid getting wet, and walked slowly back to the car. Rain soaked her hair and trickled down the neck of her jacket as she climbed into the driving seat.

She couldn't imagine what that had been like, what Harry had lived through. Barely eighteen, and suddenly he'd been alone. And the twins, too. No wonder they were so strange.

She turned her phone back on and it instantly sprang into life with a rapid succession of beeps. A voicemail from Yates and a text from Harry. *Yours tonight?* The text said. *I'll bring vodka.*

Kate stared at the message. She hadn't heard from him since yesterday and she'd told herself no, leave it be, enough was enough. With all the theories washing around in her head, she wasn't sure what to make of Harry Becker. But now he had got in touch ...

She listened to the message from Yates: they'd had the detailed results back on the rock. More than just blood type now: the DNA was a definite match to Thea. There was no doubt it was the weapon used that night. Yates asked a question to Kate's voicemail, *Where are you?* then confirmed that she and Briggs were heading home.

Kate glanced at the clock. It was getting late – she'd do the same. Pick up a bottle of wine on the way, something to enjoy while she waited for Harry. She replied to his text: *Sounds good.* So that was that, then. Something about him was addictive; she couldn't stay away. The attention, the rush, the risk? She didn't want to think about it any more. She'd have a few glasses, suppress the niggles in her head. Silence the voices telling her the one thing she knew for sure: she was playing a dangerous game, and it would only be so long before she was caught.

39

Kate knew she should have stopped hours ago. She should have put the glass away, hidden the second bottle, had a nap – anything. But she'd been bored and restless and worried; the hours had rolled around and now he was ringing on her bell. She got up from the sofa and steered herself to the front door, holding onto the backs of chairs, the table, the walls.

Harry stood on her front step, wearing a dark blue suit, light blue shirt and a navy tie. She thought he looked amazing. He pulled at the tie, taking it off and rolling it into a ball. He stared at her.

'Are you drunk?' he asked. He glanced at his watch. 'It's nine o'clock.'

Kate wobbled in the doorway. 'You're late. Are you coming in or not?'

She moved out of the way and he walked past her into the living room, draping his jacket over the back of the sofa.

'I went to check on Thea. Looks like we won't be needing this now,' he said, holding up the bottle of vodka. Kate went to take it and he moved it out of her reach.

'Who are you to say when I've had enough?' she slurred.

Harry looked at her, then shrugged. 'Fine, do what you like.' He handed her the vodka and Kate unscrewed the lid, taking a large swig straight out of the bottle. The vicious taste hit the back of her throat like a sledgehammer, and her body decided enough was enough. Hand over her mouth,

Kate ran to her downstairs toilet, barely making it in time to empty her aching stomach into the bowl.

She felt the acid burn her throat, the automatic reflex efficiently doing its job as she knelt in front of the toilet, vomiting violently.

She slumped down on the carpet, out of breath and retching, spitting the last of the sour bile away. Despite the cold of the room, her body felt hot and sweaty. She could hear Harry moving around in her kitchen, opening the fridge, probably putting away the last of the wine.

Then silence. She listened and heard the rustle of paper, then heavy footsteps walking towards her. She winced as he appeared in the doorway. Kate knew she looked a state: her hair was over her face and there were flecks of vomit on the carpet and the wall. The smell was disgusting.

'What the hell is this?' he asked. He waved the bit of paper in her face. 'Have you been to see my father?'

He had one of her police files in his hand, a piece of paper in the other. She recognised the logo of the prison in the top-right corner.

She went to stand up on wobbly legs, leaning on the sink for assistance.

'Why? You have no right to go visiting that man.' Harry stormed out into the living room, picking up his jacket.

Kate followed him. 'I'm doing my job. I wanted to know what happened to the gun.'

Harry snapped round to face her. 'Who cares? It's a murder case from fifteen years ago. You're supposed to be investigating what happened to Thea; my father has nothing to do with it.' He pushed past her into the hallway.

'Don't you want to know how he is? You should go and see him. He's not got long left, Harry.'

Harry paused, his back to her, one hand on the latch to let himself out. 'I don't want to know,' he said. 'He killed them, and that's all there is.'

'But I think there is more,' Kate continued, the last remnants of alcohol spurring her on. 'There's a connection, I know there is. And he can't remember what happened – he doesn't know where the gun ended up. We know there was no time for him to hide it, he was unconscious when the police showed up.'

'Not everything is a mystery to be solved, Kate,' Harry said, turning to face her. 'It's not all about right and wrong, black and white. Leave it alone, please.'

'Don't you want to know? Don't you care what happened that day?' She rambled, thoughts tumbling out of her mouth. 'What if your father didn't act alone? And what if he didn't kill them, Harry?'

'I was there!' Harry shouted. 'We were there. We saw him shoot them. We saw him.'

Kate took a step back. 'That wasn't in the file.'

'No, it wasn't, was it? What did it say? That we were in the garden? That's what we told them and it was all too convenient for them to believe. But we know he's guilty, we saw him do it.'

Kate grabbed Harry by the forearms. 'So where's the gun? If you were there, where's the gun?'

He moved away from her, his back to the front door. 'It was such chaos. The shouting, the noise, then Gabi and Thea crying.' He looked down at her, the pain and horror visible on his face. 'We did what we had to do, we got out of there. Just leave it be, Kate, please,' he added, quietly. 'We know he did it, and he's going to die in prison. Just leave it be.'

He turned and opened the front door, walking out into the street. Kate watched him climb into his car and drive off.

'Fuck,' she said under her breath. She closed the door and went back into the living room. The bottle of vodka lurked on the table, the lid off. She picked it up, staring at it accusingly.

With one swift movement, she walked to the sink and tipped it down the drain. She stood there, gagging from the smell, watching it glug away to nothing.

Kate went back into her living room, picking up one of the files she had taken from work, then sitting down on the sofa. If the police reports were wrong about the teenagers, if Harry and Thea and Gabi were there in the kitchen when their parents were shot, what else was missing from the file? How did they get out of the house if the doors were locked? What else had she assumed was true?

She picked up the first piece of paper and began to read.

40

Gabi was in the kitchen with Mortimer when they heard the banging on the front door.

It was Harry. He was hyperventilating, one arm supporting himself on the doorframe. He looked at Gabi, his eyes wide.

The two of them pulled him into the living room and he fell onto the sofa. He was a mess. Gabriella had never seen him like this before. His whole body was shaking, soaked with sweat. Mortimer fetched a glass of water and Gabi perched next to Harry, placing it in his hands.

Slowly, his breathing returned to normal and Harry looked at her, his face pale.

'I can see the gun, smell the burning,' he said, shaking his head. 'It's always going to follow us. We'll never get away, Gabi.'

When Harry seemed a bit calmer, Gabi went into the kitchen to make him a cup of tea. Mortimer followed her in.

'Has he ever seen anyone about this?' he asked.

Gabi glanced back into the living room where Harry was sitting with his head in his hands. 'What do you mean?'

'Has he ever seen a professional? To talk all of this through?' The kettle clicked off and Gabi poured hot water into two mugs. 'It must have been incredibly traumatic, what all of you went through.'

'We're not American – we don't go running to our therapist every time something upsetting happens.' Gabi squished the tea bags against the sides of the mugs and reached into the fridge for the milk. 'Fucked up or not,' she added bitterly, remembering Mortimer's comments at Thea's bedside in the hospital.

Mortimer winced. 'I'm sorry I said that, Gabi,' he replied. 'I was overwrought, it wasn't fair. To you or Thea.' He paused, looking at her. 'But nonetheless, you watched *your* parents be gunned down in your own home, by *his* father,' Mortimer said, pointing at Harry. 'This is exactly what therapists are for, Gabriella.'

'I know what happened, thank you.' Gabi shut the fridge and picked up the two mugs. 'Just let me talk to him, Mort, please?'

Mortimer agreed reluctantly, and sat down at the kitchen table where his laptop was open. 'I'll be here if you need me.'

Gabi went back into the living room and put the tea in front of Harry. She sat next to him and put her hand on his arm. He lifted his head and looked at it.

'What happened, Harry?' Gabi asked softly.

He looked at her, his face pale. 'She went to see my father. The detective. She went to see him in prison.'

'And?'

'She's digging. Trying to find out what happened. She doesn't think Dad did it.'

'And what did you say?' Gabi asked, cautiously.

'I told her we were there, we saw him with our own eyes. I told her to leave it alone, because we know he did it.'

'And did Harrison say anything different when she saw him?'

'I don't think so.'

Gabi stopped for a second, thinking. She barely dared to ask. 'And do the police have the gun?'

He shook his head.

'Where is it, Harry?'

'Somewhere hidden. It's safe.'

'So what's the problem?' Gabi asked.

Harry picked up the mug of tea and cupped it between both hands. He took a deep breath in and out. 'What if…' he started.

'What if, what?'

He stopped talking, shaking his head, his breath escaping out of him in bursts.

Gabi took the mug away and placed it on the table. She took his hands in hers, and pulled him round to face her on the sofa. 'So you told her we were there. So what?' Gabi spoke to him slowly. 'That doesn't change the fact that Harrison confessed. They know nothing. They don't know about the gun. There is no mystery here, and the sooner this detective realises it, the better.'

Harry nodded slowly.

Gabi looked at him, worried. 'It's getting late, and you're tired,' she said. 'Stay here tonight, with me and Mortimer. And we'll talk again in the morning.'

With the mention of Mortimer's name, Harry let go of her hands.

'No, no, I should be getting home. I'm sorry, I shouldn't have disturbed you.' He stood up, and Gabi put her hand on his arm to stop him, but he pushed her off. 'You're married now, I'm in the way. I shouldn't have dropped round unannounced.'

He walked quickly out of the living room and into the hallway. Gabi followed behind him.

'Any time, Harry, please. I mean that.'

'I'm sorry.' With a cold gust of wind, the front door opened and Harry rushed out to his car.

Gabi watched until his car had disappeared down the road. She felt Mortimer's arms around her waist.

'You did all you could,' Mortimer said. 'He's not your responsibility.'

Gabi pressed her lips together and shook her head. 'No, he is. He always has been.'

Mortimer encouraged her away from the front door and they returned to the kitchen. He had been chopping vegetables, and the room was filled with the smell of garlic and onions, cooking on the hob.

Gabi sat at the counter top and watched him, thinking about Harry. Why was she worried that the police would find out what happened? Wasn't that what she wanted? Perhaps she wasn't so sure after all.

In her heart of hearts, she didn't want anything bad to happen to Harry. She still ... what? Loved him?' Maybe so, but not in the same way as back then. Gabriella idly wondered how differently things might have turned out if she had stayed, back then, after the funeral. Or if Harry had gone with her and they'd run away together.

But there was no point in thinking about what ifs. No point in wondering. She had tried it once and it had been sweet and wonderful and perfect. She remembered that night, after. She'd watched him sleep, almost boyish, his eyelashes flickering against his cheeks. She'd run her hand across his tanned back, taking in the contours, how he'd changed. For the first time in years, she'd felt calm. In that moment, with him, everything had been forgotten and she was right where she should have been.

But it had been impossible for them to be together. It was the same now; the same as it had ever been.

Tuesday

41

DC Yates was bouncing in front of the whiteboard as Kate arrived for the day.

'Forensics report is in,' she said happily, flapping the piece of paper at Kate.

'Oh, thank fuck,' Kate said. 'Have you read it – what does it tell us?'

'Well…' Yates started talking, running her finger down the page. 'Early Evidence Kit shows…' She paused, not wanting to break the news. 'Well, nothing of note.'

'Brilliant,' Kate muttered sarcastically.

'But…' Yates pointed to the next paragraph. 'Semen on the front of Thea's dress, DNA under her fingernails…'

'So something did happen with a man that night,' Kate said. 'Any idea who?'

'Running it now. Nothing yet. But! Saving the best for last…' Yates smiled. 'They managed to find some fingerprints on the bag. Some were Thea's, as you'd expect, a few partials, but also two complete prints. And they're in the system.'

Kate punched both arms in the air triumphantly. 'And?'

'A local guy – Dave Fletcher. They're bringing him in now.'

Kate did a little dance. At last, something they could actually follow up on.

'This just backs up my theory though, doesn't it?' Yates said. 'That the attack was random, nothing to do with their parents' murder at all.'

'Maybe,' Kate conceded, as Briggs walked into the room. 'Let's wait and see. Where have you been?'

Briggs waggled his head, mocking her. 'No need to get all arsey, I've been busy.'

Kate stared at him pointedly. 'Okay, okay,' Briggs said, sitting down and pulling his notebook closer to him. 'So, I've been looking into your boy here, Mr Handsome Blue Eyes.' He pointed up at the photo of Harry on the whiteboard. 'Both him and his father are pretty dull, no records, nothing of note before 2004. But his mother – Ellen Becker – was admitted to the local funny farm in 1995, for a suicide attempt relating to disorganised schizophrenia.' Briggs held his hands out, as if expecting applause.

'And?' Yates was unimpressed. 'What does that tell us?'

'Well, what if our boy here has the same? You are ...' Briggs looked down and checked his notes '... thirteen times more likely to have schizophrenia if one of your parents has it.'

'But it doesn't mean he does have it,' Yates argued. 'And even if he does, it doesn't mean he's violent. Just because someone is schizophrenic, it doesn't make them a danger to others.'

'I know – I hadn't finished.' Briggs swivelled round on his chair. 'In 1997 she tries again, obviously learnt from previous experience and manages it this time. Hangs herself. And guess who finds the body?'

'Who? Not Harry Becker?' Yates replied. 'Poor sod.'

'I'm just saying – maybe we should look a bit more closely at him, that's all.' They both looked up at Kate. 'What do you think, Sarge? Do a bit more digging?'

Kate had been watching the exchange between the two of them nervously. She knew all this of course, but had said nothing, not wanting to receive questions about how she had discovered this potentially juicy source of information. And she felt guilty for Harry. He had confided in her, had trusted her. She hadn't heard from him after last night, and she knew she wasn't going to. Not now. It was a good thing, she told herself.

She turned back to Briggs, keeping her face as expressionless as possible, but they had already been distracted, Yates telling Briggs about the forensics report, about the fingerprints on the bag.

She swivelled around in her chair and faced the computer, typing in *paroxetine*, remembering the medication in Harry's cabinet. *Paroxetine is a type of antidepressant known as an SSRI,* she read. *Often used to treat depression and obsessive compulsive disorder, panic attacks, anxiety or post-traumatic stress disorder.* She stopped, her fingers resting on the keyboard. Would it be any wonder, she thought, given what he'd been through?

Harry had discovered his mother's body when he was just eleven. Kate had been first on the scene for a hanging case once: the man's skin red, his dry tongue protruding from his open mouth. It stayed with you, even if you hadn't personally known the victim.

Then he'd watched his father commit double homicide. It was a miracle Harry Becker was still getting up in the morning.

Kate felt guilty again and pulled herself away from Harry, switching her screen to the Police National Computer, looking up their new suspect. David Wayne Fletcher, 46. Started early in life with multiple charges of shoplifting, graduating to drunk and disorderly, common assault, then some time inside for GBH with intent. A nice guy, Kate thought grimly.

The phone rang and Yates snatched it up.

'He's here,' she said, and jumped up from her seat.

'Come on then,' Kate said, picking up the file. 'Let's go test out your theory.'

Dave Fletcher was skinny and twitchy. He had tiny eyes in an acne-scarred face, and greasy hair tied back in a ponytail. He smelt of old sweat and cheap booze and Kate was not enjoying being in a confined space with him.

He had taken the first opportunity to demand his legal counsel. The solicitor on call had arrived surprisingly fast, but gave Kate an expression that said he would rather be anywhere but there. He sat in the chair next to his client in an old baggy suit going shiny at the elbows.

'Mr Fletcher,' Kate said, placing her hands on the folder in front of her. 'Do you want to guess what we have in this file?'

'You ain't got nothing on me,' he replied, showing a row of yellow teeth.

'Ah, but we have.' Kate was enjoying herself; it was nice to be able to do some actual police work – to interview someone and be on the front foot for a change. 'Dave. You're not new to this, you know how it works. I show you what I have in this folder, you'll deny it and then I'll charge you with attempted murder anyway. Why don't you save us some time?'

The colour drained out of Dave Fletcher's face. 'Whoa there, lady. You never said nothing about attempted murder. I've not tried to kill anyone.'

'What did you think the officers said when they picked you up?'

'Yeah, but I thought you were just trying to scare me, like.' He fidgeted in the chair, hands picking at one of the scars on his face. 'Who says I tried to kill them?'

Kate pulled the fingerprint report out of the folder and pushed it in front of him. The solicitor craned his neck to take a look. 'See here, these are your fingerprints on a bag stolen from a young woman last Saturday night, a week ago. She was attacked on the common, left for dead. We don't like that kind of thing round here. Tend to frown on low lifes like you trying to kill young women.' She pushed a photo of the bag across to Dave and he looked at it.

'I want a word with my lawyer,' he said, and crossed his arms on his scrawny chest.

'Fine,' Kate replied, picking up the paper. 'Take all the time you need. But get comfortable, because when we come back in, we'll be charging you.' His solicitor looked up at her with surprise and Kate met his gaze and nodded. She turned back to Dave Fletcher. 'I can't think you're going to be getting out any time soon,' she added.

Outside the room, Yates whispered to Kate. 'Are we going to call the CPS, then?'

Kate shook her head. 'We'll need more than a few fingerprints before they'll be keen on charging him. But it's a start.'

She stopped as the solicitor poked his head back round the door and gestured them inside. 'Mr Fletcher would like to share some information with you,' he said. 'On the condition you don't charge him with attempted murder.'

'Let's see what he has to say first,' Kate said, and looked across the table at Dave. 'Start talking.'

'I was there, on the common. But I never attacked her.'

Dave got a look from his solicitor and he frowned. 'Okay, so I might have pushed her a bit, to try and get the bag off her, but no more than that.' He put his hands on the table, palms up. 'I swear. I didn't need to. She was all pissed and wobbly and pretty much gave it to me. I ran off, took the cards and cash, then tossed it in the bushes. It was shit, there wasn't even a phone in there. That was it, I swear. I didn't try to kill her.'

Kate shrugged. 'Okay, so let's say I believe you. Let's pretend that you are just a common mugger. Did you see anyone else that night on the common?'

Dave glanced at his solicitor, who nodded. 'Yeah. I might have. What are you going to do for me if I cough up?'

'Just tell them,' the solicitor said, his voice tired.

'Fine.' Dave sat back in his seat. 'Some bloke was out there too. When I threw the bag away I saw him, walking quickly. At first I thought he was afraid, bit of a pussy, big bloke like that, scared of walking that time of night, but then I thought he was looking for someone.'

'What did he look like?'

'Taller than me.'

Kate looked at Dave Fletcher; he couldn't have been more than five foot three. Everyone was tall to Dave.

'All right, all right,' Dave muttered, reading her thoughts. 'I know what tall's like. Taller than him.' He pointed at the solicitor.

'I'm six foot,' he said.

'Okay, and?' Kate gestured for him to continue.

'Long dark coat. Nice shoes. Pretty face. You know. For a bloke, like.'

'Do you think you could identify him?'

'Yeah, I think so. Yeah.'

★

Kate and Yates stood in the corridor, the excitement jumping between them.

'For once I'm glad I'm wrong,' Yates said. 'What should we do now? Get some photos?'

Kate nodded. 'Work with the solicitor to get a good impartial mix, I don't want to be accused of bias later. Use some photos off the internet as well as the usual mug shots. Include all the suspects – those nightclub owners, as well as the husband.'

'And Harry Becker?'

'Yes,' Kate said slowly. 'And Harry Becker.'

42

Thea listened to the *click click* of the central heating, of water rushing round the pipes of her house, bringing it to life. She heard cars on the road outside, the rhythmic tick of the clock by her bed. She craned her neck round to look at it: 12.32.

She moved her head gently, then stretched her legs out under the duvet. Nothing felt too bad, she thought, which was reassuring. Her head still throbbed, but it was a dull pain rather than the sharp sledgehammer she'd experienced before. She slowly pulled herself up to a sitting position.

Laughter filtered up from the floor below. She recognised it – Harry. She listened, heard him talking, then a pause. She couldn't hear an answering voice. He laughed again and she smiled.

Thea dragged herself out of bed, surprised to see she was wearing a pair of pyjamas she hadn't worn in years. She pulled a jumper over her head, slippers on her feet, and went downstairs.

Harry was sat at the kitchen table, phone to his ear, laptop in front of him. He heard the door open and turned, smiling when he saw her and ending the call.

'I'm sorry, did I wake you?' he asked, replacing the phone on the table. There were papers strewn around him, a notebook open, a pen resting, lid off.

She shook her head. 'What day is it?'

'Tuesday,' Harry laughed. 'Are you feeling better?'

'Yes. Yes, I think I am.' Thea went to fill the kettle but Harry stood and took it from her, steering her to the kitchen chair. 'How did I lose Monday? Have you been here the whole time?'

'You obviously needed the rest,' Harry said, making two cups of tea and bringing them over to the table. 'You have been awake occasionally. Don't you remember?'

'Not much.' Thea thought back. She remembered snippets, people moving in the dark. 'Has Gabi been by?'

'No,' Harry said quickly. 'I haven't seen her.' His phone vibrated on the table and he looked at it, then rejected the call.

'Are you working?' Thea asked.

'It's fine, I can phone them back later. Are you hungry? I can cook you something. There's toast, eggs, baked beans, cereal.'

'Weetabix,' Thea replied instantly. 'I need Weetabix.'

Harry fetched her breakfast and went back to his laptop. She ate it in silence, watching him. He leaned his head on his hand, his elbow resting on the table, tapping a few keys.

Harry had always been good at silence; he wasn't someone who needed to fill the space. Thea thought it was the only reason they'd been able to rattle on together for so long. He understood her need for solitude, for quiet.

Love, Thea thought, wasn't a big bang or a rush of passion. For her it was a culmination of little moments. A series of events that showed you cared, of just being there for the other person without asking for anything in return. It was sitting next to someone at the table, eating breakfast in silence, and being perfectly comfortable. For Thea, there was something rare about that feeling.

And she did feel better today. Her fingers still ached but the dirty grey tape binding them together felt uncomfortable and she pulled it off. She stretched them out and winced. Maybe she wasn't as healed as she thought she was. She reached for her pills, taking two with a big gulp of tea.

A loud bang on the door diverted their attention. Thea got up carefully and made her way to the front door, Harry following behind. Through the glass she could see the yellow and blue of the police car and the black of their uniforms. She looked at Harry and opened the door.

The police officers didn't hesitate. They caught a glimpse of Harry behind her and barrelled into the hallway, standing either side of him, blocking his exit. They were large and broad-chested; they filled the hallway and Thea backed off, moving away up the stairs.

'Harry Becker,' the one nearest the door began, and Harry nodded. 'We are arresting you on suspicion of the attempted murder of Thea Patterson on Sunday 20 January on Southampton Common.'

Thea could see DS Munro and the other woman detective watching by their car at the end of the driveway, their faces stern.

Harry looked stunned. The police officer continued his warning and Harry turned to Thea as she stood above them on the stairs. 'I didn't do this, Thea, I swear,' he pleaded. 'This wasn't me.'

The other officer took handcuffs out of his pocket, pulling Harry's arms roughly behind him. He'd gone pale, his eyes wide.

Thea watched as Harry was pushed down into the car, the police officer's hand on his head. The doors slammed and they drove away.

She slumped onto the stairs, putting her head in her hands. The front door was still open, and a cold breeze blew into the house. What had just happened? Why did they think it was Harry? She needed to call Gabi; she'd know what to do. They'd get him out.

Because it couldn't be Harry. She'd have known. She'd have noticed. Wouldn't she?

43

As the police car left for the station, Kate and Yates walked towards the open front door. Kate could see Thea in the darkened hallway, talking on the phone. She put it down as they approached.

'Can we come in?' Kate asked, and Thea grudgingly moved backwards, letting them into the hallway. 'How are you feeling?'

'Why have you taken Harry?' Thea demanded. 'It wasn't him – I'd have known.'

'Have you remembered anything?' Yates said and Thea shook her head.

'No, it's just … I'd have remembered that, I know I would.'

Yates continued: 'And was Harry aware you'd been pretending to be Gabriella?'

'No,' Thea replied curtly.

Kate wandered down the corridor as Yates persisted with her questions. She stopped in the doorway of what she assumed was the study, taking in a large desk and the back wall lined with bookcases. Kate walked to the far side and picked up one of the hardbacks, looking at the title: *Principles of Corporate Finance*.

Kate put the book back, and as she did she noticed a hollow noise as the book hit the back of the shelf. She pulled out another few, and knocked in the space. It sounded empty.

'What's behind here?' she called back.

Thea appeared in the doorway. 'Wall,' she said, scornfully. 'I think you should leave,' she added. 'That's enough snooping for today.'

Kate nodded and went back into the hallway. Thea opened the front door wide, glaring at them.

'If you think of anything else, please call,' Yates said as they left. Thea scowled, saying nothing and closing the door heavily behind them.

Yates walked over to the car, but Kate stayed outside the house, looking at the front left wall. She walked over to it, then took a few paces from the edge of the wall back to the front door. She frowned. Something wasn't adding up.

'Sarge?' Yates called, starting the engine. 'What are you thinking?' she asked as Kate climbed into the car.

Kate looked back to the house. She took in the battered brickwork, the dirty windows. Fifteen years ago something strange had been going on behind those walls. It was the same today, she knew it.

'Let's go back to the station,' Kate said. 'I want to know more about that house, and every single little sodding detail about those murders.'

44

They needed something else – anything would do. They needed more than the eyewitness testimony of a drunken known criminal wandering around at night to secure a conviction. More evidence, and preferably something that pointed towards a motive.

Now Harry had been arrested, the team could search his flat, but Yates had returned with nothing more than a pair of muddy shoes. She'd stood in the doorway as Kate looked up expectantly.

'I'm sorry,' she'd said. 'There's nothing there.' No sign of a small purple and silver button, it seemed.

Briggs glanced up from his desk. He'd been scrolling through the seemingly never-ending CCTV footage, looking at the parts the techies had sent back over from the street cameras. They were no better than before. There was no way they could definitively say the man walking was Harry Becker.

'Can't you blow it up or something?' Kate had ranted at them. 'Make the image sharper.'

The techie had looked at her, his head tilted sideways, patronising. 'A pixel is still a pixel. You make it bigger and it doesn't get any clearer. It just turns into a bigger grey pixel.'

'Should we interview him now?' Briggs asked.

Kate was on edge, and had been since Dave Fletcher's identification. All Harry Becker had to do was tell someone what they'd been up to and she knew she'd be suspended with a Professional Standards investigation on her head. But she was pissed off, too. He'd lied to her. Harry had sworn blind he had nothing to do with the attack and yet there he was – walking on the common at the same time as Thea had been attacked. The deception stung; it made her feel stupid and gullible and weak.

Kate thought of Harry down in the cells. She thought of the cold bare walls, the thin plastic mattress. The smell of piss and dirty protests that no amount of cleaning ever got rid of completely. Then she thought of Thea Patterson. Drunk and freezing and alone. Left for dead.

'Leave him,' she said. 'Let him have a shitty night in custody. We'll talk to him tomorrow. Go home, both of you – let's think again in the morning.'

They didn't wait to be told twice; Briggs and Yates had gone even before Kate had dragged herself off the floor. She was surrounded by case notes from the original murders, picking over them again, desperate to find something on Harry. Fifteen years was a long time to hold a grudge, it was true, but the twenty-four hours they had to charge him was ticking by and she was starting to despair.

Despite her fear, her police instincts were still strong. Solving the case was paramount, even if she would get fired.

The notes from the murders only confirmed what Kate had assumed: Jennings and the other detectives investigating back then hadn't been thorough. She looked at the scarce reports, the scribbled notes, the incomplete lines of enquiry. They'd had their man; why should they bother with anyone else?

She stretched her arms towards the ceiling, the search report held in her hands. As she held it above her head, a page fell out and fluttered to the floor. She bent to pick it up – it was the original warrant, dated 2004. She looked at it, the judge's signature at the bottom, and then back to the search report. It was long, more than twenty pages, detailing where the police officers had been, what rooms they had checked and how, and a long list of the evidence taken with them at the time. Clothes, shoes, an old laptop, but no murder weapon – no gun. That morning the old architects' drawing of the house Kate had requested had come in, and she now cleared the table to open it out fully. She switched another light on and studied it closely, following the route the police officers had taken, what they'd picked up and where.

The drawing had been done more than thirty years before, when it looked like the studio had been built on the back. The architects had been detailed and had included drawings of all aspects of the house. Kate looked at the photos of the front, the study and the lounge on opposite sides, then searched for a floor plan. Something seemed off. She looked again. Sure enough, the dimensions were out – the study was too small for the size of the house. She rubbed her eyes and squinted at the writing. Then she saw it. A small asterisk in the top-left corner of the wall of the study. Kate jumped, and searched around the edge of the drawing for the key. Then, there it was, in black and white: *staircase to basement hidden behind false wall.*

'There's a basement!' Kate shouted, and collapsed heavily in a chair, clutching the search report. Study, kitchen, art studio, bedrooms, bathrooms. They had ripped up floorboards, pulled apart furniture, but they hadn't found the basement. This was it! This was the evidence they needed.

They had a suspect in custody; they could search wherever

they liked. So what if it wasn't his house – it was where he spent most of his time. All they needed was approval from the DCI and they were away.

A fucking *basement*! The gun was there, she knew it.

Wednesday

45

Kate's heart was thumping so loudly she was convinced the whole room could hear. Thea had led them into the kitchen, clutching the search warrant in her uninjured hand.

'We'd like to start in the basement,' Kate said. 'Please?'

Thea looked at her, but didn't move.

'I know where it is,' she said, and walked out of the kitchen towards the study.

Kate strode confidently to the desk, standing in front of the bookcase. She could see Yates and Briggs exchange a nervous look.

Kate pointed to the bookcase. 'If you could be so kind?' she asked.

Thea pushed past her, then reached forward and pulled on one of the books. As she did so, the whole unit of shelves moved forward, and Thea heaved it to the left.

'Well, fuck me,' Kate heard Briggs whisper behind her.

She looked back to where Thea stood, her face like thunder.

'Go on then,' Thea said. 'Have a good dig around. I don't know what you think you'll find, there's nothing down there except dust and spiders.'

Taking a deep breath, Kate moved forward into the dark hole.

The corridor led downwards and Kate could see the edge

of a wooden stairway. It was narrow, the thin treads disappearing at a sharp angle into the black.

Thea reached round and a fluorescent bulb flickered into life. Kate edged down the stairwell, Briggs and Yates following carefully behind.

Thea hadn't been kidding. It was a small room, with bare brick walls and a low ceiling. Briggs had to fold himself in two to get inside. The floor was uneven brickwork, some loose and scattered across the floor. The air was cold, and filled with disturbed red dust, making Kate cough. Apart from the three of them, there was nothing in the room. Not a single box or belonging. Just four brick walls, a brick floor, the wooden staircase leading upwards and a narrow passageway leading away, under the house.

'Where does this go?' she shouted back up the staircase.

When she didn't get an answer, Kate clicked her torch on, then shuffled along the tiny corridor. The beam of light highlighted graceful spider webs and broken bricks, until she came to a wooden door at the end. She pulled the bolt across and pushed it open with her shoulder, squinting into the daylight.

The passageway had opened into the front of the garden, just under the window to the kitchen, the small door disguised with years of foliage. Kate looked out into the wilderness, then headed back to the square of light where Briggs and Yates waited.

'Let's get to work,' Kate said, directing Yates to search one side and Briggs the other. 'It must be here,' she muttered under her breath.

'I can't believe you managed to persuade Jennings to let you search the house. Becker doesn't even live here,' Yates said.

'Not to mention this case is dead and buried,' Briggs added. He scuffed his shoe across the floor, watching the dust settle across its pristine shine. 'I assume Armed Response are standing by if we find it?'

'Mmm,' Kate said. She bent down and pulled at one of the bricks. It was stuck fast, but the one next to it came loose. She poked in the dirt below it.

'Look for loose bricks,' she told the other two. 'It could be hidden below. Check the walls too.'

I bloody hope it's here, the voice said in her head, because otherwise you are in a fuckload of trouble.

The truth was the chief had not been keen, throwing her out of his office after barely five minutes. 'What's the point?' he had asked, not even letting her finish her argument. 'Who cares about a missing gun when you don't even know if these cases are related?' She knew, she did. But she couldn't tell him why and risk his wrath for not handling a piece of evidence – the button – correctly. Not to mention explaining why she'd been sitting in a pub with one of the chief suspects to an attempted murder investigation only days before.

She had stomped down the corridor, back to the operations room. Back to the whiteboard and the suspects looking out at her, mocking. If I could just find that bloody gun, she thought. If I could just get this case moving the tiniest bit of distance along...

It was early, before Yates and Briggs had made it into the office, and she sat down on one of the uncomfortable plastic chairs. She put the report in front of her, the old authorisation paperwork poking out the side.

She pulled it out and looked at it.

Your average person on the street didn't know what this documentation looked like. They didn't know that warrants had barely changed in twenty years. What if they went to the house with this one? Would Thea even bother to look, to turn the page and check the date? Who cares if it was illegal? If they found the gun, surely the end would justify the means? Surely?

A few hours on, and Kate had a sickening feeling in her stomach. They had checked every single inch of the room, scouring it for loose bricks, for anything a gun might be hidden behind. Kate had pushed and pulled but yielded no more than a bad back and the horrible knowledge that she had been very, very stupid. Yates was stood in one corner of the basement, Briggs crouched in another. They had found nothing.

'What now?' Briggs asked. 'Search the rest of the house?'

Kate shook her head. 'Time to leave.'

They drove back to the station in silence, Briggs at the wheel of the old Skoda, Yates in the back. The other two took their cue from their boss's silence, exchanging looks via the rear-view mirror. As they entered the main doors, Kate saw the chief's secretary beckon her over.

'He wants to see you,' she whispered. 'Best go up now.'

'I figured,' Kate replied, grimly.

The chief inspector sat back in his chair and drummed his podgy fingers on his desk.

'I was having a good day, DS Munro. A *quiet* day. And then what happens? One of my detectives tells me your entire team is out and about and I think, I wonder where they've gone?' He stared at her, then bent forward, picking up a small stress ball and giving it a good squeeze. 'I told you not to go digging, didn't I?' he said. In front of him, Kate stayed silent. 'And I said no to searching the house. And yet, where did you go?'

Kate pressed her lips together.

'You went to the house and poked around in their basement.' He shouted the last few words, and Kate winced. 'Didn't you?' he bellowed.

'Yes.'

'Yes, you bloody did. What did you think would happen?'

'I thought we would find the gun,' Kate said, quietly.

'And what then? What then, DS Munro?' The chief hurled the stress ball across the room, where it hit the wall and fell behind a filing cabinet. 'You find the gun, you don't have the proper paperwork, and a rock-solid fifteen-year-old conviction is challenged. Or – or! – you don't find the gun, conduct an illegal search, the press end up gettting wind of it and bang on my door. And – and! – a fifteen-year-old conviction is challenged. Fuck!'

Kate stood in front of him. He was right, of course. And she knew it.

'I told you not to dig.'

She nodded.

'And now we're faced with this shit storm. I don't want Professional Standards investigating. Christ, I hate those guys.' He took a deep breath, brow furrowed. 'And how does this make me look?' he asked her, and Kate blinked. 'I was involved in that case, and now my own detectives are trying to fuck up the conviction? I'll be the laughing stock!'

Kate opened her mouth, then thought better of it and closed it again. She didn't give a shit what people said about Jennings; surely it was more important they got the bad guys off the street? But she knew she'd made a massive mistake. She'd probably be suspended; she should be after what she'd done.

The DCI sighed, placing both of his hands on the desk, palms down. 'Can you just make yourself scarce for a while? Don't rock the boat. Don't get into any arguments until I've at least had a chance to smooth things over. If we're lucky, PR can sort it out, pretend it was all normal and above board, and nobody's legal team will go sniffing around.'

'I'm staying on the case?' Kate stuttered.

'For the moment. But dial back the investigation. Get Yates and Briggs looking at that arson from Saturday night that everyone's so excited about. It'll be fine. No one's been attacked since, have they?'

'But guv ...'

'DS Munro,' he said, a warning in his voice. 'Do as I say, and be thankful it's not any worse.'

Kate backed out of the room and stood in the corridor, battling back tears that pricked her eyes. It had been an almighty fuck-up – but something inside her just *knew* the gun was down there. Except it wasn't. There was nothing in that basement. So where the bloody hell was it?

Kate took a deep breath outside the operations room, ready to face Briggs and Yates, ready to get back to work. She went to push open the door, as Yates barrelled through from the opposite way.

'Sarge? Front desk called – said Ryan Holmes is here, and he's asking for you.'

'Again?' Kate was surprised. 'Did they say why?'

'Nope. You coming?'

'Absolutely,' Kate replied, turning in her tracks, all words from her chief inspector forgotten.

46

'Why do you think he's here?' Yates whispered. Kate and Yates were stood outside the door to the front reception desk, watching Ryan Holmes.

'Confession?' Kate said, optimistically. As usual Ryan was scruffy: jeans, trainers, sweatshirt. Grey pallor, bags under his eyes — he looked like he hadn't slept for days.

She pushed open the door and Yates followed her out.

'Mr Holmes?' Kate asked. 'Would you like to come through?'

He shook his head. 'No, no, I can't stop. I need to get to the club. I just wanted to give you this.'

Ryan reached forward and handed her a DVD, the same as the ones he had given them before.

'Not another fifteen then?' Yates asked ruefully, taking it from him and putting it straight into an exhibit bag, passing him the declaration to sign.

'No, not this time,' he smiled softly, handing it back to her. 'I'm sorry about that. What you want to see is on there.' He paused, looking at the DVD in Yates's hands, then met Kate's gaze. 'I can't turn a blind eye to this any more.'

'What do you mean?' Kate asked.

'I went to see Thea,' Ryan sighed, his shoulders slumped. 'She didn't deserve this. I know what he's capable of. I can't stand by and watch it happen again.'

'Who?' Kate asked, but he moved away from her.

'Just watch it,' he said, and walked quickly out of the police station.

'Okay, then,' Kate muttered, looking down at the DVD. They turned to leave but the desk sergeant called them over.

'DS Munro, this is James Burford,' he said, pointing to an angry man at the desk, briefcase in hand. When they both looked blank, the sergeant added, 'Solicitor to Harry Becker?'

Kate's mouth formed a perfect 'o' as the man gestured towards the door.

'And I'd like to see my client now,' he said, eschewing any formalities.

'I'm sorry, we didn't know you were coming.'

'Apparently not. And apparently you didn't take the trouble to find out a wide range of important facts about Harry Becker. Please take me to him now,' he repeated.

Kate turned and typed in the security code to the main police station, the solicitor following through the door. Unlike Dave Fletcher's legal representative, this man was smartly dressed in a well-cut suit, complete with waistcoat and bright blue tie. His briefcase was leather and expensive, his shoes clean and shiny. He turned to look at Kate.

'I'm assuming you've checked on him this morning?' he asked.

'The custody sergeant will have,' Kate said.

'And what was his mental state?' When she didn't say anything, the solicitor continued. 'So you haven't been getting regular updates? You haven't had a doctor in to assess?'

Kate stopped, open-mouthed.

'Why would we need a doctor?' Yates asked.

The solicitor stopped in the corridor, facing them. Kate suspected this day was going from bad to worse.

'Let me get this straight,' Mr Burford said, his forehead

furrowed. 'Yesterday, you arrested my client and held him overnight in a cell with no intention of interviewing him—'

'We couldn't risk him destroying evidence—' Kate started, but the solicitor interrupted.

'You don't complete a risk assessment, you don't request a doctor or any sort of medical professional.' He stopped and Kate shook her head. She could feel Yates looking at her, questioning.

'DS Munro,' James Burford said. 'What the hell were you thinking? You do not simply hold someone with PTSD alone in a cell overnight. Let alone someone with his family history. Did you even have him on suicide watch?'

'The custody sergeant would have called—' Kate started but the solicitor cut her off.

'Get me down there, now.'

Kate started walking towards the holding cells, her mouth dry. She knew. She knew what Harry had been through, she knew the medication he was on, and yet she had done nothing. But if he was so ill, why hadn't he said anything when he was booked in?

She increased her walk to a jog, pushing open doors and taking the stairs two at a time, Yates and the solicitor on her heels. She could see Yates on her mobile, trying to call downstairs to custody.

Men don't, she told herself. Men don't say anything. They let it eat them up inside, never asking for help, never wanting to seem vulnerable. Then one day ... She couldn't even think it; she wouldn't let herself imagine what he might have done.

She knew. *She knew.* How could she have been so stupid?

47

Kate ran into custody, barking at the custody sergeant to open up the cell. 'Now!' she shouted, as he hesitated at the door.

The door swung open.

'For fuck's sake,' Kate said and stopped, bent in two, her hands on her knees, trying to get her breath back.

Harry was lying on the bed, staring at the ceiling. He sat up as the door opened. He looked like shit, Kate thought. But he was very much alive.

The solicitor walked into the cell, his hand outstretched, making his introductions to Harry. Then he turned to Kate, where she stood speechless, with Yates in the corridor. 'I need some time,' he said, his voice cold. 'And then, we would like to get on with the interview, if you would be so kind. See what evidence you think you have on my client.'

An hour in, Kate fucking hated this guy and there was no doubt as to how he felt about her. He thought she was the epitome of incompetence and, to be fair, Kate could see why.

'So, you arrested my client on no more evidence than the say-so of a career criminal?' the solicitor said, sardonically. 'Who says he saw Mr Becker walking on Southampton Common, in the pitch dark, around the same time that he himself was mugging the victim?'

Kate ground her teeth together in annoyance, her fingers

rapidly tapping on the desk, barely keeping her nerves at bay. 'We have your client on CCTV walking in the area, and his voice on tape making the 999 call.'

'DS Munro.' The solicitor shook his head, letting his breath out in a long patronising sigh. 'You have *someone* on a grainy black and white video. And a crackling voice recording that could be anyone. You searched my client's flat and car and found nothing more than a pair of muddy shoes. Not to mention searching a house that has nothing to do with him.'

Kate's jaw was starting to ache from clamping it shut for so long. She stayed silent, remembering the chief inspector's words. At this point she should be grateful he wasn't aware of the illegality of that particular search. And it seemed like Harry hadn't mentioned their illicit few days together. She couldn't imagine this solicitor would keep that one close to his chest.

She looked over at Harry. Throughout the whole inter-view, he'd barely said a word, muttering 'no comment' whenever she asked him a direct question. At this point he was letting his solicitor do all the talking for him. He glared at her, his blue eyes fixed on hers.

She took a deep breath. She gripped the edge of the desk, preventing her fingers from fidgeting. It was this, or nothing. It might push Harry to the edge, but it was a risk she had to take.

'We believe Thea had sex that night,' she said, embellish-ing the evidence for the benefit of the interview. Kate saw his jaw muscles clenching, his hands contract into fists. 'We have DNA from under her fingernails, semen on her dress. We know she was pretending to be Gabi, and we know she fooled everyone into thinking she was her sister. Did she fool you, too, Mr Becker?' Harry's mouth opened, then clamped shut again. Kate kept on pushing. She knew he was hiding something. 'We took your DNA when you were arrested – it's only a matter of time until it comes back as a match. Did you think you had sex with Gabriella that night, Harry? Were you angry when you found out the truth?' Kate sat forward in her chair. She knew she was getting under his skin. 'Did you follow her? Did you catch up with her to teach her a lesson?'

'DS Munro—' the solicitor interjected.

'I did not sleep with Thea. I have never slept with Thea,' Harry snapped.

'But you have slept with Gabriella. Is that right, Mr Becker?'

James Burford laid a hand on Harry's arm, stopping him, and Harry sat back in his chair, crossing his arms over his chest.

'I think we're done here, DS Munro,' the solicitor said. 'Charge my client or release him.'

48

'Do you want me to come with you?' Thea asked. She glanced across at Harry as she drove, sitting silently in the seat next to her.

He shook his head, staring resolutely out of the windscreen.

Thea had done nothing but worry about Harry since the police picked him up. When she'd had the call from the station, she'd thought it was over, but seeing him now, she wasn't so sure.

'Thank you for getting me out,' he said quietly.

'It wasn't me, it was Gabriella,' Thea said. 'Well, Mortimer.' Harry nodded slowly.

'Are you sure this is such a good idea?' she asked. 'Why don't you come home with me first? Get some sleep? Go and visit tomorrow?'

'No.' Harry looked at her. 'If I don't go now, I won't go at all.'

'Is that such a bad thing?' Thea paused at the traffic lights, taking in his frown, his stoop, the fragility in his posture. Harry looked like he was collapsing in on himself, his body struggling to maintain normality.

She pulled up at her house and they both climbed out. Harry walked towards her, taking both of her hands in his.

'You know it wasn't me, don't you?' he said.

Thea nodded. 'I know, Harry.'

He bent down and gave her a quick kiss on the cheek, then walked to his car. She watched him pull out of her driveway, mentally castigating herself for not trying harder to convince him to stay.

Because fifteen years was a long time to wait before visiting your father in prison. A very long time indeed.

49

Harry felt eyes on him the moment he walked into the room. He felt the heat rise in his cheeks and his shirt stick to his back. The other visitors arriving at the same time as him rushed to their loved ones with kisses and hugs, but Harry felt paralysed, his feet glued to the floor.

He looked up and met his father's eyes. His dad lifted his hand in a half-wave, then lowered it again slowly. He looked older than Harry imagined he would. His hair was thin and completely grey, his face was lined and he was wearing a thick pair of unattractive glasses. But he gave Harry a hopeful smile and tentatively held out his hand as Harry approached. Harry shook it, the first touch he had had from his father in nearly fifteen years. His hand felt rough, like fine sandpaper. They sat down, facing each other across the worn table top.

'I couldn't believe it when they said you were coming,' he said. 'And here you are.'

'Here I am,' Harry replied. His mouth felt dry, his tongue sticking to the roof of his mouth. He took a sip from the cup of water in front of him.

'How did you arrange it so quickly?' Harrison asked.

'Good solicitor,' Harry said, then paused. 'They said you haven't got much time left.'

'No.'

They sat in silence. The room was featureless, humming with conversation from the other tables around them. The prison officers hovered at the edge, looking bored, their arms crossed in front of their chests. Harry fidgeted on the hard plastic chair.

'I'm sorry you're here,' Harry blurted out. He stopped, feeling his throat narrow and his eyes get hot.

Harrison breathed out. 'That's not your fault.'

Harry nodded, not trusting himself to speak.

'Why are you here?' Harrison asked. 'I mean, I'm glad you are, so glad you are, but why now? What changed your mind?'

'Thea was attacked.'

'I heard. Is she okay?'

'They arrested me.'

Harrison gasped. 'But they've let you go, right? They don't think you did it?'

Harry shook his head. 'No, I don't think so. But they kept me there overnight. Locked in one of their crappy little cells.' He looked down at his hands, threading his fingers together. 'And it was awful. I couldn't sleep. I kept on thinking of you, locked in here. One night, and the walls...' Harry shuddered. 'I thought I was going crazy. And you've been here for all this time.'

'It's okay, Harry.'

'But it's not, is it? All that happened. We shouldn't have...' Harry shook his head, stopping himself, aware of where he was, who was around them.

His father took his hands and held them in his. Harry remembered growing up, watching his dad mend a broken toy, screwdriver in those big hands, reassuring him that it would be okay, that he'd fix it. And now here they were, in the same situation. Except this time nothing could be repaired.

'You have people to look after you, right?' his dad asked. 'Yes, the twins.'

Harry saw an expression pass over his father's face. A flicker of concern, or something more. 'What?' He pulled his hands away from his father's.

Harrison looked at him. 'Don't you think it would be good to get some distance? Get away from that house and everything that happened?'

'It's a bit late for that now, don't you think?' Harry stuttered. 'They're the only family, the only home, I ever really had.' He could feel his hands shaking, the anger building. 'You were always too busy with *her* to pay any attention to me.'

'I know, and I'm sorry.' Harrison looked down and worried at a piece of skin at the edge of his fingernail. 'I loved her,' he said quietly.

'For fuck's sake!' Harry stood up suddenly, the chair screeching on the tiled floor, making the guards look over. Harry glanced at them, then leaned forward on the table, his face next to his father's. 'You should have loved me more,' he said, his voice breaking. 'And that should have stopped you picking up the gun that day. It's only ever been Thea and Gabi who mattered to me. Not you. Not ever. Never again,' he told himself, and walked towards the door.

'Harry, please. I'm here because I love you, can't you see that, son?' Harrison pleaded, calling after him.

Harry turned back. 'I am not your son,' he said.

Harry stumbled through security, out of the prison, tripping over his feet to get to his car. He fumbled with his keys, dropping them on the concrete, then climbed in, placing both his hands on the steering wheel to steady himself.

This was exactly why he hadn't been to visit his father. All this crap, all spilling to the surface. The man was responsible for ruining his life before; he wasn't going to do it again. Not now.

He started the car and drove away from the prison. But the more distance he put between them, the more he realised what he'd lost. He wouldn't see his father again. He was as much an orphan as the twins. No family, no relatives. Nobody except them.

His body started to shake and his legs struggled to make contact with the accelerator. A car coming in the other direction beeped him and he swerved back to his side of the road, hurriedly pulling into a lay-by as his eyes blurred. Tears ran down his face; his body took over, convulsing in great racking sobs.

The police digging, investigating Thea's attack and the murders; all these years on and it was like it had happened yesterday. Fifteen years of denial and therapy and cognitive behavioural this and that, and it was all coming down to tonight, crying by the side of the road, in the cold and the dark. He put his arms on the steering wheel and rested his head, crying desperate tears for his childhood, his parents, everything he had lost.

So his childhood hadn't been normal, but for a while, he'd been happy. He could cope with the strange looks from other kids in the playground, with the teasing and sniggers about his mother, as long as he had the twins by his side. But then Robert said he couldn't see them any more, and Madeleine would have taken the twins, and that couldn't happen, it couldn't, but then it didn't matter because they were dead and his father went to prison and everything had gone.

Even Gabi left. He'd resolved to track her down, but then

the world had become suffocating and he'd barely been able to leave the house. He'd been trapped in a world of triggers and flashbacks; memories that crawled into his life without warning, reducing him to a pathetic shell on the floor. Living each day in stress mode, constantly on edge, waiting for the worst to happen. And in bed at 2 a.m., shaking, sweating, nightmares worse than any horror film.

The engine idled as he cried. Headlights from the road threw strange shadows across the car, moving through an arc of black and white, but he didn't notice, too lost in the black hole.

It was never over; it could never be behind him. He would never be normal again.

50

Kate rested against the window, enjoying the cool glass against her forehead. She exhaled, and instantly the window was clouded with condensation from her breath. It was dark outside; she could see cars charging along the dual carriageway on one side, people walking down the pavement towards town on the other. She envied them with their lives to go to, their warm homes and their families. She wondered what Sam was doing at that moment.

When they were married, she'd often arrive home to tempting smells from dinner cooking in the oven, Sam sat watching the six o'clock news, waiting for her. She'd change out of her uniform and slump next to him on the sofa, muscles aching.

'Long day?' he'd ask.

'Always,' she'd reply, and they'd move on to talk about more interesting topics. What their friends had said on Facebook, what they were planning for the weekend. They'd watch television. Mundane, trivial things mostly, but the sort of chat that kept a relationship alive. They'd go to bed at the same time, clean their teeth, use the toilet with the door open. Sometimes they'd fuck; sometimes it was gentle, loving. Often they wouldn't do it at all. But that was okay. Mutual friends, mutual lives.

She wasn't sure now what he watched on TV. Their friends were now his. She had no idea who he was fucking.

The thought of Sam in bed with someone else made tears prick behind her eyes, so she turned away from her little diorama at the window, back to the ops room with the harsh fluorescent lighting and whiteboard. Harry stared out at her, accusingly.

She'd been horrible to him, she knew, but that was her job, she told herself. That was how she got results. But despite that he'd kept quiet; he could have told his solicitor what they'd been doing together and she'd have been suspended without a doubt, maybe even sacked once Professional Standards had finished with her. Harry could have done that at any time, but he hadn't. Kate wondered why.

She picked up her bag and pulled out the brown envelope. She'd been carrying it around for days. Her drunken self may have signed on the dotted line, but her conscious mind hadn't been ready to call an end to her marriage. But perhaps it was time. Harry had done the decent thing for her, despite how she had treated him, and she should do the same for Sam. She stuck a yellow Post-it note to the pages and scribbled a brief message.

I'm sorry, she wrote. *I should have trusted you, I should have listened. Kxx*

She pushed the signed pages back in and sealed the top, placing it in the post tray with the other mail.

Kate heard laughter and turned to the doorway, where Briggs and Yates were arriving back from their coffee run. Yates handed a mug to Kate, along with a packet of Maltesers.

'Thought you might need these,' she said.

Briggs sat down at his computer, flicking through the screens. He looked over his shoulder to Kate. 'Ballistics report is back,' he said.

'Thought we weren't looking at that case any more,' Yates

said, sat next to him, still working through the CCTV Ryan had given them that morning.

'We're not,' Kate replied. 'I requested the analysis on Monday.' She paused, until curiosity got the better of her. 'Tell us anyway.'

'There's nothing much here,' Briggs muttered, his eyes scanning the screen. 'Just says that the bullets that shot Madeleine and Robert Patterson were from the same gun, nine-millimetre, possibly World War Two issue. Traces of rust on the bullets. Above-average amount of black powder residue.' He looked up. 'That's it.'

'Doesn't tell us much.'

'No, and without a gun to compare it to, that's all they can say.' Briggs clicked away from the email and onto another. 'And the blood results are back from forensics,' he added, pointing to his screen.

Kate jumped up and joined him at his computer, looking over his shoulder as they read the detailed report.

'Oh, but that's weird...' Briggs muttered.

Briggs ran his finger across a line of text then looked up at her, meeting Kate's puzzled expression with his own.

'0.06?' he muttered. 'How can Thea Patterson have had a blood alcohol level of 0.06? My gran is more pissed than that on the Christmas sherry.'

Kate frowned. 'She was a mess, we can see that from the CCTV. There's no way that's right.' Her eyes continued to scan the report as Briggs scrolled down the page. 'There, there, stop there,' she said, pointing to a complicated chemical name.

'Flunitrazepam? What's that?' Briggs asked.

'I don't know,' Kate replied. 'But I bet you it's nothing good.' She looked at Briggs, a smile on her face, suddenly full of energy. 'Well, what are you waiting for? Call the lab, get someone medical to translate this waffle. And chase the rest of the forensics. Yates – keep going with the CCTV.'

She jumped up from her seat and looked at the white-board. 'It's about time we caught a break. Let's get this fucker.'

51

This wasn't a good idea, Harry told himself, this was not a good idea at all. It was dark, it was starting to drizzle, and it had been a long time since he had attempted anything like this. His head was spinning and his foot slipped. He grabbed the branches next to him, cursing under his breath as one caught him on his cheek. He slapped it away angrily, pushing upwards through the leaves.

Thea had told him about the search of the basement; he knew what the detectives had been looking for. It was here, wrapped in plastic, covered in fingerprints and hair and skin, all sorts of things that the police would love.

Back then it had been a rush job to hide it. He had panicked, and this had been the first place that came to mind. But leaving it up here had been crazy.

A hundred times he'd gone to get rid of it, and every time he'd held back. It was the only thing that could save his father, the final piece to assuage his guilt. But Harry knew what his father would say. Seeing him today had only confirmed it in his mind. Get rid of it. Now.

He pushed on, one branch after another, pulling himself up, breathing heavily. The rain had started to come down in sheets; his T-shirt was drenched and water dripped down his face. His fingers were numb. There couldn't be much further to go, surely.

He pushed branches and leaves out of the way, and there it

was. Nailed to the trunk of the tree, the wooden box looked as fragile and weather-beaten as it always had. He reached up and opened the top, feeling inside, but the nail didn't hold and it shifted, coming loose and plunging to the ground.

Harry heard it fall, his heart in his mouth. He heard the crashes as it hit the branches on the way down, then quiet. He followed it, as quickly as he could, his hands slipping on the wet branches, twigs flicking painfully against his skin.

He remembered the fear back then. He remembered all those years ago he had been fighting to catch his breath, almost hyperventilating with the shock of what had happened. The hot smell of burning; the noise loud enough to echo and bounce around the room. Searing pain in his hand. One body already on the ground, the other falling. Blood everywhere.

The shocked expression on Thea's face. Gabi screaming, turning away from the horror.

He let out a sigh of relief as his feet hit the mud at the bottom of the tree, then bent down and started looking. He dropped to his knees, sludge soaking through his jeans, and ran his hands over the soft ground. Was he looking in the wrong place? He moved slightly to the left and scrabbled around again, moving rocks and dirt, not caring how wet and cold he was.

And then there it was. A broken piece of wood, and the edge of a plastic bag. He pulled it towards him, discarding the wrecked bird box, now shattered on the ground.

He stood up, moving out of the shadow of the old oak. In the light from the moon, he rolled the plastic bag round, unwrapping what was contained inside. The last fragment came clear, and he reached inside and touched it, the cold metal coming in contact with his skin. He remembered it now.

Suddenly, he felt a rush in his stomach and bent over, vomiting into the undergrowth. He stood up, groaning, and wiped the back of his arm across his mouth. He pushed his hand into the plastic bag, wrapped his fingers round the grip and held it in front of him. Heavy, solid, cold.

He had the gun.

Thursday

52

Dressed head to toe in white paper suits, the scene of crime officers resembled ghosts to Kate. They moved in and out of the doorway of the nightclub, shifting equipment one way, plastic bags in the other. Kate stood on the empty pavement and watched them, her gloved hands thrust in her coat pockets, her scarf wrapped round her neck.

The club's doorway had been cordoned off and police vans filled the road, attracting an array of curious onlookers. The uniform guarding the line beckoned her over and she ducked under the blue and white tape, standing next to Ryan.

'I guess this is it then,' he said to her. Like her, his coat was buttoned up to his reddened nose, glasses filling the gap between collar and black woolly hat. 'No one's going to want to come here now.'

'No, I expect not,' Kate replied.

He stared grimly at his ruined livelihood. 'Someone's going to tell him soon, you know. He has friends round here, and then I can't say what he'll do.'

'We have someone watching him.'

'And are you watching me?' Ryan looked at Kate and she met his gaze. She knew he was worried. And he was right to be.

'I gave you access in good faith, DS Munro,' he continued.

'I know, and we appreciate that, Mr Holmes.'

One of the crime scene officers emerged from the club, a face mask obscuring his features. With a blue plastic glove, he waved to Kate and she left Ryan standing at the cordon.

She walked over and wordlessly the SOCO showed her two plastic evidence bags.

Kate pulled the phone out of her pocket and made a call. 'Yates? We have it,' she said. 'Arrest Steve Morgan.'

53

Kate hovered outside the interview room, her body buzzing. She was excited. She knew they had everything they needed, but she had to calm down. She couldn't mess this up.

She took two deep breaths, in and out, then turned the handle.

Steve Morgan was at the table, Briggs opposite him. She took a seat next to Briggs and placed the file in front of her.

'I'm getting bored of this,' Steve said, his knee bobbing up and down under the table. 'I can't wait to see what you think you've got on me, so I can get out of here and sue your lovely police department.'

Kate didn't say a word, and looked at Briggs. He nodded to her, slowly, showing his solidarity.

'So, DC Briggs has cautioned you, and you have turned down your right to free independent legal advice,' she started.

'I don't need it.'

'Okay,' Kate said, calmly. She felt good now. She looked him right in the eye.

'So, tell us again about your movements on the night Thea Patterson was attacked. On Saturday the nineteenth of January?'

Steve Morgan gave an exaggerated sigh. 'I was at the club, working. All night.'

'And did you see Thea Patterson?'

'Yes, except we thought she was her sister, Gabriella.'

'We?'

'Ryan Holmes and I. You should be arresting him, not me. She was his girl, you know.'

'We know. Except he was passed out all night, so it couldn't possibly have been him, right?'

'So he says,' Steve said, a scornful grin on his face.

'So your cameras say too.' Kate nodded to Briggs and he put the laptop on the table, loading up the file.

'Mr Morgan, can you describe what you're looking at?' Kate asked.

Steve leaned forward. 'That's my office,' he said, his head snapping up to look at Kate. 'How have you got CCTV from my office?'

'Mr Holmes kindly gave it to us.' Kate smiled. 'Turns out he doesn't like being accused of attempted murder when he has an alibi conveniently recorded on camera.'

The video continued to roll and Steve watched it.

Briggs filled in as Steve stared open-mouthed. 'So here, you can see the timestamp of one-thirty a.m., and here's Mr Holmes.' He pointed to the screen as Ryan rolled into view, his legs unsteady, his body reeling. He sat on the sofa in the office for a moment, a drink in his hand, then sank into the cushions, his eyes closing. 'As you can see, he's looking a bit the worse for wear.'

'Always was a lightweight,' Steve mocked. 'But what does this have to do with me?'

'Because, Mr Morgan, we were curious.' Kate pulled a sheet of paper out of the file in front of her. 'When we got the blood results back on Thea Patterson, we couldn't understand how someone who acted so drunk on camera, who could barely stand as she walked away from your club, could only have a blood alcohol level of 0.06. That's not even the legal limit.'

Steve Morgan sat back in his seat and shrugged.

'So we looked a little further down the page, and can you see what else was in her blood?' Kate pointed to a line on the piece of paper.

'Flunitrazepam?' Steve said, slowly pronouncing the syllables. 'I have no idea what that is.'

'Nor did we,' Kate said, smiling. 'So we asked our medical colleagues, and do you know what they said? It's a sort of benzodiazepine. Sometimes known as Rohypnol?' Kate saw a flicker of recognition cross Steve's face. His brow narrowed for a moment. 'You must know what Rohypnol is, Mr Morgan?'

'Someone spiked her drink, so what?'

'You're not worried that this sort of thing has been going on at your club?' Kate waved a hand, dismissing her own question. 'Never mind.' She paused, drumming her fingers on the table. 'I'd like to show you a little jigsaw puzzle that my brilliant detectives have been piecing together. But let's run it backwards, for fun.'

Briggs pulled the file on the laptop back up and Kate pointed at the screen. 'See this glass?' she said, pointing to the one Ryan was holding on the sofa. 'It has some letters on it: "Mrs", it says.' Steve crossed his arms in front of his chest and stared at Kate. 'One of a set, as you told me last week, and distinctive, I'm sure you can agree, so we can track it across the CCTV footage that you generously gave us. Here it is in Mr Holmes's hand and ...' Briggs rewound the tape, then shifted to a different perspective from a different camera. '... here it is again, in Thea Patterson's, as she passes it to Mr Holmes, hours before.'

Briggs changed view again on the tape, with a slight smile to Kate. 'And, oh look, here it is again.' She turned the screen so it was pointing at Steve. 'In the barman's hand, passing it to Thea.'

'So I'll sack him. You have my word. Job done.'

'That's what we thought, except we found that glass when we searched your office. Fallen down the side of the sofa where Mr Holmes had dropped it, and you know what we found? Traces of flunitrazepam, in high concentrations. And your fingerprints.'

'I pick up glasses every day. I'm sure my fingerprints are on half the glasses in the club.'

'Yes, but ...' Kate gestured to Briggs and he scrolled again through the video. Kate sat back in her seat, enjoying the moment. 'Here you are in your office, with that glass in your hand and a strange substance in a little plastic bag. See the timestamp on the CCTV, Steve? Twelve fifty-three a.m. And guess what we found in your office when we looked?' Kate pushed the photo of the evidence bag with the drugs inside across to Steve. 'Quite a nice little stash you have here, Mr Morgan.'

Steve Morgan frowned, pulling his handsome features into a grimace. He leaned forward over the table, putting his face close to Kate's.

'You think you're so clever, don't you? You little bitch.' Kate raised an eyebrow but didn't flinch, matching Steve's expression. She could smell his breath, sour and bitter. 'So you found my drugs. So fucking what? So I might have slipped some in that bird's drink. It's hardly attempted murder. Your beloved CPS aren't going to give a shit about this. I didn't touch that woman the whole night.'

'Not once?' Kate asked.

'No,' Steve said, smiling.

'So, how can you account for the fact that we found your skin cells, your DNA, under her fingernails?' Kate paused, as Steve opened and closed his mouth. 'You see, Steve, even though Thea can't remember anything, she fought back that night. She managed to catch you somewhere. Maybe on your hand or your arm? Who knows? But we took fingernail scrapings, and those came back to a sample of DNA we had on file from 2002. Do you remember what happened in 2002, Steve?' He looked down at the table, saying nothing. 'Let me refresh your memory.'

Kate opened the file in front of her and showed him a picture. It was a young girl, her face bloody, her eye bulging and painful. 'This is Alice Young, do you remember her? You went to university together and she accused you of rape after you'd all been drinking one night. We arrested you and took your DNA but somehow the case collapsed after she showed up looking like this and said, on reflection, what you two did that night was consensual even though her blood alcohol level was so high there was little chance she'd have been conscious. Do you remember now, Steve?'

He shook his head and stared at the table.

'So the case broke down, but we had you on file. And look who popped up this week when forensics ran the sample.' Kate leaned back in her seat and crossed her arms. 'What I don't understand, though, is why you did it. Why hit Thea over the head? Did you try it on with her and she said no? Were you angry, Steve? You don't like it when a woman rejects you, do you?'

Steve looked at her, his face defiant. 'That's ridiculous.'

Kate shrugged. 'Is it? I guess what's ridiculous is an attractive young woman like Thea Patterson wanting to be with a washed-up sleazy nightclub owner like you. She could have any man she wanted,' Kate paused, looking at Briggs and laughing. 'So why on earth would she choose you?'

'She didn't reject me,' Steve snapped. 'She wanted me. In fact, I would have had sex with her that night, if some woman hadn't interrupted us.'

Kate paused, steeling herself. 'We know, Mr Morgan. We know exactly what you were trying to do, as this camera shows.' Briggs turned the laptop round again and Kate continued. 'Here you are, dragging Thea Patterson to the toilets. At one thirty-nine a.m.' They all looked at the CCTV.

Kate had watched it a few times now, and each time her anger grew. The woman on the screen was clearly incapacitated, her head rolled to one side, hair over her face, her legs unable to support her. The man, Steve Morgan, had his arm around her tiny body as he pushed her up against the wall in the corridor. He put his free hand under her dress, pushing it up, groping her breasts, before glancing around then pulling her into the toilets. Kate fought back her revulsion, imagining him trying to screw her in a cubicle, her unable to fight back, barely aware of what was going on.

'Given the concentration when we took the samples and her body weight, the doctors estimate Thea had enough in her blood to render her almost unconscious.' Kate paused. 'Certainly not aware of what was happening to her.'

Steve Morgan looked at her, his lip curling. 'You can't prove that for sure,' he growled.

'No, but we have your semen on her dress, and a witness.' The video continued to roll, showing a blonde woman going into the toilets two minutes after Steve and Thea. 'Is this the woman you said interrupted you, Steve?' Kate asked sweetly, pointing to the screen. 'Do you remember? Because she remembers you, and she's willing to testify that there was no way in hell Thea Patterson gave consent. And that, Mr Morgan, is what we call attempted rape.'

He crossed his arms in front of him. 'I want that legal advice now,' he said.

Kate and Briggs left the room, doing a quiet high five once the door was shut behind them.

Kate shook her head. 'What a repulsive piece of shit,' she muttered and Briggs nodded. They knew they had him; they knew there was little he would be able to say now. They'd call his solicitor, who'd hopefully advise their client to come clean on what he knew.

So evidence was weak for the attempted murder but one followed the other, it was clear. Perhaps he wanted another go; perhaps she fought back this time. They knew the CPS would like it: he had previous form, no remorse or sympathy for the victim. Whatever the reason for the attempted murder, the case was closed, they had their man. They didn't care why. What did it matter now?

54

'The gun's gone, Gabriella.'

'What are you talking about?' Gabi asked, surprised at seeing Thea at her front door, relieved Mortimer was at work. Her sister pushed past her into the house without being asked, going through to the kitchen.

Gabi followed, her brain trying to catch up. 'You knew where the gun was?'

'Of course I knew where the gun was, Harry told me years ago.' Thea stood next to the kitchen table, facing her sister. 'But it's not there now. I thought I heard something in the garden last night, so I went out this morning and noticed bits of the bird box round the bottom of the oak. I checked. The gun's gone.'

Gabi shook her head. That sodding tree. Thea and Harry were always pissing about in that bloody oak when they were kids. 'So where is it?' she asked.

'Harry must have it.' Thea sat down at the kitchen table.

Gabi stared at her. 'If you knew where the gun was, why didn't you get rid of it sooner?' she asked.

'Harry wouldn't let me. He said we might need it if his dad ever wanted to appeal.' Thea shrugged. 'I guess he didn't hate his dad as much as he made out.'

'But it ...' Gabi started, but Thea cut her off.

'I know. But Harry treated it like some sort of penance. The sword of Damocles hanging over his head.' Thea stopped. 'I shouldn't have listened to him. I should have got rid of it years ago.'

'So what does Harry want with it now?' Gabi asked.

'I don't know, and that's what worries me.' Gabi saw the concern clear on her sister's face. 'Do you love him?' Thea asked.

Gabi was confused by the change of subject. 'Do I love Harry? What sort of question is that?'

'An honest one. Because he loves you. He always has, you know that. And more than just this brother-sister crap you like to hide behind.' Thea frowned, pulling the sleeves of her jumper over her hands. 'He was happy, he was okay without you. And now you're back, and he's a mess.'

Gabi took a deep breath and sat down opposite Thea at the table. 'I know. But I can't be responsible for Harry's happiness, Thea. Or yours, for that matter.'

'No, God forbid you would worry about someone else for a change.' Thea stood up and faced her sister. 'Why don't you just leave again, walk away? Stop pretending you give a shit about Harry.'

'I do give a shit. He's my friend too, Thea.'

'Is he? Really? How much do you know about him? What he's been through?' Thea's jaw clenched, her eyes aflame. 'Where were you after Mum and Dad died?' Thea confronted her, shouting. 'Where were you for the night-mares, Gabi, when Harry would wake up screaming? When he couldn't leave the house because he was afraid a loud noise would trigger a panic attack?'

Gabi reeled. 'I didn't know,' she stuttered.

'Did you know he can't go near a fireworks display? That bonfire night and New Year's Eve is a write-off? That he gets horrendous flashbacks if he hears a car backfiring?' Thea continued, her eyes narrowed. 'But why would you know? Why would you care?' She turned and walked to the kitchen door, looking back for a second, her face defiant. 'Leave him alone, Gabriella, I'll sort this out. Go back to your own life, go back to doing what you do best: caring about number one.'

Gabi didn't try to follow her. She heard the front door open. 'And you didn't answer my question,' Thea shouted back, followed by a final slam of the door.

Gabi put her head in her hands, then felt the rage build. She picked up the first thing in reach and threw it with all her force at the wall. The mug smashed with a splatter of leftover tea and shards of ceramic.

'Fuck.' The gun was gone. Thea had gone, at least for now. 'Fuck,' she muttered again, quieter this time.

A muddle of guilt and worry flooded her system. She hadn't known Harry had been so ill; he'd never said, but then, why would he? He'd always been there for her but she'd run when he'd needed her most.

Over the years she'd tried not to think about him, but every now and then when she least expected it, a memory would resurface. Snippets of their time together. The taste of salt on his skin. The feeling of him on top of her. His face when he came, and the shy, self-conscious smile afterwards.

She had never regretted it, but she knew it hadn't been fair on Harry. For years she'd fought with her feelings: the pull, her attraction to Harry, while living with the inescapable truth of what had happened that day.

And now he was struggling again. She hadn't helped him then, but she could do this now.

She picked up her mobile phone. And she pulled a small

white card out of the back pocket of her jeans, four pieces crudely taped together.

Gabriella dialled the number.

'DS Munro?' she said, when she heard the voice at the end of the phone. 'This is Gabriella Patterson. We need to talk.'

Part 3

Friday

55

Harry lay in the grass, looking up at the sky. The sun was shining down, but it was freezing. His fingers were numb; he felt the wet grass of the garden starting to seep through his jeans, stray blades scratching at his neck, but he didn't want to move.

Ever since the day of the murders, the only place he'd felt truly calm was surrounded by green. Fields, woodland, anywhere where tarmac and metal couldn't touch him. When he could he'd run off-road, enjoying the mud underfoot, trees around him, fields as far as the eye could see.

That night in the police cell he'd felt suffocated. Drowning in concrete. He couldn't imagine how his dad had been coping all these years. He couldn't imagine what would have happened if he'd had to do the same.

He heard the swishing of grass, and a figure loomed above him dressed in a long black coat, black boots on her feet, blocking out the sun. Her hair blew around her face in the wind.

'What are you doing here?' Gabi asked.

'Breathing.'

She sat down cross-legged next to him, and he pulled himself up to do the same.

'Thank you for everything you've done for me,' Harry

said. 'For getting me out on Wednesday.' He smoothed his hair down, pulling out the grass that had stuck there.

'That wasn't me.'

'It was Mortimer, I know. Still – thank you. You didn't have to do it, given the circumstances. He didn't have to.'

'The circumstances?' she asked.

'Our history. Everything that's happened between us ...' He stopped, feeling uncomfortable. Harry felt embarrassed about what had happened the other night, for being such a mess in front of her and her cool and collected husband. He pulled a pack of cigarettes out of his pocket. A light wind had started to blow, and it took two attempts to light the last one in the box. He took a drag, then offered it to her.

She shook her head and Harry took another deep breath in. 'I should give up. But there never seems to be a right time.'

'Maybe when things calm down a bit.'

'You tell me when that happens, and I'll quit.'

They sat together for a moment, listening to the wind in the leaves around them. The quiet percussion of nature. Harry felt the sun on his back, the warmth soaking through his jumper.

'Thea still sleeping?' he asked.

She paused and opened her mouth to say something, then closed it again. She nodded.

'I'm glad you're home, Gabi. I missed you.' He stubbed the cigarette out on the sole of his shoe, then put it in the empty cigarette packet. 'I still love you, Gabriella. You know that, don't you?'

She was silent, and he forced himself to look at her.

She was staring at him, her lips slightly parted, as if

wanting to say something in reply. Then she stood up, and slowly walked back to the house.

He watched her go, walking away from him again. But he sensed something was different this time. Different from the last time they'd been together, three years ago, in Bournemouth.

Harry sang a tune under his breath as he walked along the promenade on his lunch break. It was a perfect summer's day: all around him people were enjoying the sunshine – reclining on the beach, screaming as they jumped in the sea, a few ambitious joggers sweating as they ran.

As he walked, he heard a voice: his name shouted out on the breeze. He turned and there she was.

She looked different. Her hair was blonde, long, falling on her shoulders in messy waves. Her face was tanned, with a scattering of freckles across her nose.

'Gabriella.'

She hugged him. She was in a white sundress and flip-flops, barely coming up to his shoulder. After a moment he put his arms round her, bending his face to the top of her head. She smelt of suncream.

She moved away and looked up at him.

'You've barely changed,' Gabi said, smiling.

He walked her home. They moved away from the beach, past the flashing lights and electronic beeps from the arcade, the tempting smell of fried onions from the burger joints. They stopped to get ice creams and as they walked, Gabi licked the drip from the side of the 99 cone.

They stopped in front of a new-looking block of flats. 'This is me,' she said, and Harry felt his heart drop.

'How long have you been here?'

'A few weeks, it's only temporary.' Gabi stood in front of him, looking up. She reached up to his mouth and wiped something away.

'Ice cream,' she said quietly.

He paused, speechless. He couldn't let her leave, not again.

Without thinking he bent down and kissed her. She tasted of ice cream, of softness, and desire, and a childhood shared. Of all the feelings he had harboured for so long.

'Do you want to come up?' she asked, her voice soft.

He nodded, and she took his hand.

They kissed, all the time; he touched every single part of her, from her eyelids to the very tips of her toes.

And they talked. About their lives, their jobs, their friends. The words flowed freely, with teasing and mocking, their mouths wide open with laughter. As evening turned into night, they moved to the kitchen to find food and drink, raiding her sparse fridge for anything that could be turned into a meal. They had eaten in bed – basic omelettes with no filling, plain yoghurt and chunks of Dairy Milk – and Harry didn't think he had ever enjoyed a meal as much in his whole life.

Hours later he woke, his arm full of pins and needles. He tried to shift her gently, sharp spikes charging up his arm, and winced.

She opened her eyes and looked at him through the darkness. Harry smiled at her.

'What time is it?' she asked.

He pushed himself up and glanced at the clock. 'Just after three,' he said, his voice gruff from sleep.

Harry reached down and moved her hair gently away from her face.

'I wish this wouldn't end,' he said, without thinking. She

was watching him, her face serious. 'It's always been you, Gabi. I've never stopped thinking about you.'

She shook her head, dismissing what he'd said. 'Please, let's just enjoy what we have now. Why do we need to turn it into something else?'

'Because I love you, Gabi. I always have.'

'You know it's not as simple as that.' Gabi turned over, her back to him, but he pulled at her shoulder, forcing her to look at him.

'I wish everything had been different that day,' Harry said, his voice little more than a whisper. 'You know I'd do anything to turn back the clock. But I can't. Please forgive me,' Harry pleaded with her. 'I need you to forgive me for what happened.'

'I can't...' She stopped and pulled away from him, pressing her lips together. 'I'd like you to go now.'

'No, Gabi. Don't do this.'

She sat up in bed, tugging the duvet round her, her arms crossed across her chest. She shook her head. 'I want you to leave.'

Harry pulled himself up, shaking his head. 'Gabi...'

'Leave!' she shouted, and pushed at his chest. She knelt up on the bed and pushed again, her tiny frame forcing him away with surprising strength.

He stood up and backed away from her, putting on his clothes.

'I'll go now, but I'm coming back tomorrow. This isn't over, Gabi. I'm not going to let you disappear again.'

He watched as she turned her back on him, pulling the duvet over her head.

Harry resolved to go back, to apologise. Again and again, if needs be, until he made things right. Harry knew he couldn't lose Gabi again from his life, he just couldn't. But the next day the door was unlocked, keys hanging on a hook inside, no forwarding address.

She'd gone, again.

Harry lay back down in the grass. Yes, it had gone wrong then, but she was home now. For good. Things were different. He could be different: the person before the shooting. She had never seen the frightened, cowering wreck Thea had put up with for all those years. He still felt the shame, the humiliation of being such a burden to her. Of being so weak.

Gabriella hadn't known that Harry. She remembered him how he was. He wanted to be that again. He pushed all thoughts of her husband out of his head. He and Gabi had history. There was more between them than the few short months Mortimer had known her.

Gabriella had loved him before; she could love him again.

He felt sunshine fall on his eyelashes and his face. He closed his eyes.

56

Kate was surrounded by paper: search reports, witness statements, photographs. So many photographs. Some stuck up on the wall, some covering the table, others discarded on the carpet. She was sat in the centre, cross-legged, notebook in hand.

Since Gabriella's call yesterday she'd been frantically sifting through the case again. Kate wanted to know everything before she sat down with her. She didn't want to miss any opportunity.

'Bring what you have on the murders,' was all Gabi had muttered on the phone, then refused to say any more. But Kate had no idea what Gabriella could possibly add. For hours all she'd done was read the file, going through the slightest detail over and over again. And she couldn't see any holes in the conviction of Harrison Becker. Other than the fact Harry had told her that he and the twins were there when the murder took place, there wasn't a single discrepancy. Harrison was guilty.

Regarding Thea's attack, Steve Morgan was locked in a police cell while they waited for confirmation from the CPS to make the charge. But he was silent. His solicitor had been and gone; he was expected back today. Until then things were on pause.

Kate started moving round the room, collating the paper. She grabbed the main summary file to take with her, adding the post-mortem report and the transcripts of the interviews to the death certificate already in there. She picked up the filing box, about to put the pile of photos back into it, when a few pieces of paper caught her eye. They were caught in the bottom, obviously stuck when she'd initially dumped the contents onto the floor.

She picked them up. *Southampton General Hospital*, they said in big bold letters. There were three reports, dated the day of the murder. She flicked through them: *Thea Patterson, Gabriella Patterson, Harry Becker*. Okay, so all three teenagers had been admitted to hospital the day their parents were killed. So far, so unsurprising. *Shock, dehydration, recommend counselling. Displaying extreme emotional blunting and potential derealisation. Possible warning signs of PTSD.* Thea's detailed superficial scratches to her forearms, Gabi's talked about grazes to her elbows and hands, but otherwise they were the same. The twins were discharged the day after, Harry following them two days after that. Two days? She looked closer at his report, taking in the same diagnosis as the girls and then, at the bottom, an additional note: *second-degree, partial thickness burn to fingers and palm of right hand.*

She stood up straight and put the report down. Why would he have a burn on his right hand? What was he doing...? Unless... She took a sudden breath in, then looked up at the clock. Shit! She threw the hospital reports into the file and shoved it all into her bag.

It was time.

Gabriella was late. The meeting had been agreed for midday at the local coffee shop. Gabi had wanted somewhere busy, a generic location where they wouldn't stand out, and Kate had to come alone. But she wasn't here. Kate had chosen a table on the far side of the room, away from the main bustle, and waited impatiently, drinking one coffee then another as the minutes ticked by. And then, there she was. As always, her hair was immaculately blow-dried, but she looked tired and drawn, grey smudges under her eyes, her face pale. She joined Kate at the table, taking off her coat, then waiting, her hands clenched together in front of her.

'Would you like a coffee?' Kate asked and Gabriella shook her head.

'This won't take long,' she said. She looked at the file in front of Kate. 'Is that it?' she asked.

'Yes, but I can't just hand over a homicide file,' Kate replied. Ever since Gabi had asked her to bring the notes with her, Kate had wrestled with what she was going to do with them. As much as she had screwed up this investigation so far, she knew giving confidential information on an investigation to someone at the heart of the conviction was a big no-no. 'Tell me why you're here, and I might be able to help.'

Gabriella shook her head. 'I shouldn't have come,' she muttered and went to stand up again, but Kate caught her arm.

'Gabriella,' Kate said firmly. 'Something made you call me yesterday, something important, I'd guess. It's obviously been playing on your mind, so tell me what it is and I guarantee you'll feel better.'

Gabi paused, and to Kate's relief sat back down. She looked at Kate and she could see tears in her eyes. 'It's not as easy as that, DS Munro,' she said. 'This is my family you're talking about.'

Kate paused. Perhaps sharing what she suspected would encourage Gabi to talk. 'Harry Becker is not related to you,' she said quietly.

'Family isn't just about blood and DNA, DS Munro,' Gabriella said. She looked at her hands, picking at the edge of one of her nails. Kate remembered her doing the same the first time she'd met her, in the interview room at the police station, while she was pretending to be Thea.

'So how do families behave, Gabriella?' Kate asked, pushing at her, trying to get a response. 'Is it lying to them, like you did, Gabi, when you pretended to be Thea? Is it obsessively stalking someone, like your husband did to you?'

Gabi looked at her, her eyes narrowed. 'You wouldn't understand, Kate,' she said, her nose wrinkled with disgust, leaning forward in her chair. 'You probably grew up in a nice little cul-de-sac, with two parents who doted on your every move. I bet you never had your teachers ask why your mum and dad didn't turn up for parents' evening, or knew what it felt like to come home from school and find nobody there, day after day. Harry and Thea were all I ever had, growing up.' Gabi took a juddering breath in, then let it out slowly. Kate could see her gathering herself, before she continued: 'Family is about trust, and love, and doing the very thing you don't want to do, even though you know it's the best thing for them. Even though it breaks your heart to do it.'

Kate made a split-second decision. 'I'm going to get up now,' she said, slowly. 'And go to the toilet. I'm going to leave this file here, and trust that you won't look in it. And when I get back, I want to hear everything you know. Otherwise, Gabriella, I'll have no choice but to arrest you for obstructing a police investigation.'

She stood up without another word and left Gabriella at the table. Kate didn't look back as she shut the door to the bathroom, knowing that this could be it, this could be the

decision that finally ended her career. If she opened that
door again and the file had gone, she was in deep shit.

She counted thirty seconds, then, with her heart in her
mouth, did it again, forcing herself to take her time. To let
Gabi do whatever she needed to do. But after the second set
she couldn't wait any longer, and opened the door.

'Fuck,' Kate muttered.

Gabriella had gone. But the file was still there.

She walked back to the table and sat down, pulling the
folder towards her, thumbing through the paperwork. She
looked at it and frowned. The contents were all inside,
but the pages were in a different order. Where before the
summary document had been on the top, now there was
something else. *Post-mortem*, it said in big letters. *Madeleine
Patterson*. The pathologist's report for Gabriella and Thea's
mother had been pulled out, the punched holes ripped, and
placed on the top.

Kate knew that whatever Gabriella wanted her to see was
hidden in the pages of that report.

In front of her, her mobile rang. It was Yates.

'Sarge, where are you?' she asked, but before Kate could
answer, Yates cut back in. 'We've got a problem with the
charge for Steve Morgan. And the chief wants to see you.
Now.'

57

Thea couldn't concentrate. She was trying to work, flicking through photographs on the screen.

The last job had been a corporate shoot; formal, boring, but good solid money. Thea had resolved to get the shots finished as soon as possible, knowing how delayed they'd already been, but she couldn't focus.

She was worried about Harry. He had the gun, and Thea didn't like to think about why. To get rid of it, to give it to the police? Or what? To use it? On himself? Thea tried to quash the churning in her stomach. He'd gone back to work that afternoon, a good sign, Thea thought, so she'd call him when he got back. She wouldn't let things get that far.

Thea turned her attention back to the computer and saw the few photos she had taken the other day at the house. They were darker, and the natural light had cast weird shadows across Gabi and Harry's faces. She clicked on one of Gabi, studying it closely. As a child she used to stare at photos of the both of them, looking for differences, looking for the subtle changes that made one of them more attractive than the other. Back then, she'd not seen much – the identical features were still striking; only their expressions were different.

In this photo, Gabi was looking away from the camera, out of the window into the rain outside. Her expression was pensive; she looked like she was considering something far deeper than a mere mortal could comprehend. Thea knew that when she wore the same expression it was more like a scowl. 'Stop sulking, Thea,' her mother used to say. 'It doesn't suit you.' It did suit Gabi, it seemed.

She moved on to a shot of Harry. He was standing in the doorway, looking away from the camera, towards something in the kitchen, out of shot. The light from the open door caught his cheekbones and lit up his eyes, showing him to his best advantage. His hair was longer and tousled, just the slightest bit of stubble on his jaw. She'd never considered him handsome before, but here in this photo there was no mistaking it, especially given the look on his face.

He was smiling, his eyes creasing on the edge of laughter. It was clear he adored the person he was talking to. And it had been Gabi.

Thea had known, of course. She'd known from the beginning, but she'd accepted it, in the same way she tolerated that everyone was more attracted to Gabriella, boys and girls alike. She remembered things changing between Harry and Gabi. That summer, that last fateful summer, Gabi had been teasing Harry, tickling his ribs, both of them play-fighting, pushing each other into the long grass. She had watched them, puzzled at the time, everything clear now.

She was tired of being alone. She missed Harry. Before the attack he'd been a constant resident of her home: after work for dinner, sometimes staying the night in the spare room when he'd had too much to drink. But now there were gaps. There was space in the house he'd normally be there to fill.

Thea felt the silence suffocate her.

She wondered what had changed. She wondered if it was something she had done, if he was angry with her for going out that night. She raised her hand to the back of her head and felt the last bit of scab, the slight bump that remained. She didn't have the bandage any more, and the few bits of shaved hair were barely noticeable. And Thea was feeling better, there was no doubt about that. Her headache still clung on, but she was getting strength back into her bones. Her initial fear after the attack was fading. Gabriella was home; everything could go back to how it was, just the three of them. That was all she'd ever wanted.

And Harry was going to be okay. She would make it right. She couldn't watch him fall again. She just couldn't.

58

Kate shifted from foot to foot outside the chief's office. She flipped through the pages of the file in her hand, excited.

The door opened and DCI Jennings looked at her.

'DS Munro,' he said, sighing. 'Just what I need at the end of a long, tiring week.'

He grudgingly held the door open and Kate went inside, standing in front of his desk. She waited until he had settled his large bulk back in his chair.

'Guv, I—' she started, but he held up his hand and silenced her.

'I don't want to hear it,' he said. 'This whole episode with the house search has been a total nightmare. Professional Standards got back to me this morning; luckily nobody outside has caught wind of what you've done so they're prepared to overlook it, just this once. I assured them you've dropped the case from fifteen years ago and will be on your best behaviour from now on.' He placed his hands on the desk and leaned towards her. 'Because that's what's happened, isn't it?' he said slowly.

Kate took a deep breath. Here was her opportunity to roll back the clock. To restore good graces with the boss, all sins forgotten. But something niggled; the file felt heavy in her hands.

'Guv, I appreciate everything you've done for me ...' she started and he leaned back in his chair, satisfied. 'But I've been reviewing the files and I found something.' She thrust the piece of paper from A&E in front of him.

'What am I looking at here, Kate?' he asked, through gritted teeth.

'It's a report from the night of the double homicide,' she said quickly, words rushing out. 'See here, it says Harry Becker had second-degree burns to his right hand.'

The chief looked at her, his head on one side, his lips pursed. 'And the boy burning his hand means what, exactly?'

'It means he had the gun. It means he picked it up.'

'A gun fired twice wouldn't cause second-degree burns—'

'No, but an old World War Two gun, malfunctioning, might. They would have been old bullets. What if it misfired? What about muzzle flash? What if—'

'*Might*?' the chief thundered, hauling himself out of his chair. '*What if*? Now you listen to me, and you listen well. This case is closed. Got it?' He waved a fat finger in front of her face. 'I don't give a flying fuck if that bloke has the gun shoved up where the sun don't shine, you are not to go near it any more. Now get the hell away from me before I change my mind.'

He stopped and Kate nodded slowly, her breathing shallow.

'Get out of here.' He held out his hand and she reluctantly went to pass him the file. But then she paused, remembering her conversation with Gabriella, knowing there was more to this case than they were seeing. She pulled the folder back and he looked at her, astonished, his hand still outstretched.

'Sir,' she said, her voice bitter. 'With all due respect, I am a good detective. I work hard, I solve cases. Yes, I have made mistakes but because of me and my team, we have a solid case against a nasty sexual predator and I won't stop until we have him for attempted murder as well.' Kate spoke deliberately, determined to get the words out. She needed to say this. She wanted to be heard. 'But I know how to do my job. I know when something isn't right and I will pursue it all hours of the day until it's sorted. And if that affects an old case of yours, or whether your buddy from school gets his burglary solved, I don't give a shit. From this point on, if you prioritise your own personal gain over the needs of our victims, I will report you to Professional Standards.' She stopped talking, feeling her face go red, her body sweaty.

Kate could see him clamp his lips together, then take a deep breath in, letting it out of his nose with a high-pitched whistle. 'Your comments have been noted,' he growled at last and she turned, retreating quickly out of the room.

She fled down the corridor, pushing the toilet door open with a bang. She sat down in one of the cubicles and locked the door as embarrassing tears started to flow.

'Damn it,' she muttered. She'd really fucked up this time, talking to her boss in that way. But at least if she was going to go down, she was going in a blaze of glory. It felt good, telling him exactly what she thought after all this time, although – shit – she wasn't sure she was going to have a job by the end of the day.

But he had made her mad. So mad. She wanted to know what had happened fifteen years ago, she wanted to know what Gabi had indicated about that post-mortem report, and most of all she wanted to know what had happened to that damn gun. Kate pulled out a piece of toilet roll and dabbed at her eyes. She tried to get control of her emotions, flooding over into hot, snotty tears, and looked at her shaking hands.

What had Harry said? *Not everything is a mystery to be solved. It's not all about right and wrong, black and white.* Maybe he was right. Because that's what she had always believed, and look where she was now. Career in ruins, marriage destroyed.

She stood up and left the toilet, standing at the mirror and wiping off misplaced mascara. Kate heard another cubicle door open.

'Sarge?' Yates stood behind her. 'Are you okay?'

Kate sniffed loudly and stood up straight. 'Yes, I'm fine, Rach. Just been in to see Jennings.' She smiled with a sincerity she didn't feel.

Yates reached over and gave her a hug. Kate was surprised by the contact, standing stiff in her embrace. 'What did he say, the grumpy bastard? Is he whingeing about the attempted murder charge? Because, you know, I'm not feeling so great about it either.'

Kate cleared her throat. 'Why? What's the problem?'

Yates washed her hands in the sink, looking at Kate via the reflection in the mirror. 'The solicitor called, he's been with Steve Morgan again and it looks like he's prepared to cop to the attempted rape. But the attack?' She shook her head. 'He says he's got nothing to do with it. Says he was nowhere near the common. And he's got evidence to prove it.'

'What?'

Yates rested her bum on the sink and faced Kate. 'Something about a speeding ticket. Somewhere miles away from The Avenue.'

'Fuck,' Kate muttered. 'Check it out, see what the hell they're talking about. I'll be back in a moment.'

Yates swung out of the toilets and Kate heard the door slam behind her.

She looked at herself in the mirror. She looked like shit. Kate dug in her bag and pulled out her hairbrush, running it through her hair, then tying it up neatly in a ponytail. She slicked some lipstick on, and looked again. Better. If she was going to be fired – and it was probably going to be today – she'd better get this case solved. And quick.

She frowned. 'Get your shit together, Munro,' she muttered to herself. 'You've got work to do.'

'Fuck.'

An hour later, Kate stared at the photo in her hand.

'We've still got him for the attempted rape,' Yates said, tentatively.

Kate sighed. 'Fuck,' she said again.

In her hand was a grainy black and white photo. On it was Steve Morgan's Jaguar, his scowling face in the front seat, captured by the speed cameras on the M27. The photo was stamped with the time 3.40 a.m.

Dave Fletcher had put his mugging at about quarter past three. The 999 call was made at 3.53 a.m. Roughly at the time Thea Patterson was being attacked, their prime suspect was nine miles away, doing a hundred and two on the motorway.

There was no doubt about it: Steve Morgan was not going to be charged with attempted murder.

Kate looked at the dejected faces of her colleagues. Briggs and Yates were sitting at their desks, swivel chairs pointed towards her, waiting for a way forward. Waiting for some indication of what to do next. Kate didn't have a clue.

'You've both done some amazing work this week,' she began. 'Okay, so we don't know who attacked Thea Patterson, but at least we've taken one sexual predator off the street.'

'And closed a dodgy Southampton nightclub,' Briggs added.

Kate pointed at Briggs. 'That too. And I'm sure if we pass the CCTV footage to the drugs squad, they'll nail a few others on narcotics and prostitution charges. So go home. Have a nice weekend and we'll pick up again on Monday. See what else we can find, see what we've missed.'

Briggs and Yates started gathering papers together, tidying up files and notes left from their week putting together the case against Steve Morgan.

'Leave it,' Kate said. 'I'll sort it all out.'

As soon as they were gone, Kate pulled the beige file from the double murder in front of her. She hadn't mentioned it to them, not wanting to put her team in the firing line too, but she'd been desperate to take a look at the post-mortem report. Was this the key? What did Gabriella Patterson know?

Kate sat back in her chair and started to read, quickly growing frustrated in the face of the medical jargon. She looked down to the name on the bottom of the report and smiled – Dr Albert Adams.

Kate picked up the phone and dialled the morgue at Southampton General Hospital. She imagined Albie cursing at the intrusion, looking up from whatever body he was working on and ignoring the call. Sure enough, the call rang out, so she dialled again. This time someone answered.

'What?' came the voice at the end of the line.

'Albie? It's Kate Munro. I'm sorry to disturb you.'

'Ah, Katherine. Forgiven, because it's you. Why have I not seen you lately?'

Kate smiled, imagining her friend at the other end of the line. Years ago, when she was a fresh new recruit, the tutors decided to take all the probies down to the morgue to view a post-mortem being carried out – get them used to the grim side of the job. Kate had been the only one to hold onto her lunch. Albie had been the pathologist, and a grudging friendship had been forged.

'I know, and I'm sorry. But I have a case you could help with. Do you remember the Patterson double homicide back in 2004?'

'I don't remember what I had for breakfast this morning – what makes you think I could remember some dead bodies from the last decade?' His voice was gruff but Kate could hear tapping on the other end of the phone, 'What's the case number?' he asked and Kate reeled it off. 'Yes, here it is. But wasn't this one convicted?'

'Yes, but we don't think it was as straightforward as it seemed. Could you talk me through what you found?'

'Of course, but I'm up to the armpits in offal right now,' he said and Kate grimaced at his black turn of phrase. 'Come by tomorrow, I'll be here from eight.'

'But…' Kate tried, but the line was dead.

She sighed and slumped back in her chair. Tomorrow it had to be, even though it was Saturday. She'd find out more then.

She pulled herself up and moved back to the whiteboard, perching on the table in front, looking at the photos. Harry Becker, Gabriella Patterson, Steve Morgan, Mortimer Breslin. She picked up a pen and drew a big red cross through the face of Steve. Alibied out. That left Harry, Gabriella and Mortimer. Or maybe someone completely different.

'What have you all been up to?' Kate muttered to herself. 'What the hell am I missing?'

59

Gabi stopped in the doorway, watching him. It was the end of the day and Mortimer looked tired. He had a shadow of stubble, his shirt was uncharacteristically creased, his feet bare. She watched him as he made the coffee: taking a mug out of the cupboard, assembling the different pieces of the machine, ready to go. Any time of day, always coffee; caffeine didn't keep him up at night as it did other people. She took in the smell of freshly ground beans, and liked the way his hair touched the collar of his shirt at the back. She felt something warm in her. A strange sense of belonging, of contentment.

Mortimer looked over and jumped.

'There you are!' he said, smiling. He loosened his tie with one hand, then undid his shirt cuffs, rolling the sleeves up to mid-forearm. 'Where have you been?'

She'd been wandering for hours. After meeting Kate, her mind had been racing so she'd started walking to calm it down. She'd talked about family, yet there she was, helping the police incriminate the people she loved. She hated herself, but she couldn't deny she'd felt something lift. She didn't have to decide any more, to think or to worry – that was it. She knew that detective wouldn't stop now.

As Gabi had walked, she'd thought about all those years ago. Her parents' funeral, once the police had deigned to release their bodies, had been in October in a deluge of cold rain. She remembered the three of them standing there, hand in hand. She'd sensed Harry's stoicism; he'd seemed so immovable that day, determined to stay resilient for her and Thea. She remembered how she'd felt. The guilt, the concern. She'd been barely holding it together. In contrast to her own grief, Thea had seemed almost absent, an empty shell where some emotion should have been. It had scared her then, and it worried her now.

And the one person she wanted to talk to was Mortimer. Right now, watching him in the kitchen, all she wanted was to sit down and tell him everything, but something was stopping her. The detective's words haunted her. Kate had described Mortimer as obsessively stalking her and true, she knew he'd been following her when she'd pretended to be Thea. And he'd been there that night, so the police said. So why hadn't he said anything? What did he know?

'Where were you?' she asked, standing in the doorway to the kitchen. 'When Thea was attacked?'

He turned away from her, still fiddling with the coffee machine. 'I was here, at home,' he replied.

'Why are you lying to me?' she said slowly.

Mortimer turned back quickly. 'What do you mean?' He was uncomfortable, turning the mug round in his hand.

'I know you were there that night, the police told me, so why are you lying?' Gabi asked again. She felt herself get louder, a trace of hysteria creep into her voice. 'What are you not telling me, Mortimer?'

He paused, his hands going up to his face, covering his mouth. 'I was at the club, but I went home, I swear,' he muttered. He walked over to where Gabi stood in the doorway, but she raised her hands in front of her, forcing a barrier between them. 'Please, Gabi,' Mortimer said again. 'I promise, I had nothing to do with what happened to Thea.'

She pulled away from him, backing into the hallway. 'So why were you following me? Why did you have to do that? Why couldn't you have let me be?' she pleaded.

Mortimer shook his head. 'Ever since I met you, I knew I had to be with you. I couldn't just let you go. It was selfish and weird and scary, I know, and it's not a side of me I'm proud of. I'm so sorry, Gabriella.'

He reached out to her and for a moment, she let him take her hands in his. She felt the warmth, and looked up at him, meeting his gaze. He was worried: about her, about what she might do.

'Please, Gabi, don't push me away,' he said quietly. 'Tell me what's going on.'

But she couldn't trust him. She couldn't let go of the thought that one day he would betray her, too, and then he'd be gone and she'd be alone again. If she left now, she could stop the heartbreak before it got really bad, before she let her guard down and properly fell in love. Because she couldn't do that again, she couldn't. She couldn't lose another family.

She pulled away from him and ran to the front door, one hand on the latch, pulling it open.

'Stay, Gabriella,' Mortimer said calmly and she turned. She took in the look on his face: the desolation, the concern.

'Don't run. Not this time. If you always do the same thing, if you always let your anger get the better of you, push people away, you'll never know what good might happen if you stay.'

She knew he was right but her reaction was too ingrained. She felt that fear, and every part of her body told her to run.

'Stay, Gabriella.'

She felt the cold wind rush in through the open door, the night sky dark, the day nearly over. She looked at the open door, at the wedding ring on her finger.

And she paused.

60

Harry lay on the sofa, one leg hanging off the end, the other resting on the coffee table. He had the television on, football blaring out and a beer in front of him, but he couldn't concentrate. All he'd wanted was a distraction, something to take his mind off the visit with his father, the prison cell, Gabriella, the mistakes he'd made with Kate.

'Fuck,' Harry muttered under his breath as another goal trickled into the English net. These guys weren't even fucking trying any more. He hadn't been able to watch television properly for years, needing to avoid the gunfire and loud bangs omnipresent in any drama. So sport was the only safe zone for him, but this was just depressing.

He picked up his beer from the coffee table, and put it back down again. He looked over at the pile of work accumulated from too much time off, abandoned when his mind couldn't focus.

The doorbell rang and he looked up. Harry debated ignoring it. After all, who was it going to be? Kate? Maybe. And that wouldn't be a good thing.

At any time while he'd been arrested, he knew he could have told all to his solicitor and he'd have been out of there. At the very least he wouldn't have had Kate coming at him like a possessed woman on a mission. But as much as he'd thought about it, he couldn't do that to her. He'd liked her. Seeing her alone in the bar had been coincidence but, if he was being honest, everything after that point had been him taking advantage of her emotional state. Maybe not cold, hard calculation as such, but he had seen she was vulnerable, and it wasn't something he was proud of. Confessing all to his solicitor would have been an admission of his own complicit actions, and he wanted that second chance to be a better person, as much as he wanted it for her.

The doorbell rang again and he sighed.

He could see a figure through the glass. Far too short to be Kate. He opened the door, and took in the sight of her.

Gabi was wearing a short black skirt and knee-high boots, with a turtle neck jumper. A long purple coat was thrown over the top. Her hair was poker-straight, her eyes dark. She had never looked so beautiful.

Harry cleared his throat. 'What are you doing here?' he asked.

She stepped into his flat, closing the door behind her. Without a word, she put one hand on his chest and pushed him against the wall in his hallway. She stood on her tiptoes and pulled his face towards her, kissing him hard.

Harry was taken by surprise at first, then swept along by the strength of his lust. This was different to anything he had experienced with Gabi before; she was demanding, forceful, rough even. She pulled him into the living room and pushed him down onto the sofa, straddling him and kissing him again. He pushed his hands up her jumper, feeling soft, warm skin, surprised by her lack of bra. She pulled her jumper off in one quick move, then did the same with his T-shirt, kissing him in a mess of bumped teeth and lips.

As much as Harry was enjoying it – and he really was enjoying it – he took her face gently in his hands and moved her away from him.

'What's brought this on?' he asked.

'Why does that matter?' she replied, and went to kiss him again.

'What about your husband?'

'I don't care about him.' She sat up, her hair falling around her face, glaring at him. 'He means nothing to me.'

'Yes, but—'

'But what? Your whole life you've wanted me, and now you finally get a chance to have me, you're hesitating?'

He looked at her sitting on top of him, topless, her hair ruffled, her skirt pushed up around her waist. She was right: what the fuck was he thinking?

He reached up and grabbed her, flipping her over and kissing her, hard. She responded, her hands on his face, in his hair, moving down his back, pushing them into his jeans.

They fumbled over belts and zips, pulling clothes off, desperate to get rid of anything between them. Harry wanted to feel her skin on his again; he wanted to touch every part of her, kissing her breasts, her belly button, and she seemed to want the same, not holding back.

She was right. It was everything he'd wanted, and more.

'Fuck, Gabriella.' Harry lay on the carpet of his living room, out of breath, staring at the ceiling. She lay resting on his chest, her arm draped across him, her cheek against his collarbone. 'I can't feel my toes.'

He ran a finger from the nape of her neck down the middle of her spine. He took in the curve at the base of her back, then looked into her eyes, pushing her hair away from her face.

She met his eyes for a moment, her cheeks flushed, then pulled herself forward and kissed him. 'That's a pity,' she said, a small smile playing on her lips. 'I was hoping we could do that again. But you know,' she shrugged, 'if you're not able…'

In one quick move he stood up, pulling her up with him, and carried her into the bedroom, her laughter filling the air.

Saturday

61

The morning was arctic as Kate locked her car and walked to the morgue at Southampton General Hospital, two large takeaway cups of coffee in her hands. She took the lift to the bottom floor, then awkwardly pressed the doorbell, the buzz sounding to let her in without question.

She walked down the corridor, the smell of disinfectant getting stronger with every step, and pushed her way through the double doors into the laboratory where she knew Albie would be waiting.

Dr Albie Adams was as tall as he was wide, with an accent honed from a lifetime of public school and redbrick universities. He was precariously balanced on a stool in front of a computer screen, his spindly legs dangling, giving him a somewhat froggy appearance. He pointed at the monitor.

'What do you see?' he asked, taking one of the coffees out of her hand.

Kate squinted at the photo. It was a shot of a closed eye, marked with red spots on the pallid skin around it. 'Petechial haemorrhage,' she said confidently and he smiled. 'Is this the Patterson case?' she asked.

Albie nodded, taking a sip. 'I started reading last night, it was quite a fascinating one.' He pointed to the stool opposite him and Kate sat down, cradling her coffee. It was cold in the lab, and her hands needed the warmth. Behind her she could see the stainless-steel tables used for autopsies, and the rows of small metal doors. Kate imagined the bodies lurking behind, preserved in their refrigerated purgatory.

'Robert Patterson was straightforward.' He pulled the notes up on the screen and ran a finger along the text. 'Gunshot injury to chest, with the round transecting his descending aorta, resulting in exsanguination.' He looked up at Kate. 'He would have bled out in a matter of minutes.'

'And Madeleine Patterson?' Kate asked.

'Well, that's where it gets interesting. She was shot in the abdomen and her injuries were less catastrophic. The bullet caused damage to her stomach, colon and liver, but she had other pathological features that gave me pause for thought.' He scratched his head, making his grey hair stand up on end. 'She had petechial haemorrhages on her face, as you correctly said, but also in her conjunctiva and oral mucous membranes.'

Kate frowned. 'Which means?'

Albie waggled his head from side to side, debating. 'Unfortunately, there's no specific diagnostic marker at autopsy, but my guess at the time was that as well as being shot, she'd also been asphyxiated.'

'Why wasn't that given as cause of death?' Kate said, astonished.

'As I said, there is nothing pathognomonic for asphyxiation. Was there anything found at the scene that indicated suffocation or smothering?'

Kate shook her head. 'There was nothing noted.'

'Then that's probably why. I remember debating it with the coroner at the time. You had a confession and there was pressure from above to get this one sorted. I thought there was something weird, but you know I'm not one to argue with those in charge.' He smiled at Kate. 'That's more your bag, I hear.'

Kate shrugged. 'Trouble finds me,' she said with a wry smile. 'So how might we know for sure?' she asked.

Albie screwed his face up. 'You can't, but take a look back at the evidence. You're probably looking for a pillow or a cushion – something soft, because there wasn't much other damage to the soft tissue on her face, only slight abrasions on the inside of her lips where they pressed against her teeth.' He flicked through the pages on the screen. 'Here it is, I thought so.' He pointed to the text. 'Small red fibres were found in her nose and mouth, and sent down to the lab for analysis, along with the fingernail scrapings. Did you get any DNA from those?'

'There was nothing in the file,' Kate said slowly, thinking back.

'Looks like you have a few things to track down, DS Munro.' Albie sat back precariously on the stool, finishing the last of his coffee and dropping the cup in the bin. She leaned forward and kissed him on the cheek.

'Thank you,' she shouted as she ran out of the lab.

'Any time, Katherine,' she heard Albie call after her, but she was already gone, rushing back to the station, her mind going at a hundred miles an hour.

Back in the office, her suspicions were confirmed. There were no DNA results on file and the lab was closed, everyone at home for the weekend. She looked through the paper around her, picking up the itemised list of seized evidence from the case, running her finger down the list.

Harrison Becker's laptop, containing photos of Madeleine Patterson, naked. The clothes worn that day by Thea and

Gabriella and Harry. Bullet fragments and shell cases, back from ballistics. Then, at the bottom of the page, a list of miscellaneous items from the kitchen, including a red velvet cushion.

Kate pulled out the crime scene photos, searching each one; then, there it was. Lying underneath the kitchen table, no doubt pushed away by the paramedics but nonetheless close to Madeleine's body. She took a deep breath, staring at the photo. Madeleine Patterson had been shot, but someone had smothered her.

The revelation nagged at Kate's mind. Why would you go to that trouble? Madeleine was dying. Albie said the injuries sustained from the gunshot would have been life-threatening, so why the overkill?

There had only been a few people in that kitchen: Gabriella and Thea Patterson, Harrison Becker and his son, Harry. Kate looked over at the whiteboard, and the face of Harry stared back. Handsome, disarming, damaged. She had a theory he'd fired the gun, and they knew he'd been on the common on the night of Thea's attack. What else had he lied about?

Kate glanced at the clock, then swore under her breath. The one thing she had intended to do that day was update Thea on the events in the case, and now it was nearly evening and she'd completely forgotten. She picked up her coat and keys and ran out to her car.

The route from Southampton Central Station to Thea's house took her up Hill Lane. Past the common on her right, past the pub and the phone box where the 999 call had been made. It had been two weeks to the day since Thea's attack. Kate couldn't imagine what the poor woman had gone through. It must be terrifying to have no memory of what had happened to you.

She indicated and pulled slowly into the gravel driveway, surprised by the presence of another car alongside Thea's red Micra. She looked up at the house. The afternoon was closing in and it was shrouded in darkness, looking down intimidatingly. She shivered. The eerie surroundings felt appropriate, she thought, to the dark nature of the crime.

Kate rang the doorbell, and heard footsteps and the bolts being pulled back. Thea smiled when she saw her, opening the door to let her inside.

'Here, let me take your coat,' she said.

Kate took it off and handed it to her, Thea draping it over the banisters at the bottom of the stairs. She showed her down the corridor to the kitchen.

'You seem much better,' Kate said, following behind her. Thea was wearing her usual uniform of black jeans, and looked tired, but had on a clean ironed T-shirt and cardigan over the top. Her hair was washed and neat. 'Have you had a haircut?'

'Yes, I thought I'd better.' Thea self-consciously pushed her hair behind her ears, a gesture that reminded Kate of Gabi.

They walked down to the kitchen, and as they got there Ryan Holmes stood up from the kitchen table.

'I should be going,' he said. 'Nice to see you, DS Munro.' She nodded in return, surprised to see him there.

'I'll show you out,' Thea said and the two of them left Kate alone in the kitchen.

She looked around the room, taking it in properly for the first time. The dark afternoon did the house no favours. Even though the main light was on, there were corners of shadows throwing odd shapes up the walls.

'Do you want anything?' Thea asked her as she came back into the room. 'Tea, coffee?' She seemed nervous, the sleeves of her cardigan pulled down over her hands.

'Tea would be good. I didn't know you were still friends with Mr Holmes,' Kate said.

'Yes, well, not for much longer, it seems. He's going away. Death threats.' Thea turned to fill the kettle from the tap. 'It seems people don't like it much when you turn your business partner in to the police and shut down your club. He thought it best to disappear for a while.'

Kate nodded. 'Listen, Thea, I wanted to give you an update on where we are. With your case.' She waited until Thea had made two mugs of tea and joined her at the table. 'We've arrested someone.'

'For my attack?'

'Well, kind of.' Kate was accustomed to giving bad news, but it wasn't easy. She would never get used to it, and hoped she never would. She needed that empathy to keep her human, to avoid the desensitisation that often came with jobs like hers. 'Through the evidence we've been gathering over the last few days, we've got a better picture of what happened to you that night.' She stopped and looked at her. 'We're sorry, Thea, but we believe you were sexually assaulted.'

Thea chewed the inside of her cheek. Kate could see tears in her eyes. 'Was I raped?'

'No,' Kate said quickly. 'But he tried. And he's in police custody now. We have a witness who is prepared to testify and DNA evidence against him.'

Thea thought for a moment, then looked up at Kate. 'Was it Steve? The man that owned the club?'

'Yes. I'm sorry,' Kate said.

Thea took a deep breath in. 'I started to remember bits. Not much, but little fragments. Sort of, flashes, you know?' Kate nodded. 'But I couldn't piece it all together. I remember him, and being in the toilets and ...' She tapered off. 'I just feel like such an idiot.'

Kate reached across and put her hand on Thea's arm. 'Nothing that happened that night was your fault. Nothing.' Thea stared at Kate's hand. 'He spiked your drink, and the drug will have contributed to your memory loss that night. We believe you drank some, then Ryan finished off the rest. You did nothing wrong, Thea.'

'And did Steve attack me on the common?'

Kate took a deep breath. 'No, he didn't. He has an alibi. But please be reassured, Thea, we are doing all we can. We haven't stopped investigating, and won't until we find who was responsible.' She took a notebook out of her bag and wrote down a number. 'These are the contact details for a helpline for people who have been through the same thing as you.' She ripped off the page and passed it to her. 'Call them.'

Thea took the piece of paper and pen. She made a note next to the number and underlined it twice.

Kate frowned. 'You're left-handed,' she said.

'Not usually,' Thea replied. 'Since my fingers were hurt, I've been using my left more.' She held up both her hands. 'I'm ambidextrous, we both are. At school we were told to choose which hand to write with so we chose the right, but we can still use either.'

'You both are?' Kate repeated. 'Gabi too?'

Thea cocked her head to one side. 'Yes. Why?'

'In the notes from the attack it says you're right-handed. That you sustained injuries to your right hand, fighting off ...'

She tapered off. 'It's not important, it doesn't matter,' she said, but her eyes had started scanning the room, her police instincts kicking in. 'I should go. I've taken up too much of your time already.'

She stood up and Thea followed her to the front door. Kate picked up her coat from the banister and the one underneath it fell to the floor. Kate picked it up.

It was dark purple, and velvet. The bright patterned lining was lavishly made and luxurious, the coat distinctive and recognisable.

'It used to be my mother's,' Thea said, noticing Kate looking. 'I forgot we had it.'

'We?' Kate asked.

'Well, Gabi really. She used to wear it. She must have left it here.' Thea smiled. 'Pretty, isn't it?'

Kate nodded and ran her hand down the row of silver buttons, each one beautiful, unique, with a purple stone in the middle. Two of them were missing.

Thea saw the look on the detective's face. She saw the speed she rushed away from the house.

Thea picked up the coat, running her hand down the soft velvet. She remembered an argument. She remembered the coat, the silver buttons shining in the darkness. She thought about what the detective had said, how she'd reacted when Thea had said they were both left-handed. Thea knew now. She knew what had happened.

She walked back to the kitchen and sat down at the table. The night was closing in, the rain pouring in torrents, the wind blowing it viciously against the window.

She picked up her mobile phone and dialled. A voice answered.

'Meet me at the south entrance of the common, now,' she said. She paused, listening to them protest. 'Park on Cemetery Road. I'll give you ten minutes.'

Thea hung up the phone, picked up the purple coat and left the house.

Harry drew up outside Mortimer's house and turned the engine off, watching. His windscreen wipers divided the night into snippets through the rain. On the seat next to him, the gun lay wrapped in its plastic bag; a portent of doom, foreboding and ominous.

The night before, Harry hadn't been able to sleep after Gabriella had left. Her absence had left a gap: a dent in the pillow where her head had rested only hours before; where she'd looked at him in the dim light and said she loved him; that she was sorry for everything that had happened, and she wanted to be with him.

But then she'd got dressed, and no amount of convincing from him could persuade her to stay.

Her departure had left him nervous. He'd lain there for hours, tossing and turning, before giving up to watch more late-night television. NFL, bloody American football, the only thing on at that time of night.

Morning had arrived and he'd woken scratchy-eyed on the sofa. He'd phoned her mobile and it rang out. He hadn't left a message.

He'd got dressed and gone for a run, the crisp winter air numbing his hands, his muscles stiff. Harry realised he didn't know where Gabriella had gone, or even how she had got to his in the first place. He knew she had a flat somewhere, separate from her husband, and then there was *his* house, of course. Had she gone back to Mortimer? The thought of it started a burn of jealousy in his chest and he ran faster, pushing it to the back of his mind.

He ran further than he had in a long time. It started to rain but he barely noticed. His brain replayed snapshots of their night, their whispered conversations, faces barely inches apart. He'd forgotten aspects about her that he now loved: the slight imperfections in the dark of her eyes, the scar on her forehead, practically hidden in her hairline.

His breath caught in his throat. He stopped in his tracks, doubled up by the side of the road, struggling to breathe. The scar on her forehead. That day after school, with the bullies. It had been Gabriella who started the fight, but Thea was hit with the stone. It was Thea who'd needed stitches. Thea who had the scar.

Harry felt the bottom drop out of his world. He remembered her words when she first arrived at his flat: '*Your whole life you wanted me, and now you finally get a chance to have me, you're hesitating?*' Thea hadn't known about him and Gabi in Bournemouth; she didn't know they'd slept together before.

His chest heaved and he rested his hands on his knees, light-headed, forcing himself to take gulps of oxygen. He felt sick. How could she have lied in that way? How could she do something so cold? He started the walk back to his flat, soaked to the skin, tired and shivering, crossing roads without looking, nearly getting hit by cars, horns blaring. But he didn't care. He didn't care about anything any more.

He opened the door to his flat, pulling off his wet clothes and leaving them where they fell. He turned the shower on full and stood under it, letting the scalding water burn his skin. Harry felt dirty and used. How could he have been so *stupid*? The things he'd said, the things they'd done. He faced the torrent of water, trying to wash away the humiliation and shame. Deceived by the person he trusted more than anyone in the world.

But then something inside him switched; the hurt curled up and hid, replaced by a burn he'd only felt one time before, fifteen years ago. He turned off the shower, got dressed and opened the drawer next to his bed.

He'd meant to get rid of the gun. But something had stopped him, and it wasn't because he wanted to take it to the police. Holding the gun in his hand, standing by the tree in the dark and the rain, Harry had remembered how he'd felt all those years ago. It had been scary and terrifying and horrible. But it had also been powerful. He'd been in charge.

Harry picked up the gun, unwrapping it from the plastic bag, and held it in front of him, feeling its weight, the cold metal in his hand.

He wouldn't be a victim any more. It was time to take back control.

He'd driven first to Thea's, but finding the house empty he'd gone to Mortimer's, his next best guess as to where the twins would be. The house was shrouded in darkness, but Harry could see a dim glow from one of the front windows.

As he waited, the outside light turned on and the front door opened. Gabriella emerged, pulling a long black coat around her shoulders, ducking her head in the pouring rain. Harry went to open the car door, then stopped as Mortimer followed her out of the house. They were clearly arguing. Lights flashed on the black BMW and Gabriella climbed in, Mortimer waiting behind, his arms crossed, sheltering in the doorway. The BMW sped off down the road and Harry started his engine and followed.

The BMW was going at speed and Harry struggled to keep up, cursing the cars that got in between them, aggressively pushing his way out onto the roundabout and following her down The Avenue. He saw the common on his right, frowning as she turned down a side road. Why on earth was she going here? And why the urgency?

Gabriella parked up and Harry followed her in a few cars down. He watched her climb out, then walk quickly towards the common. The rain had stopped but it was completely dark now and freezing cold; it reminded Harry of that night, two weeks ago.

He'd known Gabriella was back in town. He'd seen her on the society pages, out and about with other men, knowing she hadn't called him. So he'd gone to the club to see her, to talk, nothing else, but before he'd had a chance to go inside, she'd come out and he'd followed her. But it hadn't been Gabriella, had it? Like last night, he'd got the twins confused. It had been Thea, drunk, alone, and he'd followed her onto the common.

Like now, he'd been a mess: confused, tired, angry, his emotions torn to shreds. But unlike then, tonight he had a gun.

64

Gabriella walked deeper down the paths of the common. She heard nothing more than the rustle of the leaves and the sound of the cars on the road; it was pitch black and the streetlights had little effect on the murky night. She cursed her sister for making her come here. She should have said no, she should have refused, but how could she?

She could feel the cold reach under her coat, freezing her to her core. She thought about turning back, but pushed on, her eyes straining to see into the darkness. She knew she was getting close to the place Thea had been attacked.

Eventually, she saw a figure on the path ahead, partly hidden by the trees.

Gabi took a deep breath, trying to quell her nervousness. She stopped and stood in front of her sister.

'Why are we here, Thea?' Gabi asked.

There was a long pause, then Thea started talking, her voice solemn. 'I know what happened,' she said. 'That night, I saw you.' Thea lifted her arm and subconsciously stroked the back of her head. 'I don't remember much, but I remember seeing you. I remember this coat.' She looked down at what she was wearing and Gabi recognised it as her old purple velvet coat, the one that used to belong to their mother. 'You've had it all this time, and that night you were wearing it.'

Gabi didn't reply, the words caught in her throat.

'Why can't we just be a family again,' Thea said, sadly. 'It's all I've ever wanted, Gabriella. You, me and Harry. Why can't you leave the past alone?'

'I'm sorry, Thea,' Gabriella started, but before she could say any more, a figure in the darkness caught her attention.

'I know it was you,' a male voice said.

Harry was standing behind them. 'How could you do it, Thea?' he said, slowly.

Gabi looked from Thea back to Harry, confused. 'What are you ...?'

'You told me you loved me, you let me believe ...' Harry started. Gabi saw his eyes narrow and his jaw contract.

She looked back to her sister. 'What did you do, Thea?' she asked, a wave of dread creeping across her body. 'What have you done?'

'I did it for you, Harry,' Thea pleaded. She took a step towards him, her hands outstretched. 'You were so miserable, I just wanted to make you happy, to give you what you wanted.'

'I wanted Gabi, not you!' he shouted, backing away from her.

Gabriella's mouth dropped open. She turned back to Harry. He was wearing his black coat and in the darkness, she didn't see it at first. But then, there, black against black, a gun in his hand. The gun. He raised it, slowly, pointing it at Thea.

Thea held her hands out in front of her. 'Harry, please ...' she started, glancing across at Gabi. 'Put the gun down, you don't want anyone to get hurt.'

'Why not?' he shouted. 'After what you did last night?' He shook his head in disbelief. 'Everything you said, everything you did. That was you.'

Gabi could see his arm trembling, the gun shaking in the

moonlight. She could only guess at what had happened, but she could see the hurt clear on Harry's face. Deceiving him in that way – it was cruel.

'And why is that so terrible?' Thea asked, and Gabriella turned back to her sister. Thea was angry, her mouth twisted in a grimace. 'I've never been good enough, have I? I've been your best friend,' she shouted. 'I've been there with you, every day, when *she* was off travelling the world. And I wanted...' Thea stopped, then turned to Harry. 'I wanted you. You ... You're my everything, my whole world, Harry. But the moment Gabriella's back, it's all about *her* again.' Thea spat out the words. 'Despite everything she's done. To you. To me. Lied to us both.'

Gabi could see Harry's aim waver. Thea looked at Gabriella, pointing a defiant finger in her direction.

'It was her who attacked me,' Thea hissed. 'It was your precious Gabriella who tried to kill me – that night, out here.'

'What's she talking about?' Harry shouted. He glanced at Gabi, then moved the gun to point it at her.

Gabi saw the black metal shine in the darkness. Her focus narrowed, the barrel of the gun her only concern. She held her hands up in an automatic reaction.

'Harry, please,' she begged.

'Tell me!'

Gabi felt her body trembling. 'I wasn't trying to kill her, it was an accident,' she pleaded. She turned to Thea, watching the gun out of the corner of her eye. 'I'd worked out what you were doing, pretending to be me, and I just wanted you to stop. So I followed you. Out here.'

'And you attacked me,' Thea said. Gabi could see the anger flicker behind her eyes. 'You wanted me dead.'

'No!' Gabi cried. 'I didn't, I swear.' She turned back to Harry. He was watching her, the gun still pointed at her face. 'Please, Harry, please put the gun down.'

He shook his head, a frantic movement to and fro. 'Not until you tell me. Not until I know what's going on.'

'Okay, okay.' Gabriella's body was shaking. She didn't know whether it was the cold, the anger, or the fear, but she felt every muscle in her body contract. 'We fought. About you going to the club, about...' Gabi paused, choking back a sob. 'About what happened to Mum and Dad. What I wanted to do. You were drunk, you were a mess, Thea. You started hitting me, you wouldn't stop and I got angry. I was furious – with you, with everything that had happened. You were hanging off me, slapping my face, out of control, so I pushed you and you fell.' Gabi started crying, the tears rolling down her face. 'I thought you'd just get up, but you didn't. You must have hit your head on something. There was blood, so much blood, so I just ran. I called the ambulance, but I had to get away. I'm sorry, Thea, I'm so sorry.'

Gabi wiped the tears away from her eyes and looked at her sister. Thea was staring at her, her eyes cold.

'And have you done what you said you were going to do?' Thea asked, slowly. 'Have you told the police about what happened to our parents? What *really* happened?'

Gabi stopped, perfectly still. She could see Harry pointing the gun at her. She could see the look on his face – the confusion, the misery. But she didn't want to lie any more. There had been enough lies.

Gabriella nodded.

Next to her, she heard Harry make a strangled sob. Gabriella saw the gun move, flashing in the moonlight, and flinched, raising her hands to her face. But it didn't fire; there was no gunshot. It was far worse. Gabi saw Harry raise the gun, pointing it at himself, the muzzle at his temple.

'Harry, no,' she shouted, and he looked at her, his face creased with despair.

'I can't go to prison, Gabi, I can't,' he cried.

She held out her hands to him but he backed away from her, the gun still pointed at his head. 'Please, Harry, no,' Gabi begged. 'We can make this better. I can help you.'

'How?' he sobbed. 'How? Madeleine's dead. I shot her, and she's dead, nothing is going to change that.' Harry's arm tensed but then, from the corner of her eye, Gabi saw Thea move. Her sister flew at Harry, grabbing his hand and pulling it away. She saw them fall together to the ground. She heard the gunshot.

It was loud. Louder than she remembered, louder than anything she had seen since on television or at the movies. It deafened her, stunned her into silence, leaving her body quaking. She smelt the gunpowder, reminiscent of fireworks and bonfires.

Gabriella ran to the bodies on the ground. Thea rolled onto her back, away from Harry, the gun now in her hand.

'I'm okay, I'm okay,' Thea gasped.

Gabi fell to her knees at Harry's side. He lay on the grass, staring up in shock. She floundered, unsure of what to do, running her hands across his chest.

'Are you okay? Harry?' she pleaded. 'Please talk to me.'

Harry shook his head. Gabi looked at his hands covering his stomach, and gently went to hold them. But then she felt the wet. It was warm, and she held her hand up to the light. Her palm was bright red, her hand covered in blood.

Harry winced, his face crumpled with pain. He looked at Gabi; she could see tears in his eyes and she held his hand.

'I always wondered how this was going to end,' he said quietly, his blue eyes locked on hers. His face was pale, his lips turning grey.

'You're going to be okay,' she whispered to him. 'Everything's going to be okay.'

But she didn't know how it could be.

She looked up at her sister. Thea took off her coat, then her jumper, rolling it into a ball and kneeling next to Gabi on the grass.

Thea held the gun out to Gabi, the muzzle pointing down. Gabi recoiled at the sight of it but Thea pushed it into her hand. 'Take it, and go,' she said, her voice steady. She seemed unnaturally calm.

Gabi shook her head, over and over again, staring at the gun, frozen in shock. 'I can't just leave him, I can't.'

Thea looked down at Harry, opening his coat and putting her jumper against his stomach, trying to stop the bleeding. 'I'll stay here, but you need to get rid of the gun and your coat.' She looked up at her twin. 'The police will arrest you if you stay.'

'So let them,' Gabi cried out. 'I deserve it. You tell them what you remember, what I did to you.'

'No.' Thea met Gabi's gaze, her eyes red and angry. 'I won't. Unlike you, I have loyalty to my family. I don't want you to go to prison.'

Gabi shook her head frantically. 'It was never about loyalty, Thea. It's about being human. It's about drawing a line between what's right and wrong and telling the truth.'

'Fuck, Gabi, what's wrong with you?' Thea shouted. She held Harry's hand tightly, the other still pushing against his chest. Gabi could see a red stain widening across his stomach, blood soaking the grass where they were kneeling. 'You're supposed to love us, you're supposed to do anything for us,' Thea cried, her voice desperate. 'We did, all those years ago, for you, why can't you do the same?'

Gabi backed away from Harry, her hands shaking. She felt her anger build. She remembered what had happened between them all, fifteen years ago.

'Because I can't stop thinking about it, Thea,' Gabi cried. 'Every time I close my eyes, there it is. I see you, Thea!' She put her hands over her face, sobbing. 'I see what you did.'

July 2004. Fifteen Years Ago.

65

The sun beat down relentlessly, sending ripples of heat from the concrete path. Gabi was hiding at the back of the garden in the shade, earphones shoved in, pumping the latest Chili Peppers album at full volume.

She hadn't seen Thea or Harry all morning, but that was her aim. She thought about the night before, after the prom, kissing Harry. She'd liked it. She wanted to do it again, but knew it was going to create a change in their lives she wasn't sure she was ready for yet. It had always been the three of them and now – what? How would Thea feel if it was just Gabriella and Harry? For the moment Gabi wanted to enjoy her own little perfect memory. Without the complication.

Gabi felt a drip of sweat roll down her stomach. She reached for her drink and, finding it empty, looked down towards the house. The air was still. The laundry hung limply on the line; the sky was oppressive and stifling.

She couldn't see Thea or Harry; perhaps she could make it to the kitchen for an ice cream then out again without anyone seeing her. She took her earphones out. Back at the house she could hear voices, loud and shouting.

It seemed to be all three of them this time – her parents and Harrison – and her curiosity was raised. For days all they'd heard was her mum and dad, alternating between bellowing at each other, then living in a deathly silence. The addition of Harrison was new.

She left her Walkman in the grass and crept towards the house, coming to a stop by the kitchen window. She looked up and saw the three adults: Harrison standing at the door, her mother and father at opposite corners of the room.

'This is ridiculous,' her mother was shouting. 'How can you give me such an ultimatum?'

'How can I not!' her father responded. 'We can't stay here, living next door to the man you've been sleeping with all these years. The two of you, creeping around behind my back. How can I possibly trust you if we stay?'

Thea saw her mother scoff, and look away. Their father turned to Harrison, still standing in the doorway.

'I don't even know why you're here. This has nothing to do with you any more, you've done your damage. You need to leave.'

'What's going on?'

Gabi jumped as Thea came up next to her, crouching low, Harry behind her. Harry was almost bent in two to keep out of the way of the window, and now sat down on the path, crossing his legs under him. He was wearing a baseball cap, shorts, and a slightly grubby T-shirt with a black and white Oasis logo across the front. Seeing Harry made Gabi feel a little surge of excitement, a tingle of warmth that went all the way to her toes.

'They're fighting again,' Gabi said. 'Dad wants us to move.'

They paused for a moment, and listened to the argument continue.

'She's not going to stay with you!' their dad was shouting. 'We've discussed this, Madeleine and I. It's over between you two.'

'Maddy, please ...' They saw Harrison reach out to Madeleine, holding his hands out, pleading. 'I love you. Let's leave here, let's be together.'

'What do you think you can offer her?' Robert mocked. 'A waster like you, living off your widow's pension and state benefits.' He laughed cruelly and Harrison looked at him.

'You're not so fucking perfect. You're a shitty husband and a neglectful father.' Harrison turned, and Gabi saw him walking out to the studio, then coming back with something wrapped in a cloth. 'Maddy told me – this damn thing is still hanging around the house, after you promised to get rid of it.'

Gabi gasped as Harrison unwrapped the gun, dangling it between two fingers in front of Robert's face. Gabi exchanged looks with Thea and Harry, their eyes wide.

'It's dangerous,' Harrison shouted. 'They found it once before, who says they won't find it again. And then who knows what would happen.'

'This has nothing to do with the sodding gun,' Robert said. 'And it has nothing to do with you. We are leaving. We're getting away from this house, from you and your son.'

'Leave Harry out of this,' Harrison growled, but Robert couldn't be stopped.

'Your precious son ...' he pointed to Harrison '... is a bad influence on my daughters. Who knows what they've been doing together all these years? The sooner he's apart from them, the better. I'll make sure he never sees them again and that this ridiculous plan of theirs to go to university together doesn't happen.'

Gabi saw their father step forward towards their mother. 'Let's move. Let's sell this place and get out of here.' He took one of her hands, pulling her towards him. 'We'll move away from him, we'll take the girls and go far away. Start afresh.'

Gabriella shook her head. She couldn't believe what her father was saying. What their mother had been doing had nothing to do with them. How could he blame Harry? How could he say those things?

Furious, Gabi pushed into the kitchen and stood in front of the three grown-ups, hands in fists by her side. 'Stop! Stop all this fighting!' she shouted. She saw Thea join her, Harry's hand in hers.

The three adults stared at the teenagers. Robert turned to his daughters, plastering a smile on his face. 'What do you think, girls?' he asked. 'Where would you like to go? We can be a family again, all together. Anywhere you like, just name the place.' He reached across to Gabriella, but she pulled away.

'I want to go where we planned!' Gabi shouted. 'To uni, with Harry and Thea. Why does that have to change?'

Robert took a deep breath. Gabi could tell he was still angry, fighting to keep it under control. 'Some things have been going on long enough. And as your father, I have the right to put a stop to it.' He looked over at his wife, and Madeleine slowly nodded. 'To it all.'

Maddy glanced at Harrison, then turned back to Gabi. 'We'll all be together, I promise. You and Thea, me and your father.' She took Robert's hand and looked up at him. 'Nobody else.'

It all played out in seconds. Gabi saw Harrison raise his arm, the gun still in his hand. She saw his muscles tense.

She saw Harry dive forward to stop him. His hand grabbed his father's but it was too late.

She heard the gunshot. The sharp bark was sudden, so

recognisable but strange in the familiarity of their kitchen. A high-pitched ringing echoed in Gabriella's head, her hearing muffled. Her mother screamed.

Gabi saw the blood bloom across Robert's chest as he collapsed. Harry wrestled with his father and Harrison slipped, falling and banging his head on their kitchen table with a sickening thud. The gun fell to the ground and Harry picked it up.

Gabi saw Harry look at it, slowly, then raise it up in the same way his father had done. Madeleine saw him, her screams escalating, eyes wide as Harry pointed the gun her way. He pulled the trigger, a second gunshot ringing out, the bang louder, a huge fireball projecting out of the gun, grey smoke filling the room. The gun clattered to the floor and Harry doubled up in pain.

Gabi blinked, her mouth open in disbelief, then ran to her parents, now fallen on the floor in the kitchen. She knelt next to their mother, the red spreading across her stomach, tentatively going to touch her then pulling away. She felt panic take hold in her chest, forcing her breath out in staccato bursts.

Blood pooled out from under their bodies, unnaturally twisted where they fell, widening across the white tiles of the kitchen floor. Her father lay face down next to Maddy, his body broken.

Gabi couldn't look away. She could feel Harry pulling at her, but she was hypnotised by the blood. So much bright red blood. Harry tugged at her arm again.

'We need to go,' he said, his voice strained. Gabi could hear the wail of a police car in the distance. 'Pick up the gun. We need to go now.'

Gabi bent down and grabbed the gun, wrapping it quickly

·in the cloth. Harry dragged her out of the house, blinking in the sudden sunshine, pulling her through the grass and wild flowers, to the oak tree, until Gabi realised Thea wasn't with them.

'I have to go back for her,' she cried.

She ran back to the kitchen door but it was closed. She couldn't get through. She tugged at it with all her might, panicking, peering through the glass panels, then running to the side of the house, pulling open the old oak door to the basement.

Gabriella almost fell down the steps, crouching low as she ran through the darkness, feeling bricks and dust move under her bare feet. She climbed the stairs into the study, running back into the kitchen.

Gabriella stopped dead in the doorway, the devastating scene hitting her full force, knocking the wind out of her.

The shattered body of her father lay to her right. On her left, Harrison was still out cold, a large angry cut bleeding on his forehead.

She saw Thea on the far side of the room. She was bending over something on the ground. Gabi saw her mother's feet and Thea's back, Thea straddling her body and bending over her face. Gabi assumed Thea was trying to help her, and leaned forward to pull her away, but then realised. Something wasn't right.

Her mother's legs were moving, weakly, her heels pushing into the ground, trying to get purchase on the tiled floor. Her mother was reaching up, her hands wrapped round Thea's arms.

And Thea ... Thea was leaning forward, a cushion in her hands, pushing it down, using all her body weight to hold it over their mother's face.

Gabriella froze. Her body locked. Her brain couldn't make sense of what she was seeing, what her sister was doing. As Gabi watched, her mother's arms dropped limply to her sides. Thea turned, the cushion still in her hands, and saw Gabi standing in the doorway. Her face was sweaty, her hair plastered to her face. Her mouth fell open.

'What did you do?' Gabi whispered to her twin. 'What have you done?'

66

The instant Kate saw the coat in the hallway, all the pieces fell into place. She had already connected it to Madeleine, but she hadn't known that Gabriella had owned it for the last fifteen years. Kate had found the silver and purple button at the crime scene; it had been worn that night on the common, then left at the house by Gabi, while pretending to be her sister.

Kate could see it now. The shadowy figure on the CCTV Kate had assumed was Thea, then dismissed. Gabi was ambidextrous. She'd fought with Thea with her left hand, and Thea had defended herself with her right. The DNA results from under Thea's fingernails connected them to Steve, along with Thea's own genetic profile. But it could have been Gabriella's. It could have been her identical twin's.

All that time, focusing on the men in Thea's life and it had been Gabriella — the very first person they'd interviewed.

Kate had rushed out to the driveway, then cursed as she realised that she had brought her own vehicle rather than a police car — there was no bust box in her boot, no evidence bag to seize the coat. She didn't want to make the same mistake she'd made with the button, so she jumped into her car. She needed to get back to the house before Thea realised. Before the coat disappeared.

She drew up at the police station with a screech of brakes,

where one of the uniforms waited in his car, engine idling. She threw herself into the seat next to him.

'Do you have evidence bags in the boot?' she shouted and he nodded. 'Then just drive.' He put the car into gear, blue lights flashing as they charged back towards the house.

Normally she relished the thrill of being in a police car, blues and twos blaring. But this time Kate couldn't enjoy the ride, too nervous about recovering that coat, knowing exactly what it meant for a conviction. Knowing how much she needed it to charge Gabriella Patterson.

The officer called in their movements as they made their way towards the house. But when they got there it was completely dark, windows looking down disapprovingly.

Kate climbed out of the car, blue lights flickering across the brickwork. She felt a sinking feeling as she looked round, peering through the windows at the empty hallway, the deserted living room.

'Sarge?' The officer called to her from the car. 'Are we done here? It's just there's another call – all hands on deck on the common.'

Kate turned towards the uniform, a bad feeling washing over her. 'What's the call?'

'Shots fired,' he said. 'Ambulance dispatched. Armed Response moving towards scene.'

Kate ran back to the car. 'Let's go,' she shouted. 'Now.'

67

Thea stared at her sister through the darkness, her eyes cold. Fifteen years on, her resolve was the same.

'I did what I had to do,' she said.

'You killed our mother!' Gabi shouted.

'Our mother was a selfish, vain woman who couldn't accept the fact she wasn't the most beautiful person in the room any more. She wanted everything for herself. She wanted...' Thea stopped herself.

'What?'

'It doesn't matter.' Thea shook her head slowly. She looked down at Harry. His eyes were flickering, his breathing laboured. 'We couldn't take the risk she would survive. She would have told the police. All that was important was that Harry didn't go to prison. Harrison knew that – why don't you?'

After the gunshots, Thea remembered Gabi and Harry running from the room. She remembered turning towards her mother's body, surprised to see her mother looking at her, her lips moving. In that moment, despite the heat of summer, Thea felt her body turn cold. The most important thing was the same as it had always been: they were her family, just her and Gabriella and Harry.

She walked quickly towards the kitchen door, turning the key in the lock. She picked up the cushion from one of the chairs. She leaned down to her mother's face.

'Gabriella,' she heard her mother whisper. She was dying. She was looking her daughter right in the eye, and she still couldn't tell them apart. Thea pushed the cushion onto her face.

She felt her mother struggle, but she didn't relent. This was how it had to be, she told herself. It was how it should be.

Thea looked back at Gabriella. She could see Gabi's body shaking, convulsing with sobs. Thea could hear sirens in the distance.

'You need to get out of here, please,' Thea pleaded. 'Go!' she shouted, and at last Gabi ran. Thea watched her disappear into the darkness, then looked down at Harry. He was silent, his eyes closed, his head turned to one side. She couldn't tell if he was still breathing. Thea took his face gently in her hands, stroking his cheek, blood from her fingers leaving garish streaks on his skin. She felt the panic take hold, the fear of losing him gripping her tightly, making her heart race. She started to cry.

'I did what I had to do,' Thea whispered to Harry, through her tears. 'I promised you.'

Sunday

68

Gabi stood in the doorway. She remembered the stifling heat from two weeks before, the smell of disinfectant and bleach. She knew she had to go in, but she was afraid. Scared to face him after everything that had happened.

She walked in slowly. Unlike Thea's ward, this one was full. Some people sat up, gaze fixed on the middle distance, others sleeping, the curtains pulled around them.

The cushion made a soft sigh as she sat down next to the bed. He seemed to be sleeping, his eyelids flickering. His arm was free of the covers and Gabriella saw the line linking him to the array of drips behind him.

He stirred and opened his eyes.

'Hi Harry,' she said.

Harry turned in the bed and winced. He reached for a small controller by his side but he didn't press the button to activate the pain relief, just held it in his broken hand.

'Does it hurt?' she asked.

'Fuck, yes. But the morphine makes me sleepy and I'd like to see you. While you're here,' he added.

'They said you'll be okay,' she said and Harry nodded.

The doctor had been there when she'd arrived, and had been quick to reassure her. 'Your friend was very lucky,' he'd said. 'The bullet entered on the left-hand side from a downward angle and lodged in his iliac crest. His hip bone,' he explained. 'We had to remove his spleen, so he'll probably need to be on antibiotics for the rest of his life, but otherwise the prognosis looks good.'

Harry's skin was grey, his eyes dark and sunken, his lips cracked. But he was alive, and Gabriella had never been so pleased to see him in her entire life.

'I feel like such an idiot,' Harry said softly. He stared up at the ceiling. 'I was so quick to believe it was you. It didn't even cross my mind it was Thea.'

'Why would you?' Gabi took his hand and held it in both of hers. 'You had no reason to think she would trick you in that way.'

'She did it before, too,' Harry said. 'In her garden. She just looked so much like you, her clothes, her manner.'

'If it helps, I don't think she did it out of malice, Harry. She loves you, she thought she was helping.'

He nodded, and winced at the movement.

'I followed Thea that night,' he said. 'When she was attacked. I thought it was you. I knew you were back, and I wanted to see you so I went to the club.'

'What did you see?' Gabi asked.

'Not much. By the time I caught up with Thea on the common, she was lying on the ground. But I didn't know what to do. I ran. I was scared they'd arrest me. And then they'd go digging and they'd find out...' Harry stopped himself. 'I couldn't face them investigating your parents' murders again. So I left her there.' He paused, his face crumpled with pain.

An alarm started ringing on the other side of the ward. Nurses rushed over, curtains were pulled round the bed.

Gabi was distracted by the commotion and turned towards the noise. When she turned back, Harry's blue eyes met hers.

'Do you think you'll ever be able to forgive me?' He closed his eyes again. 'I wish we'd never found the gun, I wish I'd never picked it up ...' He carried on, and Gabi watched him as he spoke. 'I was so scared, of losing you both. I thought ... I thought that Maddy would take you away and I'd never see you again and I just reacted. I hated her, I hated her so much. She ...' Harry stopped talking, his face collapsing.

'Harry,' Gabi said, quietly. She took his hand, preparing to tell him the very worst. 'I'm sorry, but your dad died last night.'

Harry nodded, his eyes still closed. 'He shouldn't have died in there.' A tear escaped and ran down his cheek. 'Alone.'

'I know,' Gabi whispered. 'But he loved you, he was protecting you.' She paused, debating what to do. 'But that's it now, Harry. The only people who know what happened that day are you, me and Thea. It's over, you don't need to worry any more.'

Harry opened his eyes and looked at her. 'The police were here. That detective. She knows I had the gun back then. She thinks I had something to do with Madeleine's death.'

Gabi felt the guilt. This was her fault. She'd pushed the detective; she'd encouraged her to keep looking. And now she was sniffing around Harry.

'What did you tell her?'

'Nothing. And that I couldn't remember anything about last night. That I didn't know who shot me.' A small smile crept across his face. 'I really pissed her off.'

'Then she can't prove anything,' Gabi said. 'There's no gun, no evidence ...'

'And what about Thea? What about you, Gabi?'

Six months ago Gabriella had come home to put things right. She'd run, all those years ago, because she'd been afraid – of her sister, of her feelings for the man who had shot her mother – but now? She'd done things she'd previously thought unimaginable. She'd nearly killed her sister. She'd lied to the police; she'd faced what happened on that day, years ago. And she'd disposed of the evidence that any of it had ever happened.

Thea's pleas had jolted Gabriella and she'd run down the path, back to the car, the gun a heavy weight in her hand.

She'd driven through Portswood and St Denys, parking the car and walking quickly to the water's edge. She had been nervous; she didn't want to be seen, but the pavements were empty. Gabriella had stood next to the disused buildings and looked out across the river, the Northam Bridge towering above her on her left, the wind whipping round her coat, the cold now ingrained in her bones. She didn't think she'd ever be warm again. She looked at the gun in her hand.

Now she had it, she couldn't remember why finding it had seemed so important. She'd wanted to restore some feeling of control in her life. Somehow she'd thought that if they told the truth about what happened that day, she would feel better, when the reality was that that would never happen. She'd only made things worse.

With a cry, she hurled the gun with all her strength towards the river. She saw it twisting and turning into the darkness until it was gone. For good.

She'd driven back to the house in a daze, falling through the door into Mortimer's arms. The shock of the evening hit her like a tsunami, an onslaught of images and emotion, stopping her breathing. He'd held her close as she cried, rocking her gently like a child.

After what seemed like an eternity, Mortimer had put his hands either side of her face, gently forcing her to look at him.

'Gabriella,' he said, carefully. 'I don't understand what happened tonight. I don't know what happened all those years ago to your parents, or even to Thea two weeks ago. And I don't need to know. But what I will say is this. I love you. I've loved you since the moment I met you, and I will follow you to the ends of this earth. I always knew we were in this together, but I never realised just how much until today.'

Gabriella had nodded, and Mortimer had slowly leaned forward and kissed her.

'Now, what do you need?' he'd asked quietly.

'We have to burn this,' Gabriella whispered and they both looked at the purple coat. It was time it all came to an end. They had all been through enough.

Gabi squeezed Harry's hand tighter. 'You don't need to worry, Harry. It's over.'

'You're leaving, aren't you?' Harry said.

'Yes.'

'Where are you going?'

Gabi shrugged. 'We don't know at this point. Mortimer can work from anywhere, so we'll see where we end up.' She paused. 'I'll send you a postcard.'

Harry nodded. His finger twitched over the green button in his hand but he didn't press it.

'When you're better,' Gabi said, 'perhaps you could join us?'

'I'd like that.'

Harry closed his eyes and she saw his finger press the button. The muscles in his face relaxed and he lay back in the bed. His hand let go of hers.

Gabriella leaned over and kissed him on the forehead. Then she walked away to join her husband.

69

The hospital was surrounded. The police were watching her.

Briggs was parked outside the front entrance, Yates in a squad car next to the multi-storey. The hospital was sealed tight. She was not getting away, not this time.

They'd found the black BMW in the car park and saw Mortimer return. Kate had made them all keep their distance, watching the ward. Waiting for Gabriella. Kate knew there was no way Gabi would leave without saying goodbye to Harry.

From the doorway of the ward she carefully kept an eye on Gabi seated at Harry's bedside, the affection obvious between them.

The night before, when they heard the call, gunshots on the common, Kate had known who it had been. They'd sped to the scene, arriving at the same time as the Armed Response vehicle, by then full of grumpy redundant officers. They hadn't found a gun, she was told, and the victim had been taken to hospital. Alive.

Kate hovered as Gabi and Harry finished their conversation. Harry had been less than forthcoming about what had happened last night. Amnesia, my ass, Kate thought. And Thea had described an unknown gunman dressed in black in a hoodie. She'd wanted to arrest her but the chief had said no, a warning frown on his face. 'You have no evidence to the contrary,' he'd said and she'd been forced to admit that he was right.

But he'd been unable to deny what she'd found out about Madeleine Patterson and the evidence of suffocation. They'd pulled more boxes out of storage and sent the red cushion to the lab. High-priority this time.

'We're going to have to raise this to the coroner,' he muttered, shuffling the paperwork round his desk. 'They'll have to open another inquest.'

Since their exchange on Friday, DCI Jennings had been wary, circling Kate like a fat tomcat, bitten on the nose for the first time by a feisty mouse. But he seemed to have accepted defeat; their conversations were short but polite, letting her do what needed to happen on the case.

Kate was relieved. As much as it took over her life, she loved her job, and more than that, she wanted to know what had happened. Determination burned in Kate's veins. She knew Gabriella was responsible for the attack on Thea, and she'd rallied the team, updating them on everything she'd found on the way to the hospital.

Kate's phone vibrated in her pocket. She looked towards Harry and Gabriella, still talking, and pulled it out. It was a message from Sam.

I got the paperwork back, thank you, the message said. *But can we talk? Tonight? Sxx*

Kate frowned, and typed her reply. *I thought we were past talking. What's changed?*

She looked up quickly as Gabriella walked away from the bedside and Kate followed her, pushing her phone back in her pocket. They walked towards the main entrance, Gabriella's pace increasing until they rounded a corner and

Kate cursed under her breath – she'd gone. Kate reached for her radio, desperate to call Briggs and Yates for an update.

'Stop following me, detective,' Gabriella said. She stood in front of Kate, determined, her eyes dark.

'You need to come with me,' Kate said, taking Gabi's wrist in her hand. 'You can come quietly now and not make a scene, or I can put you in handcuffs – it's up to you.'

'On what grounds?' Gabi asked, calmly.

'You know exactly what – you attacked your sister,' Kate said. 'Stop playing games with me, Gabriella.' She started to give the standard warning but Gabriella cut her off.

'What evidence do you have, Detective Sergeant Munro?' Gabi's voice was slow and measured. 'Tell me what you have and I'll admit it, here and now. Save us all a lot of time.'

Kate hesitated. She knew she should take her into the station but Gabi's arrogance made her blood boil. 'We know you were wearing the purple coat that night. We know you were walking down London Road...' she began.

Gabi shrugged. 'What purple coat?'

'We'll search your house, Gabriella. We'll search Thea's. We'll find it.'

'You can try, DS Munro. Please do. But I think you'll discover no such coat exists. And as for walking round Southampton at night, well. That's no crime.'

Kate stopped, her brain scrabbling for the evidence that proved what her instincts knew to be correct. But Gabriella was right. They had none. Gabriella pulled her wrist out of Kate's grasp.

Without the coat, without the continuity of evidence for the button Kate had found on the common, she couldn't prove Gabriella had been there. They'd searched the CCTV looking for Gabriella but it was patchy at best, the girl on the screen indistinguishable from her sister or indeed any other woman out there that night.

But they had the new bullet, the one from last night. When the surgeons had removed it from Harry Becker, they'd sent it straight to ballistics and it had come back a match to the same ones used fifteen years ago. Kate knew they were all involved. But could she prove it?

'I know how your mother was killed,' Kate said.

Gabi clapped, slowly. 'Well done you,' she said sarcastically. 'It took you guys long enough.'

'Come in to the station, Gabriella, tell us what you know,' Kate said. 'Do the right thing.'

Gabriella laughed – a sharp outburst in the quiet of the hospital. 'The right thing,' she smiled. 'What exactly is that? We all think we know. We're all lying and sneaking around and betraying the ones we love because we think we're right. But what if, Detective Sergeant Munro,' Gabi said, mocking her name, 'there is no right answer? What if we're all wrong?' Gabi paused, adjusting her coat round her shoulders and tucking her hair behind her ears. 'I've done all I'm going to do,' Gabriella said, shaking her head. 'This is yours now.'

Kate knew that was it. She knew she wasn't going to get any more out of Gabriella Patterson.

'Just tell me, where's the gun?' Kate said quietly.

Gabi tapped the side of her nose and smiled. 'You're a good detective, DS Munro. I can see that. But sometimes you have to accept you'll never know what happened.' Gabriella walked away from her, towards the black BMW now pulled up outside. 'Some secrets are destined to stay buried,' she said.

Gabriella opened the door to the BMW and looked back at Kate. She nodded, slowly, then climbed into the car, next to her husband.

Kate took a deep breath. She heard the frantic chatter over the police comms, Briggs and Yates asking what to do, what did she say, should they go in for the arrest?

She felt her phone vibrate in her pocket again and pulled it out.

Your note said you were sorry, her husband replied. *You seemed different. You've never apologised for anything before.*

Kate stared at the message. Was she different? No case had ever affected her like this one. The attack on Thea Patterson and the murders of their parents fifteen years ago had pushed her to the edge. Locked in a relentless pursuit, she'd done things she never imagined doing – conducting illegal searches, mishandling evidence, sleeping with suspects, risking her career – and for what? To put away a woman who had clearly gone through enough in her life already?

Maybe it wouldn't hurt to leave this one be. Maybe here there was no such thing as right and wrong; for once in her life she would look for the shades of grey.

'Let them go,' Kate said into her radio. 'Just let them go.'

As she stood watching the black BMW drive away, her phone rang. Kate answered it, dejectedly.

'Katherine,' said the posh voice at the end of the line. 'It's Albie. I've been following up on your Patterson case.'

'Go on …' Kate said, slowly.

'After you left, it pricked my conscience, so I called one of my colleagues who works in the lab …'

'They're still shut, it's Sunday,' Kate interrupted.

'Not if you know the people I know,' Albie chuckled. 'They looked up the results on the fingernail scrapings, the ones from Madeleine Patterson, and it's the most curious thing. There were skin cells under the nails. The DNA wasn't on file but they came back as a familial match. Fifty per cent of the markers matched Madeleine's.'

'What does that mean?' Kate asked, the hairs on the back of her neck standing up on end.

'They were related,' Albie said. 'My guess – the person that suffocated Madeleine was most likely her child.'

Kate hung up the phone, her brain racing. She stared up the now empty road, listening to the exclamations of annoyance coming over her radio.

Maybe Gabi was right. Some secrets were destined to stay buried. But it wasn't going to be this one.

Friday 8 February 2019

Epilogue

Thea looked around the bare room. She looked at the cream walls, the wooden table screwed to the floor, the black box videoing their conversation. She looked at the detective sitting opposite her. She seemed smarter than usual. Her hair was shiny and hung loose around her shoulders; her shirt was ironed. She was wearing lipstick. Thea wondered what had prompted the makeover.

To her left was a window, looking out from the police station into the night sky. Outside, the rain continued to fall. It had been pouring all week, a biblical flood, echoing the disquiet in Thea's mind. She hadn't heard from Gabriella since she'd left. She hadn't dare contact Harry.

DS Munro was going to end the day disappointed. She would never betray her family. Whatever happened, however they behaved towards her, they were the most important thing in her life. Tell the truth now, and all she could see was a gaping hole where loneliness and rejection and regret looked back at her. She'd never see them again. At least this way, there was a possibility. She had a chance for their forgiveness.

Thea thought about her sister. She'd lied to Gabriella about their mother. It was true, she had killed her to protect Harry, but for a different reason, one Gabi could never know about. Thea had sworn never to breathe a word. She'd promised Harry, all those years ago.

The morning after the prom, Thea woke to the sound of Gabriella's snoring. Already the summer's day was making itself known; their bedroom was muggy and smelt of stale alcohol, oozing out of her sister's pores. She climbed out of bed and padded down the corridor to the stairs.

The door was open to their parents' room and Thea peered through as she passed. She could see her father's foot sticking out of one side of the bed, and wondered whether their parents had made up. Of her mother, there was no sign, her nightclothes in a pile on the floor.

At the bottom of the stairs a noise caught her attention. She could hear her mother's voice, low and calm, then male tones, coming from the living room, and she paused in the hallway. She'd been in this situation years before, listening to her mother and Harrison carry on their affair, but she was older now. She wouldn't put up with it again.

She felt anger burn in her stomach and pushed the door open with a bang. Thea saw her mother facing away from her in the middle of the room, naked, her dressing gown pooled on the floor around her feet. A man was sat on the sofa in front of her wearing a T-shirt and boxer shorts. As Thea came into the room her mother turned, surprise on her face.

Because the man in front of her mother wasn't Harrison. It was Harry.

He was on the far side of the sofa, his legs pulled up to his chest, his arms wrapped round them, his knees almost touching his face.

Thea's mother sighed, then bent down and picked up her

dressing gown, swinging it round her shoulders and pulling the cord tight at the front.

'You can't blame a girl for trying,' she said and pushed past Thea.

Thea stood in the doorway, her mouth open. She heard her mother's footsteps on the stairs, then the door to the master bedroom slam.

'I wasn't... We weren't...' Harry gabbled. His eyes were wide, every inch of him tense. 'I was sleeping, she came in, she ...'

Thea slowly walked over to the sofa and sat next to him.

'Did you have sex with my mother?' Thea asked carefully and Harry shook his head. A quick movement, emphatic, over and over.

'But she's always around, she always manages to get me by myself. She's kissed me, she's ...' He stopped and shook his head. 'I've told her to leave me alone but she won't let it go. She says we need to ... Says I need to experience a real woman.' Harry pulled his legs closer to his chest, the words flying out of his mouth. 'You believe me, don't you, Thea?' he pleaded, and she nodded.

Thea leaned over and pulled Harry to her in a hug. She felt him relax, his arms go round her and his face rest on her shoulder. 'Please don't tell anyone, don't tell Gabi,' he said into her hair.

'I won't,' Thea replied. 'And I promise I'll fix this.'

'How?' Harry murmured.

'I don't know,' Thea said, slowly. 'But I promise I will.'

A flash of lightning lit up the sky outside the police station. Thea started counting, looking out of the window, waiting for the soft rumble of thunder to follow seconds later.

She turned back to the detective. 'Whatever you think you know about my mother, DS Munro, I assure you, you're wrong. She deserved everything that happened that day.'

'She deserved to be shot by her lover's son, then smothered by her own daughter?' DS Munro asked, her voice calm.

Thea slowly shook her head. 'You can't prove anything. Harrison confessed. He's dead. You'll have a hard time convincing any jury otherwise.'

'That may be the case, Thea,' the detective said. 'But you know what? I'm willing to try. We have saliva and blood from your mother on the cushion. We have a medical report detailing Harry's injuries from the gun. We have DNA from either you or Gabriella under her fingernails. And I've learnt a little something about DNA recently.' DS Munro sat back in her chair, putting her arms behind her head. 'Do you want to hear it?'

Thea scowled, and the detective carried on, a slight smile on her face. 'A normal test just looks at a short sequence of the DNA, a part known to be highly variable between individuals. So for identical twins, this comes back the same.' She pointed at Thea. 'No use for you two. But...' she said. 'If we sequence your entire DNA genome, everything that makes up who you are, then subtle differences show up where environmental factors over the years have slightly changed your profile.' She nodded. 'Good, huh?'

Thea shook her head. 'So do it, what's stopping you?'

DS Munro frowned. 'Well, it's super-expensive and takes forever.' She shrugged. 'But if we have to, we will. In the meantime, the media will love this. I can see the headlines already – the press have always been fascinated by the three of you.'

Thea bristled with anger. She remembered the newspapers

when their parents were murdered; she remembered the reporters constantly hounding them. This wasn't fair. 'Leave them be,' she growled. 'Leave Harry and Gabriella out of it.'

'And I will, I will, Thea.' DS Munro slowly took a sip of water from the cup in front of her. 'I believe it was you.' She pointed a finger at Thea's chest. 'I think you killed your mother. Because of the hospital report from that day, because of the scratches on your arms. But, you know ...' She shrugged and Thea felt her rage build. 'If you don't tell me what you know, then what choice do I have? We'll ask for the test, but while we wait, maybe I'll go after your sister. Maybe I'm going to have to charge Harry, petition for no bail, leave him to rot in prison like his father did, while we wait for a court date. You know how long these things take, don't you, Thea? You do know what happens in prison? To people with a mental illness like Harry's?'

Thea glared at the detective. She couldn't let her ruin their lives. Harry would not go to prison. She had to protect them, as she always had. As she always would.

Outside, the rain continued to fall. Lightning flashed, a sudden burst of brightness through the dark. Thea asked herself the question. Then she slowly started to count, waiting for the thunder. Waiting to give the answer.

A slow rumble echoed through the room. And Thea started to talk.

Author's Note

I have lived in and around Southampton most of my life, so when I needed a home for Kate, it was my obvious first choice. And anyone who lives in Southampton will recognise many of the places mentioned in this book: Bassett, Southampton Common, Hill Lane and The Avenue are very real. However, Gabi and Thea's childhood home and the nightclub, Heaven, are a complete figment of my imagination and the depiction of a few locations have been skewed to suit the story.

In addition, while Hampshire Constabulary exists, the version in Kate's world is, of course, complete fiction, and not a true depiction of the many dedicated (and rule-abiding!) people who work there.

Acknowledgements

Thank you, as ever, to my agent, Ed Wilson, for his continuous faith, endless support and introduction to the world of gin.

To my editors Harriet Bourton and Ben Willis: thank you. I am so fortunate to work with you both and be at the receiving end of your incredible knowledge and insight.

And thank you to the rest of the amazing team at Orion Fiction: to Alainna Hadjigeorgiou, Jessica Tackie, Lucy Frederick and, of course, Bethan Jones for her work on the early stages of the manuscript.

A special mention must go to PC Dan Roberts and Dr Matt Evans. Thank you for taking time out of your incredibly busy lives to answer my questions with tireless patience – and for responding to the weirder queries without comment or judgement. And thank you to the other experts for your advice: particularly to Susan Scarr, Laura Stevenson, Charlie Roberts and Hannah Leggett. All mistakes made and liberties taken with the truth to fit the plot, are entirely down to me.

Thank you to Meenal and Seetal Gandhi, Alec Bennett and Madeline Taylor, for providing me with your unique experiences of being an identical twin.

Thank you to Teresa Andrews and Janet de Lange – readers of the very first draft and dispensers of ever-valuable honest feedback.

To Ryan Mortimer, James Burford and everyone else who

allows my shameful habit of stealing names – thank you. Please consider it a compliment – even if it turns out you're naming a baddie.

And last but not least, thank you to Chris Scarr and Benjamin: for always being there for me, and tolerating the crazy that comes with this bizarre profession.

COMING AUTUMN 2020:

NOWHERE TO BE FOUND

Louisa de Lange

★★★

SHE FOUND THE BODY.
NOW LUCY BARKER IS MISSING...

Lucy Barker has disappeared, and her distraught husband
Scott says he has no idea where she is.

But rumours abound about this seemingly perfect couple.
Why is Scott behaving so strangely? And why was Lucy
lying to him about where she went every Tuesday night?

Then, while investigating the recent murder of man found
floating in a lake, DS Kate Munro learns that it was Lucy
Barker who discovered the body and called the police.

Now she must find out if the two crimes are connected.
Before Lucy's time runs out...

Nowhere to be Found is the brilliantly twisty second
thriller in the DS Kate Munro crime series.

Credits

Louisa de Lange and Orion Fiction would like to thank everyone at Orion who worked on the publication of *Ask Me No Questions* in the UK.

Editorial
Harriet Bourton
Bethan Jones
Ben Willis
Lucy Frederick

Copy editor
Clare Wallis

Proofreader
Jenny Page

Audio
Paul Stark
Amber Bates

Contracts
Anne Goddard
Paul Bulos
Jake Alderson

Design
Debbie Holmes
Joanna Ridley
Nick May

Editorial Management
Charlie Panayiotou
Jane Hughes
Alice Davis

Finance
Jasdip Nandra
Afeera Ahmed
Elizabeth Beaumont
Sue Baker

Marketing
Jessica Tackie

Production
Hannah Cox

Publicity
Alainna Hadjigeorgiou

Frances Doyle
Georgina Cutler

Sales
Jen Wilson
Esther Waters
Victoria Laws
Rachael Hum
Ellie Kyrke-Smith

Operations
Jo Jacobs
Sharon Willis
Lisa Pryde
Lucy Brem